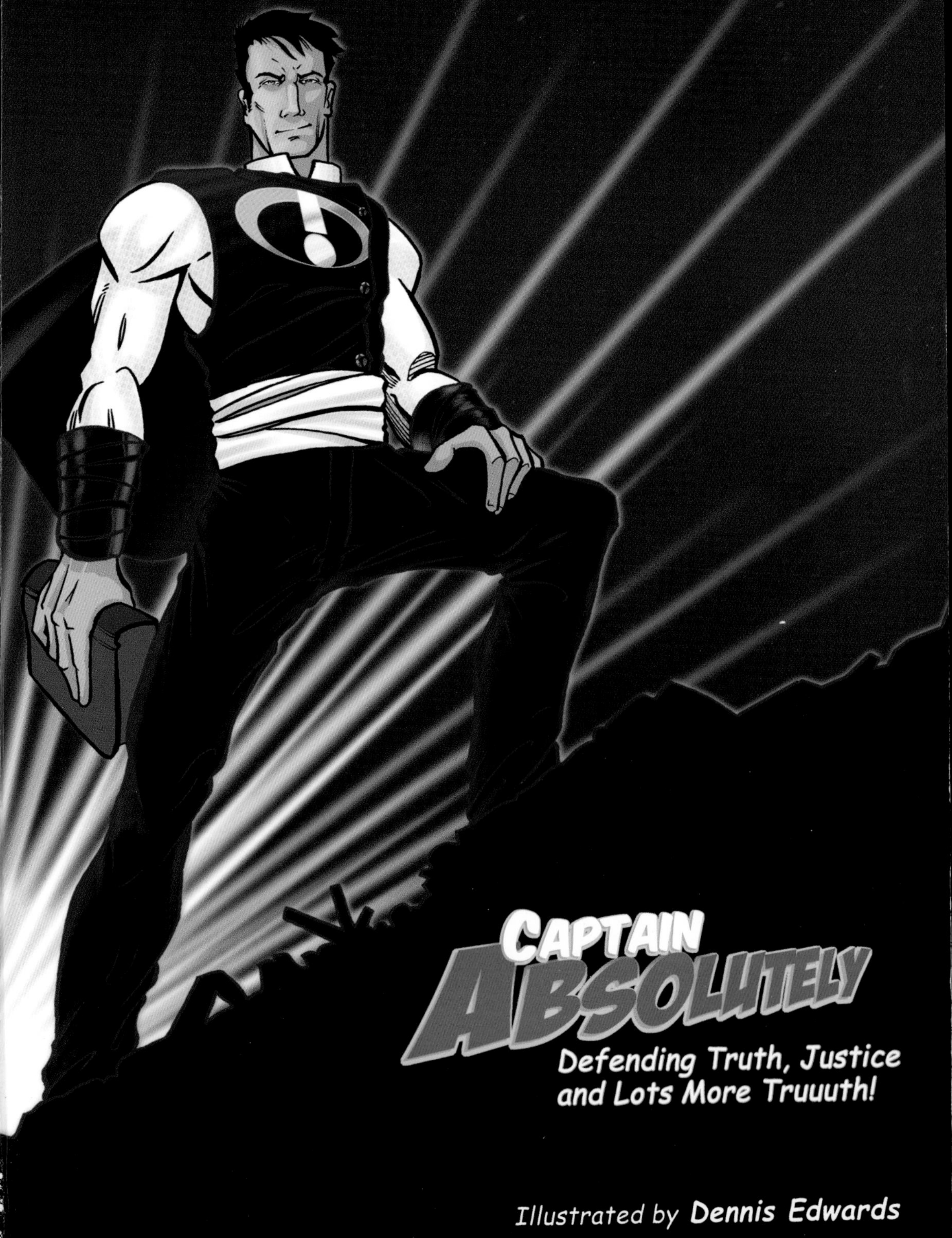

CAPTAIN ABSOLUTELY

Defending Truth, Justice and Lots More Truuuth!

Illustrated by Dennis Edwards

Captain Absolutely

A Focus on the Family book published by Tyndale House Publishers, Inc., Carol Stream, Illinois 60188

Written by Stephen O'Rear and Christopher P.N. Maselli, based on a character created by Paul McCusker

Illustrated by Dennis Edwards

Wooton illustrations by Gary Locke

Cover design by Mark Anthony Lane II

Library of Congress Cataloging-in-Publication Data can be found at www.loc.gov

Printed in China

23 22 21
7 6 5

KEEP YOUR EYE ON THE BALL

by Wooton Z. Bassett —
Mailman, Licorice Enthusiast,
and Creator of ***CAPTAIN ABSOLUTELY***

I'M NOT VERY GOOD at softball. After dozens of strikeouts, I had a brilliant idea. I figured if I could see the ball sooner, it would make me a better player. So I strapped a pair of binoculars to my head before the next game.

Boy, was that a mistake!

Suddenly, everything looked too close. I opened my glove to catch a pop fly, and the ball landed 20 feet in front of me. I swung at the same pitch three times before it crossed home plate. What's worse, the binoculars limited my peripheral vision, so I couldn't see who was standing right next to me. Sorry, Jason!

That's what this comic is about. Not softball—worldview. Just like those binoculars impacted my game (and Jason's nose), your values, priorities and perspective change how you see life. Some people see the world as a battlefield, where only the strong survive. Others say the rules don't really matter, so just do whatever makes you happy.

As Christians, our worldview is shaped by the absolute truth found in the Bible. God gave us detailed instructions: Love your neighbor. Be honest. Worship no one and nothing but Him. And through it all, keep your eyes on Jesus (Hebrews 12:2).

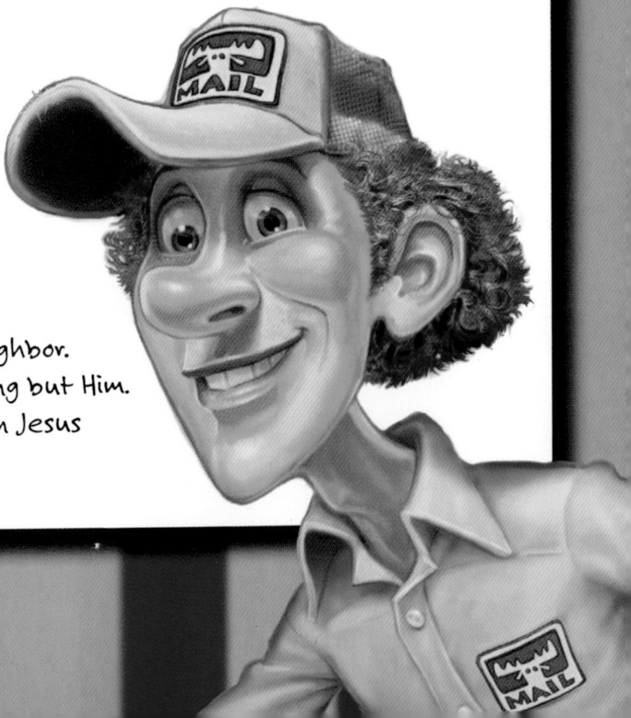
MAIL
MAIL

I wrote ***Captain Absolutely*** to show how bad guys try to mess with your vision—and how to combat those lies.

The book you're holding took five years to complete, written and illustrated two pages at a time for ***Focus on the Family Clubhouse*** magazine.

A ginormous, fudge-covered thank you goes to Paul McCusker, Dave Arnold, Nathan Hoobler, and Jess Harnell for helping me find Josiah's voice. Christopher P.N. Maselli, Stephen O'Rear, and Jesse Florea filled Metropolitanville with quirky characters. Jenny Dillon, Peg Mamalakis, Liz Duckworth, and Mike Harrigan worked extra hours to make up for the deadlines I constantly missed.

Most of all, thanks to Dennis Edwards, whose amazing illustrations brought ***Captain Absolutely*** to life. Seriously, look at this book. Dennis is the best!

I hope you enjoy this comic. As an added bonus, look for my extra comments and jokes throughout. I hope this book makes you explore your faith more deeply. Finally, I hope it inspires you to be a hero in your community, defending truth, justice and lots more truuuth!

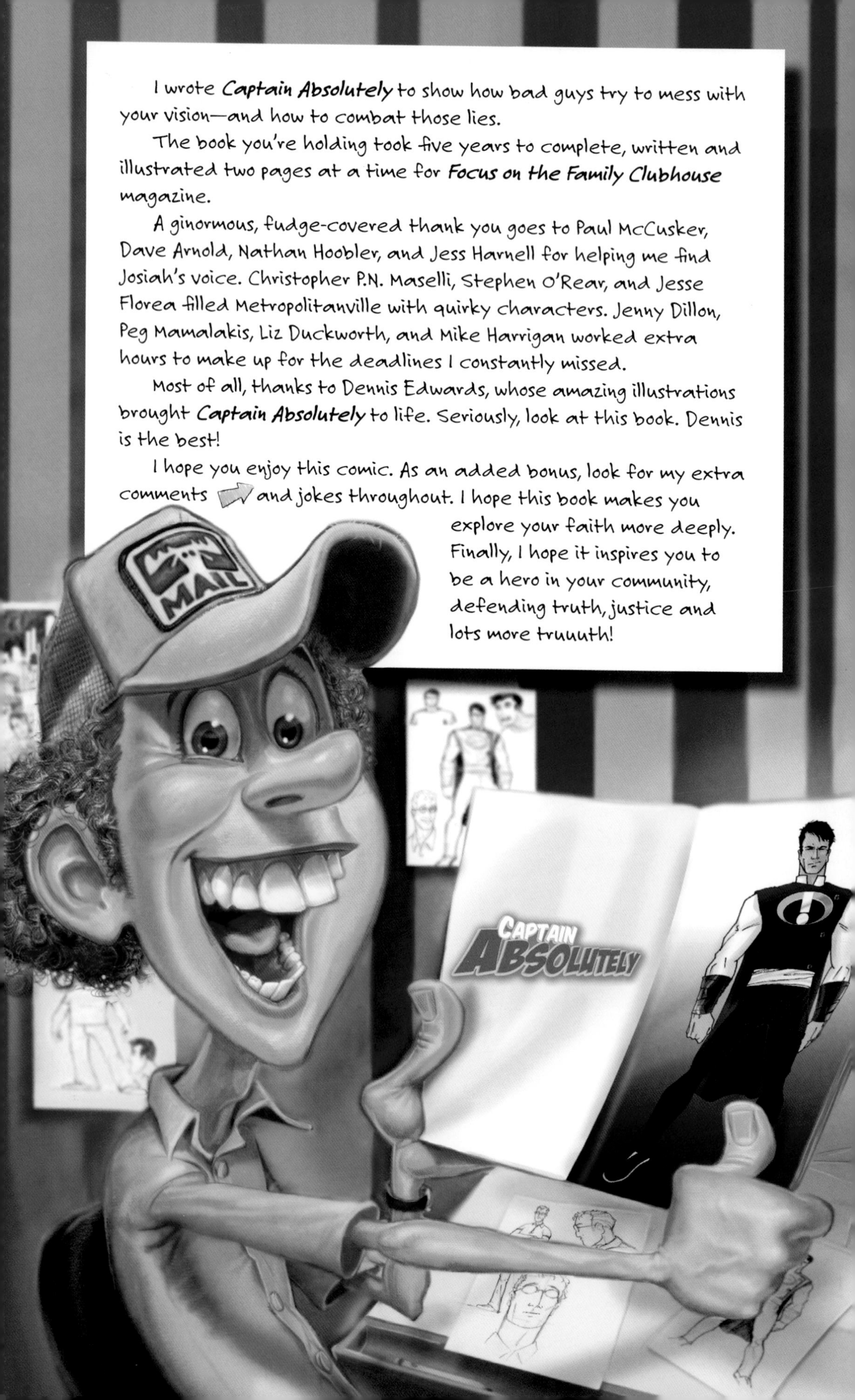
MAIL
CAPTAIN ABSOLUTELY

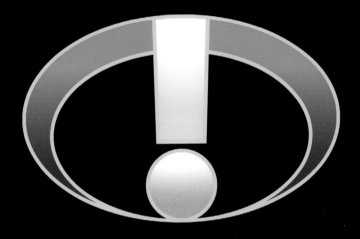

OUR STORY BEGINS . . .

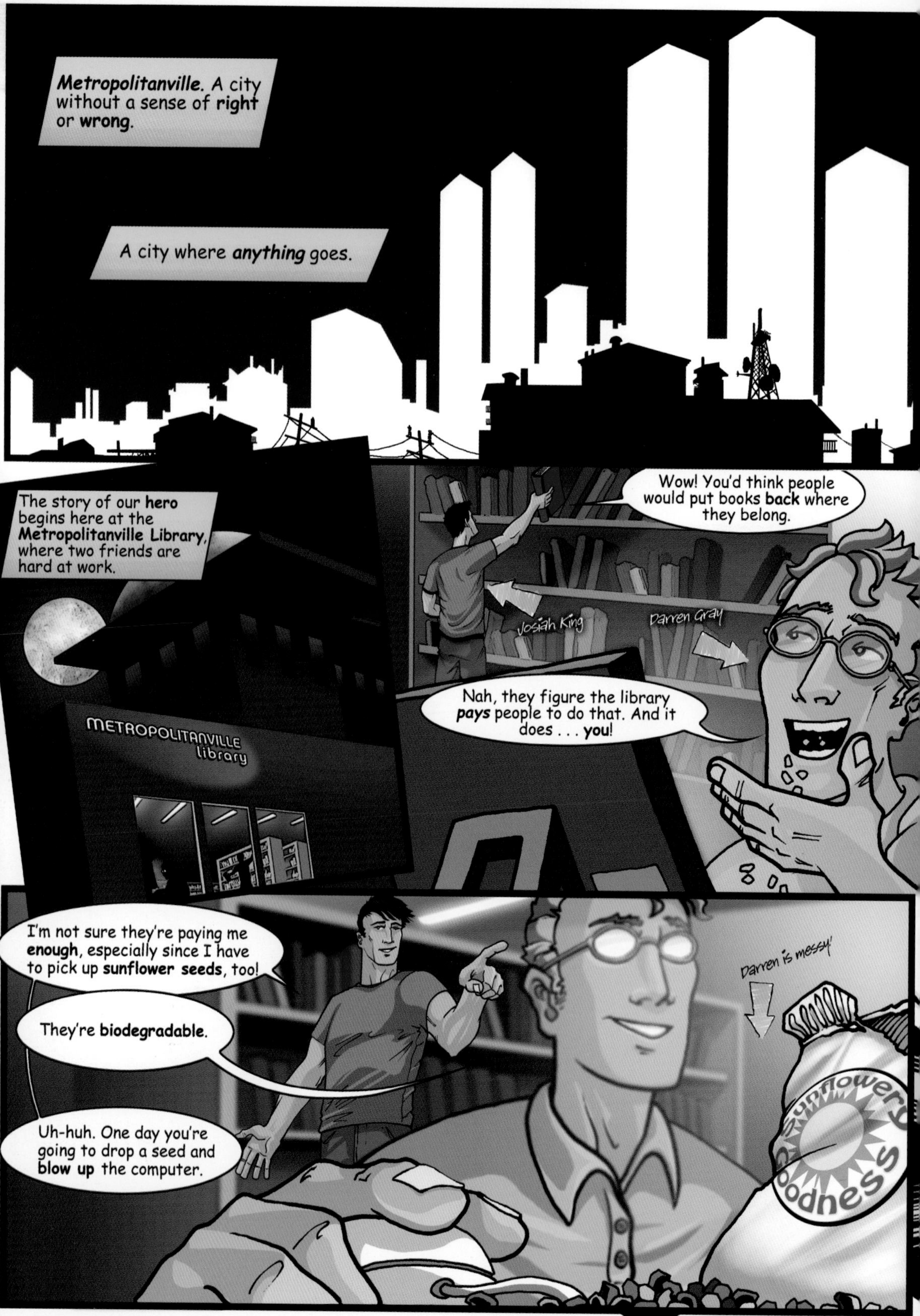
Metropolitanville. A city without a sense of right or wrong.
A city where anything goes.
The story of our hero begins here at the Metropolitanville Library, where two friends are hard at work.
METROPOLITANVILLE library
Wow! You'd think people would put books back where they belong.
Josiah King
Darren Gray
Nah, they figure the library pays people to do that. And it does . . . you!
I'm not sure they're paying me enough, especially since I have to pick up sunflower seeds, too!
They're biodegradable.
Uh-huh. One day you're going to drop a seed and blow up the computer.
Darren is messy!
Sunflowery Goodness

Sunflower seeds are my **fuel**, man! I need them as I work on this much needed **upgrade** to the **Dewey Decimal System**.
Suddenly, just as Josiah predicted only two frames ago, one of the seeds falls into the computer!
Never underestimate the power of a seed! Read Mark 4.
TIC
CLACK
Merciful motherboards!
What?
ZZZZTTT!
Isn't this the central computer for the **entire** library network?
Yeah.
And isn't it run by **nuclear power** from the city's main reactor?
Yeah, so . . .
ZZIT!
ZAP!
ZZIT!
RUN!!!
But the **books**!
Josiah really likes books
And so the story of **CAPTAIN ABSOLUTELY** begins like all hero stories begin—with two friends . . .
. . . and one spectacular **explosion**.
Ouch.

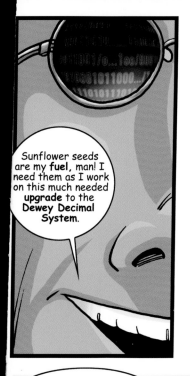

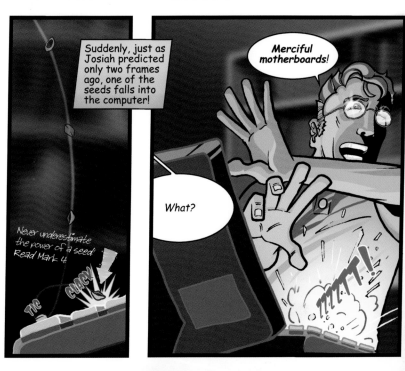

The greatest **heroes**…

… are those who **rise** from the rubble.

COUGH.

Hello? Darren? **Anyone?!**

I must've been thrown during the exlosion. I'm **trapped!**

But I'm alive.

keychain flashlight

Where am I?

WARNING
THESE BOOKS ARE BANNED BY THE METROPOLITAN LIBRARY COUNCIL. **NOT** READ WITH PROPER FORMS AND CLEARANCES.

That's **odd**— I've never seen these books before.

They're all different copies of the **same book!**

THE BIBLE

Holy Bible

THE HOLY BIBLE

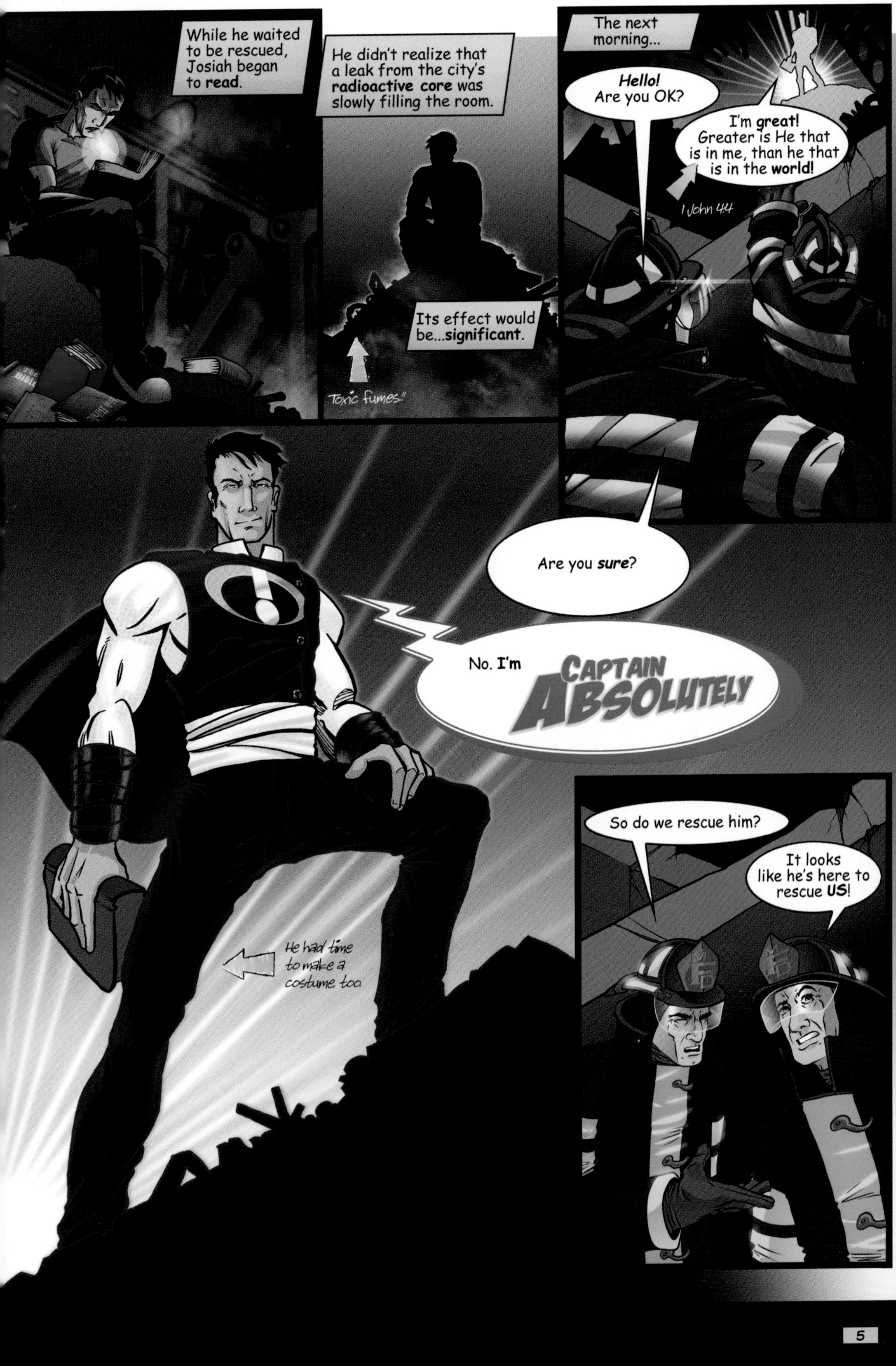
While he waited to be rescued, Josiah began to read.
He didn't realize that a leak from the city's radioactive core was slowly filling the room.
Its effect would be...significant.
Toxic fumes!!
The next morning...
Hello! Are you OK?
I'm great! Greater is He that is in me, than he that is in the world!
I John 4:4
Are you sure?
No. I'm CAPTAIN ABSOLUTELY
He had time to make a costume too.
So do we rescue him?
It looks like he's here to rescue US!

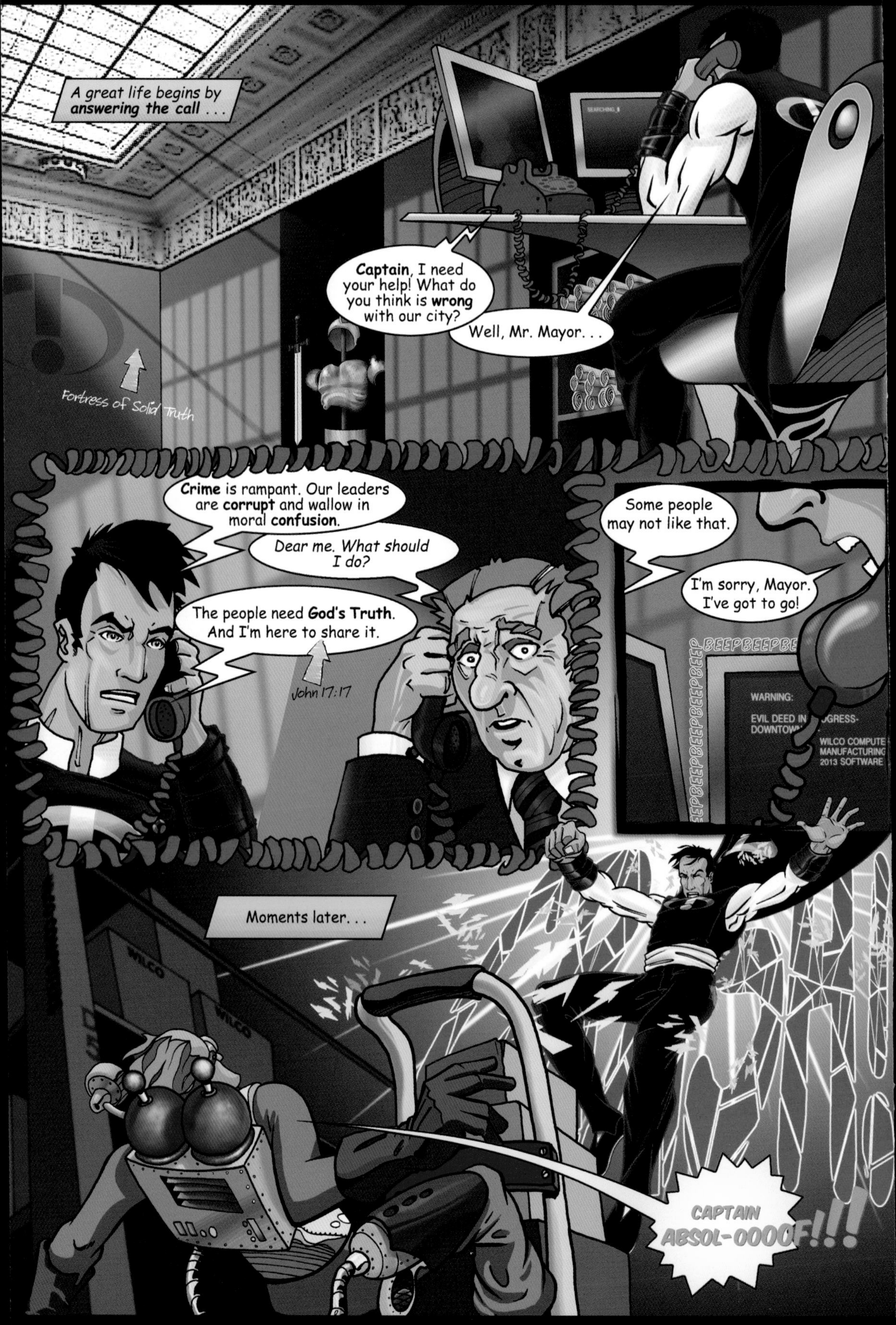
A great life begins by **answering the call** . . .
SEARCHING
Captain, I need your help! What do you think is **wrong** with our city?
Well, Mr. Mayor. . .
Fortress of Solid Truth
Crime is rampant. Our leaders are **corrupt** and wallow in moral **confusion**.
Dear me. What should I do?
The people need **God's Truth**. And I'm here to share it.
John 17:17
Some people may not like that.
I'm sorry, Mayor. I've got to go!
BEEPBEEPBE
WARNING:
EVIL DEED IN PROGRESS-
DOWNTOWN
WILCO COMPUTE
MANUFACTURING
2013 SOFTWARE
Moments later. . .
WILCO
CAPTAIN ABSOL-OOOOF!!!

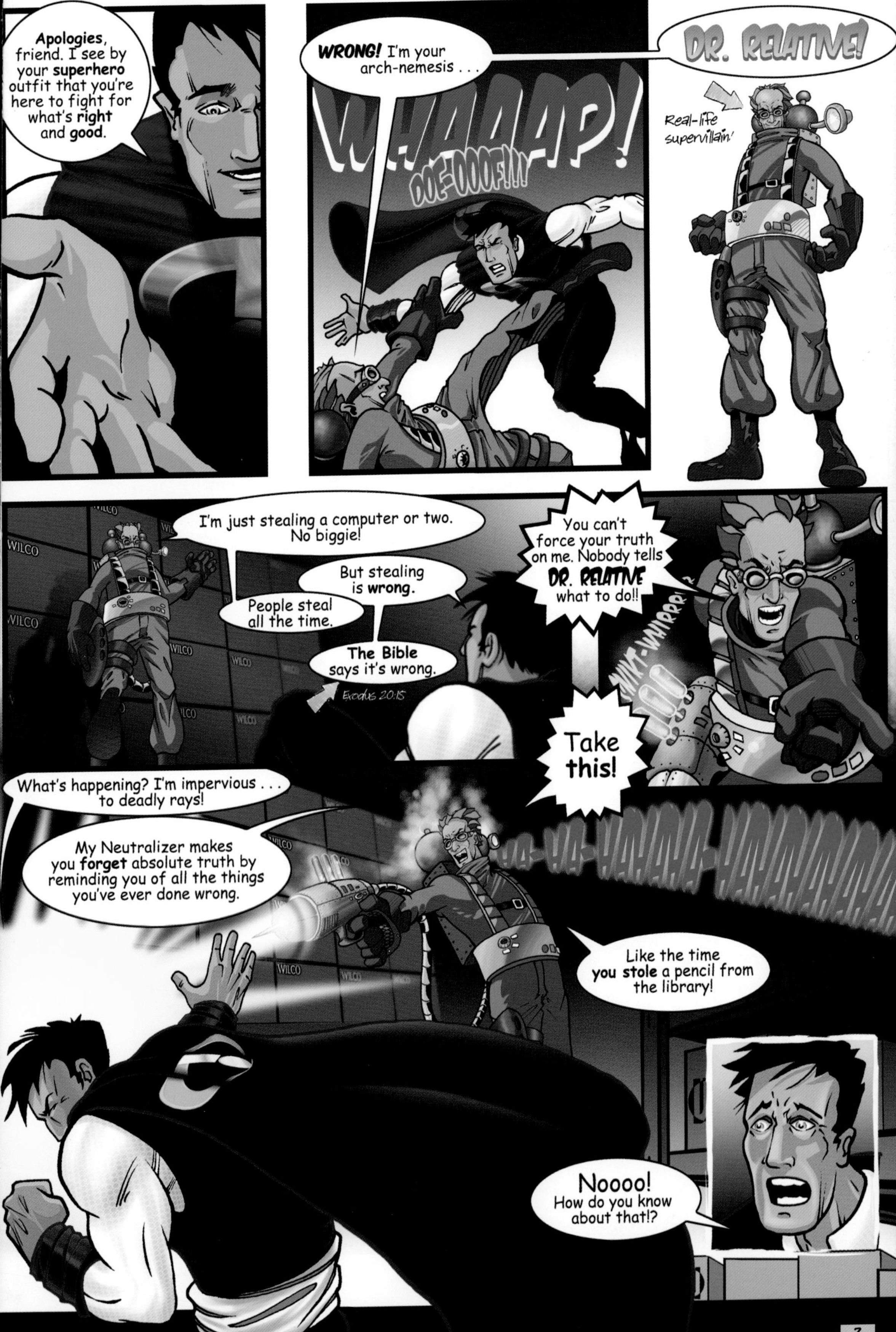
Apologies, friend. I see by your superhero outfit that you're here to fight for what's right and good.
WRONG! I'm your arch-nemesis . . .
WHAAAP!
DOF-DOOF!!!
DR. RELATIVE!
Real-life supervillain!
I'm just stealing a computer or two. No biggie!
But stealing is wrong.
People steal all the time.
The Bible says it's wrong.
Exodus 20:15
You can't force your truth on me. Nobody tells DR. RELATIVE what to do!!
Take this!
What's happening? I'm impervious . . . to deadly rays!
My Neutralizer makes you forget absolute truth by reminding you of all the things you've ever done wrong.
HA-HA-HAHAHA-HAHAHAHAHA
Like the time you stole a pencil from the library!
Noooo! How do you know about that!?

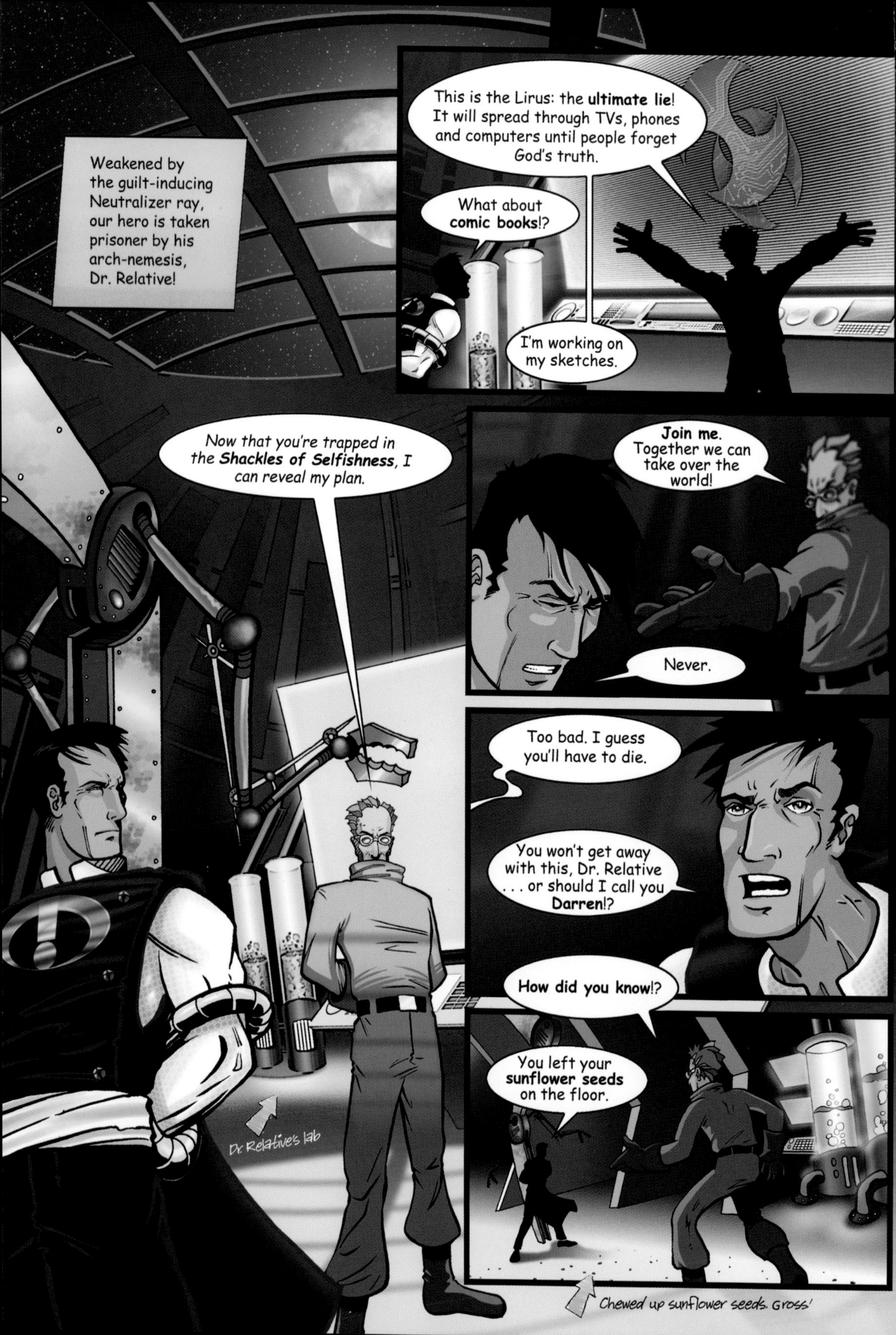

Weakened by the guilt-inducing Neutralizer ray, our hero is taken prisoner by his arch-nemesis, Dr. Relative!
This is the Lirus: the **ultimate lie**! It will spread through TVs, phones and computers until people forget God's truth.
What about **comic books**!?
I'm working on my sketches.
*Now that you're trapped in the **Shackles of Selfishness**, I can reveal my plan.*
Join me. Together we can take over the world!
Never.
Too bad. I guess you'll have to die.
You won't get away with this, Dr. Relative . . . or should I call you **Darren**!?
How did you know!?
You left your **sunflower seeds** on the floor.
Dr. Relative's lab
Chewed up sunflower seeds. Gross!

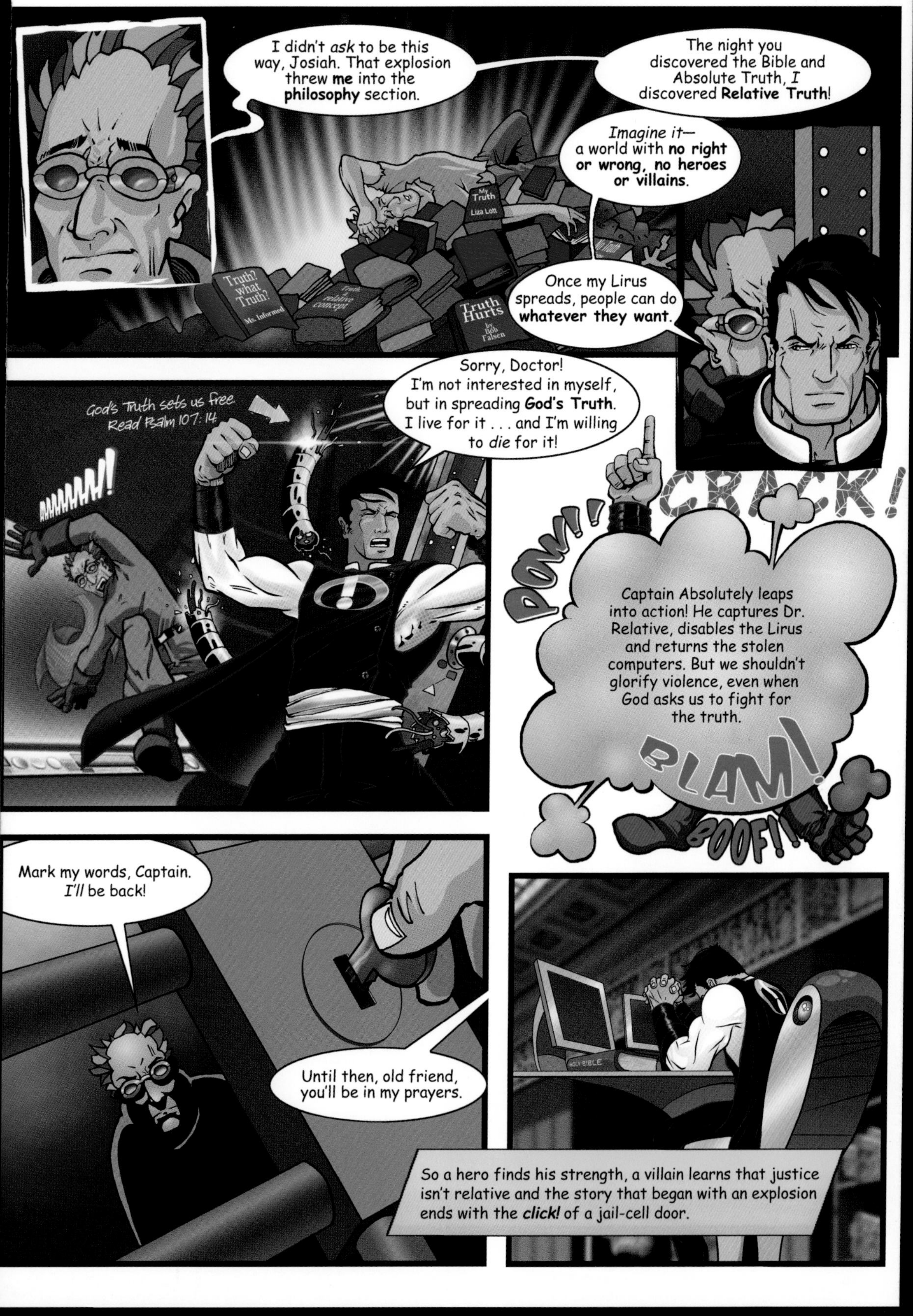
I didn't *ask* to be this way, Josiah. That explosion threw **me** into the **philosophy** section.
The night you discovered the Bible and Absolute Truth, *I* discovered **Relative Truth**!
Imagine it— a world with **no right or wrong, no heroes or villains**.
Truth? what Truth? Ms. Informed
Truth a relative concept
My Truth Liza Lott
Truth Hurts by Bob Falsen
Once my Lirus spreads, people can do **whatever they want**.
Sorry, Doctor! I'm not interested in myself, but in spreading **God's Truth**. I live for it . . . and I'm willing to *die* for it!
God's Truth sets us free. Read Psalm 107:14
AAAAAAAH!
POW!!
CRACK!
Captain Absolutely leaps into action! He captures Dr. Relative, disables the Lirus and returns the stolen computers. But we shouldn't glorify violence, even when God asks us to fight for the truth.
BLAM!
BOOF!!
Mark my words, Captain. *I'll* be back!
Until then, old friend, you'll be in my prayers.
HOLY BIBLE
So a hero finds his strength, a villain learns that justice isn't relative and the story that began with an explosion ends with the ***click!*** of a jail-cell door.

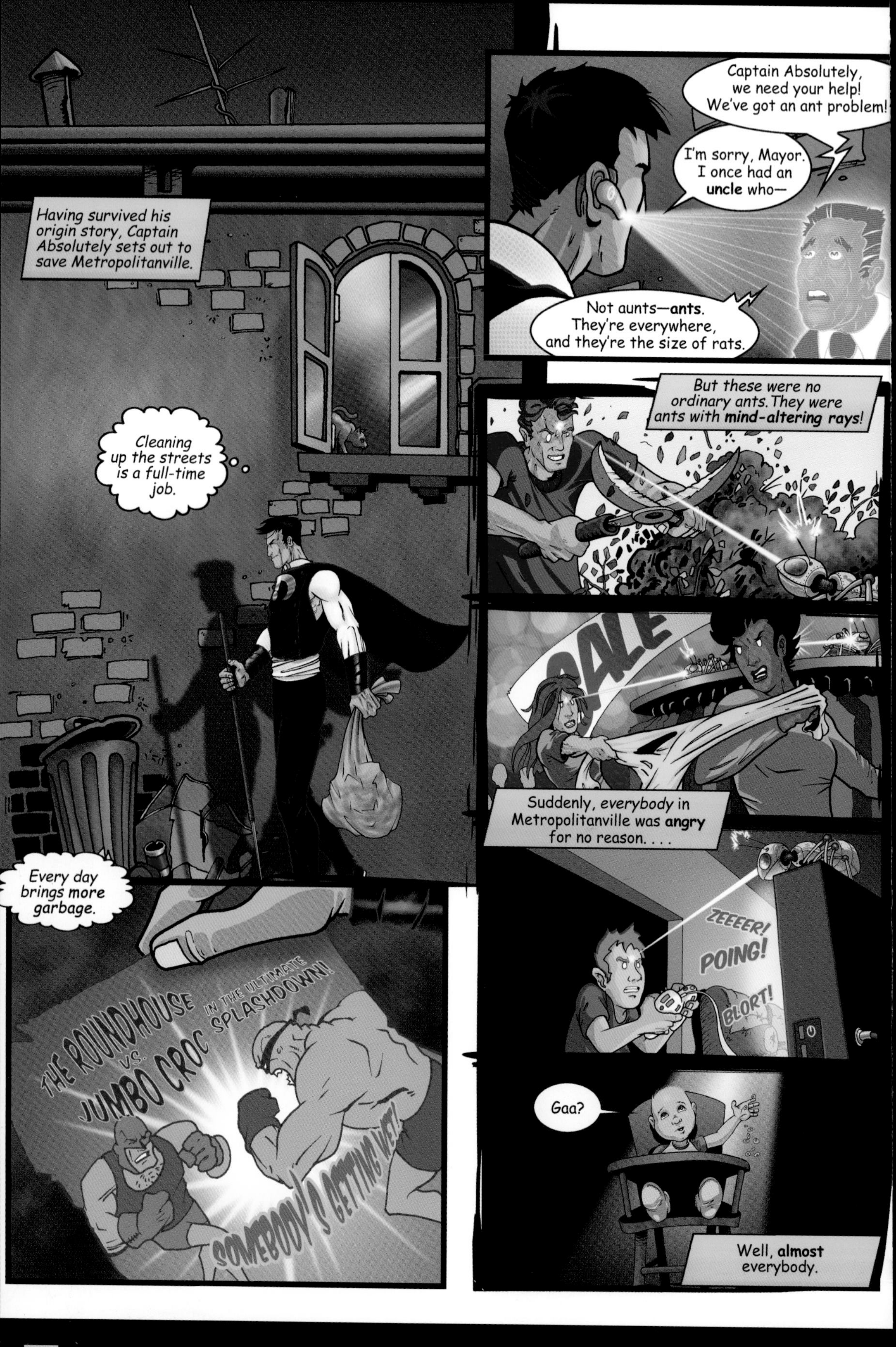
Having survived his origin story, Captain Absolutely sets out to save Metropolitanville.
Cleaning up the streets is a full-time job.
Every day brings more garbage.
THE ROUNDHOUSE VS. JUMBO CROC
IN THE ULTIMATE SPLASHDOWN!
SOMEBODY'S GETTING WET!
Captain Absolutely, we need your help! We've got an ant problem!
I'm sorry, Mayor. I once had an **uncle** who—
Not aunts—**ants**. They're everywhere, and they're the size of rats.
But these were no ordinary ants. They were ants with **mind-altering rays**!
Suddenly, *everybody* in Metropolitanville was **angry** for no reason. . . .
ZEEEER!
POING!
BLORT!
Gaa?
Well, **almost** everybody.

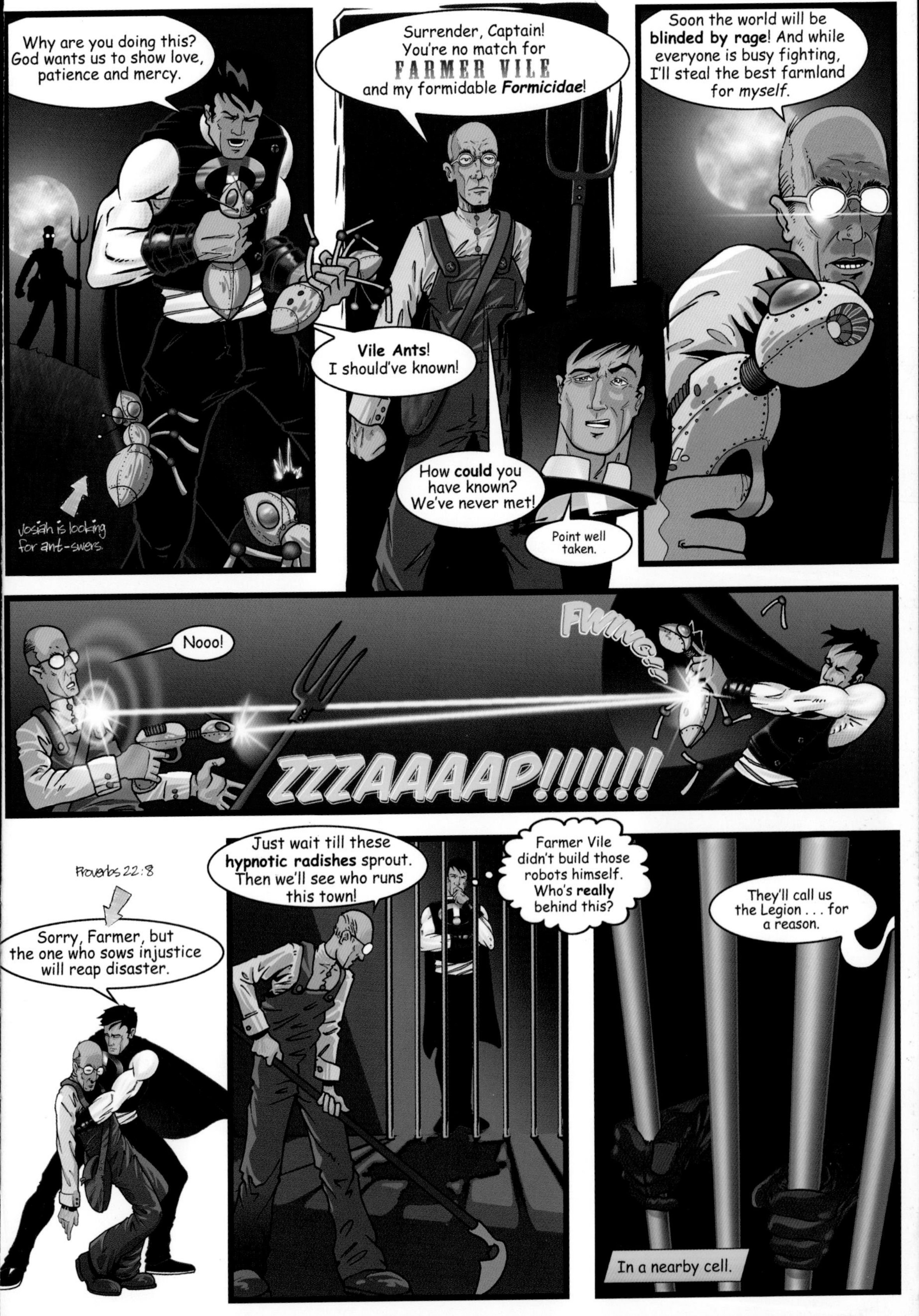
Why are you doing this? God wants us to show love, patience and mercy.
Surrender, Captain! You're no match for FARMER VILE and my formidable Formicidae!
Vile Ants! I should've known!
How could you have known? We've never met!
Point well taken.
Josiah is looking for ant-swers.
Soon the world will be blinded by rage! And while everyone is busy fighting, I'll steal the best farmland for myself.
Nooo!
FWING!!
ZZZAAAAAP!!!!!!
Proverbs 22:8
Sorry, Farmer, but the one who sows injustice will reap disaster.
Just wait till these hypnotic radishes sprout. Then we'll see who runs this town!
Farmer Vile didn't build those robots himself. Who's really behind this?
They'll call us the Legion . . . for a reason.
In a nearby cell.

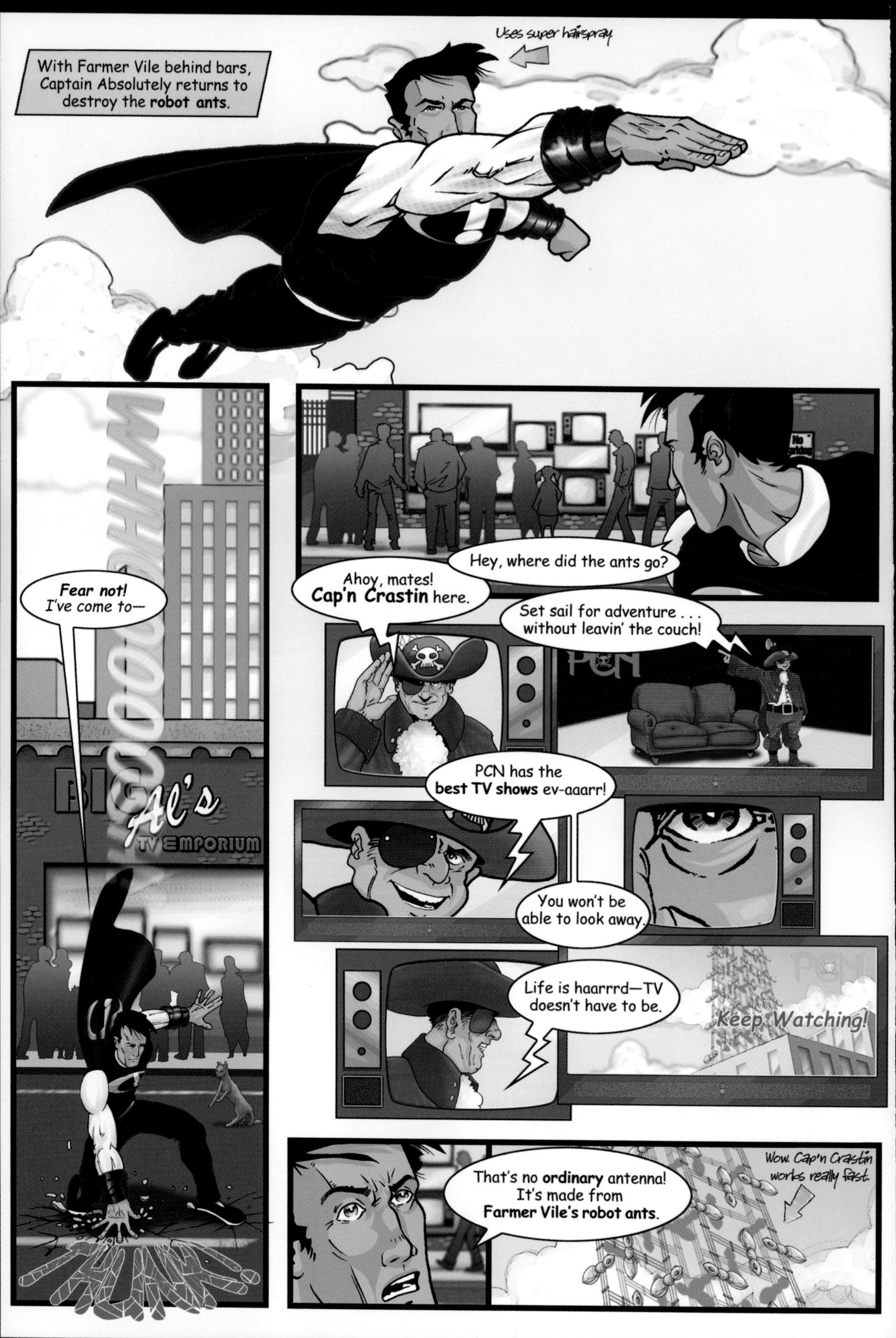
Uses super hairspray
With Farmer Vile behind bars, Captain Absolutely returns to destroy the **robot ants**.
BIG Al's TV EMPORIUM
Fear not! *I've come to—*
Hey, where did the ants go?
Ahoy, mates! **Cap'n Crastin** here.
Set sail for adventure . . . without leavin' the couch!
PCN
PCN has the **best TV shows** ev-aaarr!
You won't be able to look away.
Life is haarrrd—TV doesn't have to be.
Keep Watching!
That's no **ordinary** antenna! It's made from **Farmer Vile's robot ants**.
Wow. Cap'n Crastin works really fast.

Our hero follows the signal back to its source.

PCN Network—can I help you?

Yes. I need you to shut down your evil, **mind-controlling** broadcast!

I just answer the *phones*, sir.

Ye can't stop me, Captain Absolutely. People **love** PCN! They don't have to work, they don't have to think. *They just watch.*

Soon this will be a **pro-Crastin-nation!**

You've got it all wrong. TV should bring families together. It can be a tool to broadcast God's Truth.

If you won't change, then I'm taking you *off the air!*

FWOOOSH!!!

VARGH!

The LORD . . . is . . . my . . . strength!

Psalm 118:14

These villains keep trying to distract the town.

What are they hiding?

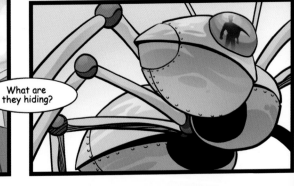

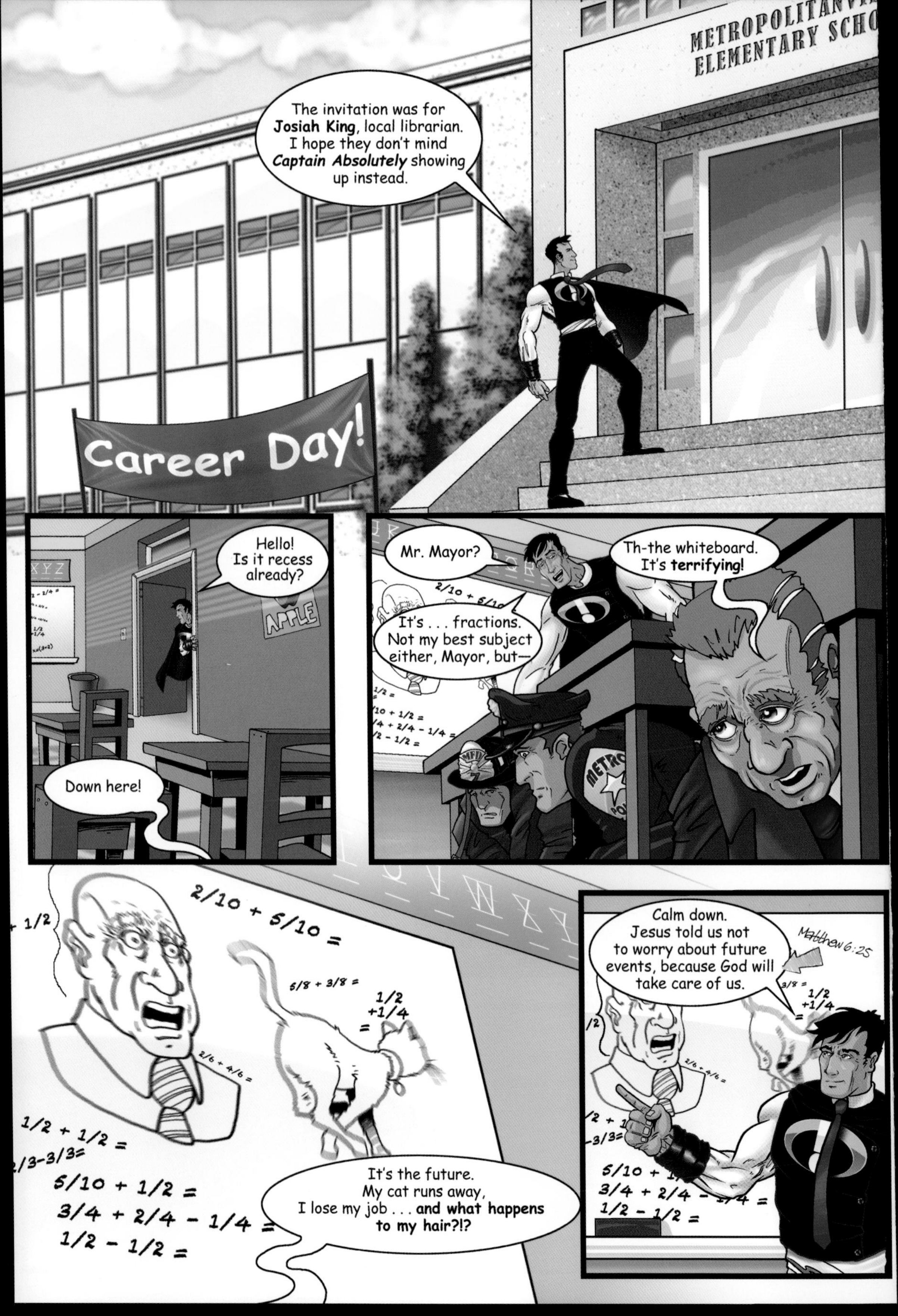
ELEMENTARY SCHO
The invitation was for **Josiah King**, local librarian. I hope they don't mind *Captain Absolutely* showing up instead.
Career Day!
Hello! Is it recess already?
APPLE
Down here!
Mr. Mayor?
Th-the whiteboard. It's **terrifying!**
It's . . . fractions. Not my best subject either, Mayor, but—
2/10 + 5/10 =
5/8 + 3/8 =
1/2 + 1/4 =
2/6 + 4/6 =
1/2 + 1/2 =
5/10 + 1/2 =
3/4 + 2/4 - 1/4 =
1/2 - 1/2 =
It's the future. My cat runs away, I lose my job . . . **and what happens to my hair?!?**
Calm down. Jesus told us not to worry about future events, because God will take care of us.
Matthew 6:25

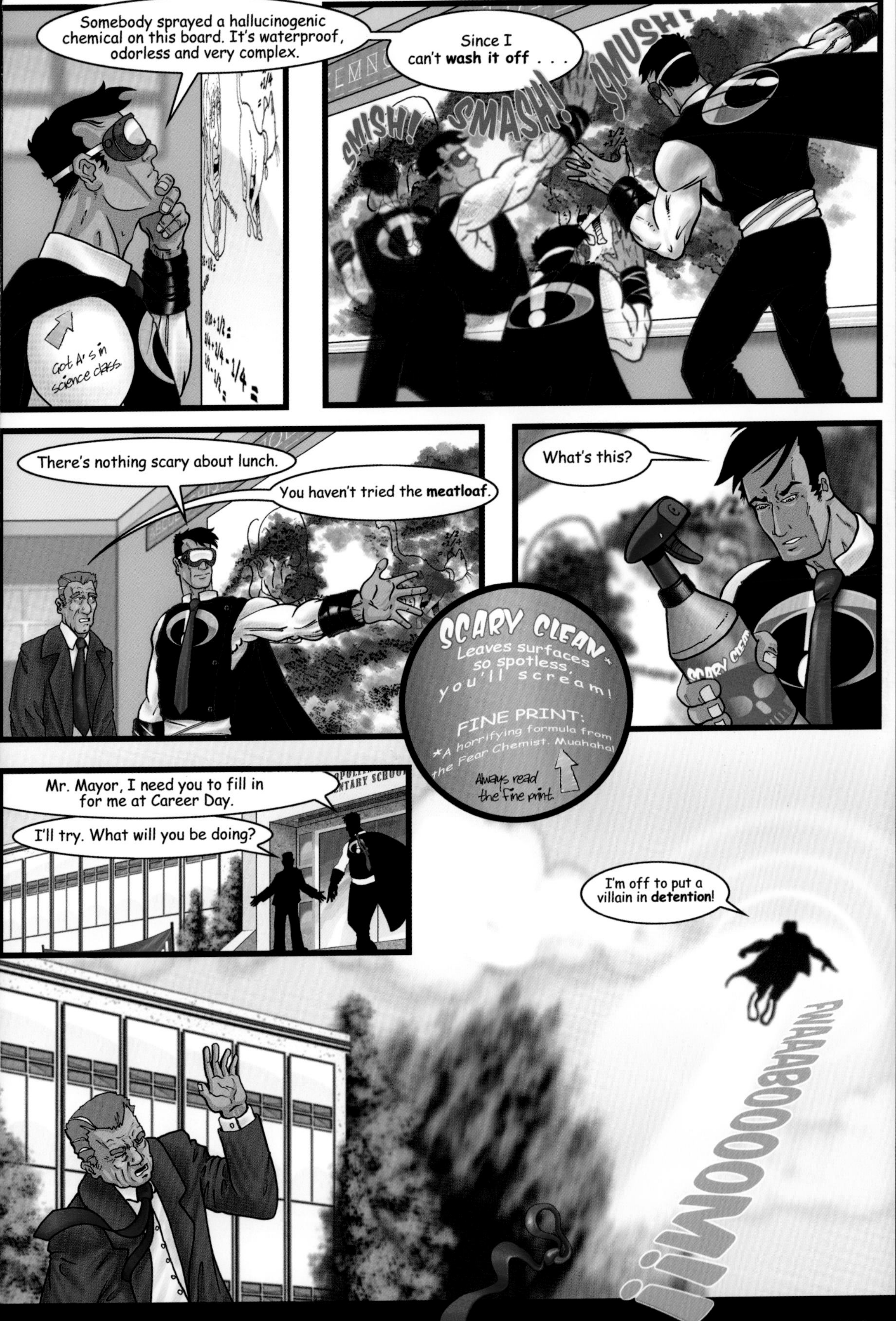
Somebody sprayed a hallucinogenic chemical on this board. It's waterproof, odorless and very complex.
Got A's in science class
Since I can't wash it off . . .
SMISH!
SMASH!
SMUSH!
There's nothing scary about lunch.
You haven't tried the meatloaf.
What's this?
SCARY CLEAN
Leaves surfaces* so spotless, you'll scream!
FINE PRINT:
*A horrifying formula from the Fear Chemist. Muahaha!
Always read the fine print.
Mr. Mayor, I need you to fill in for me at Career Day.
I'll try. What will you be doing?
I'm off to put a villain in detention!
FWAAABOOOOOM!!!

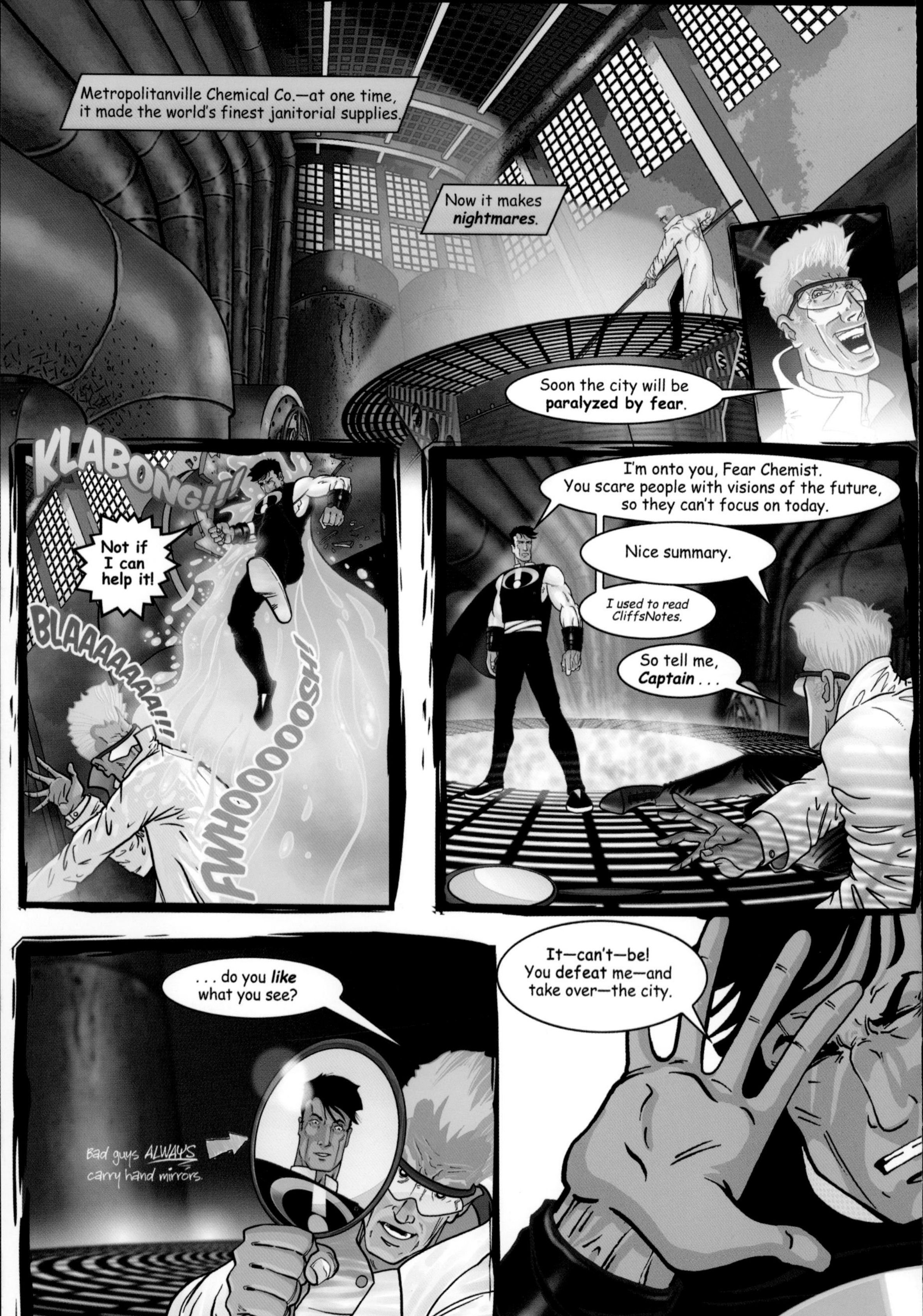

Metropolitanville Chemical Co.—at one time, it made the world's finest janitorial supplies.
Now it makes *nightmares*.
Soon the city will be **paralyzed by fear**.
KLABONG!!!
Not if I can help it!
BLAAAAAAAA!!!
FWHOOOOOOSH!
I'm onto you, Fear Chemist. You scare people with visions of the future, so they can't focus on today.
Nice summary.
I used to read CliffsNotes.
So tell me, ***Captain*** . . .
. . . do you ***like*** what you see?
Bad guys ALWAYS carry hand mirrors.
It—can't—be! You defeat me—and take over—the city.

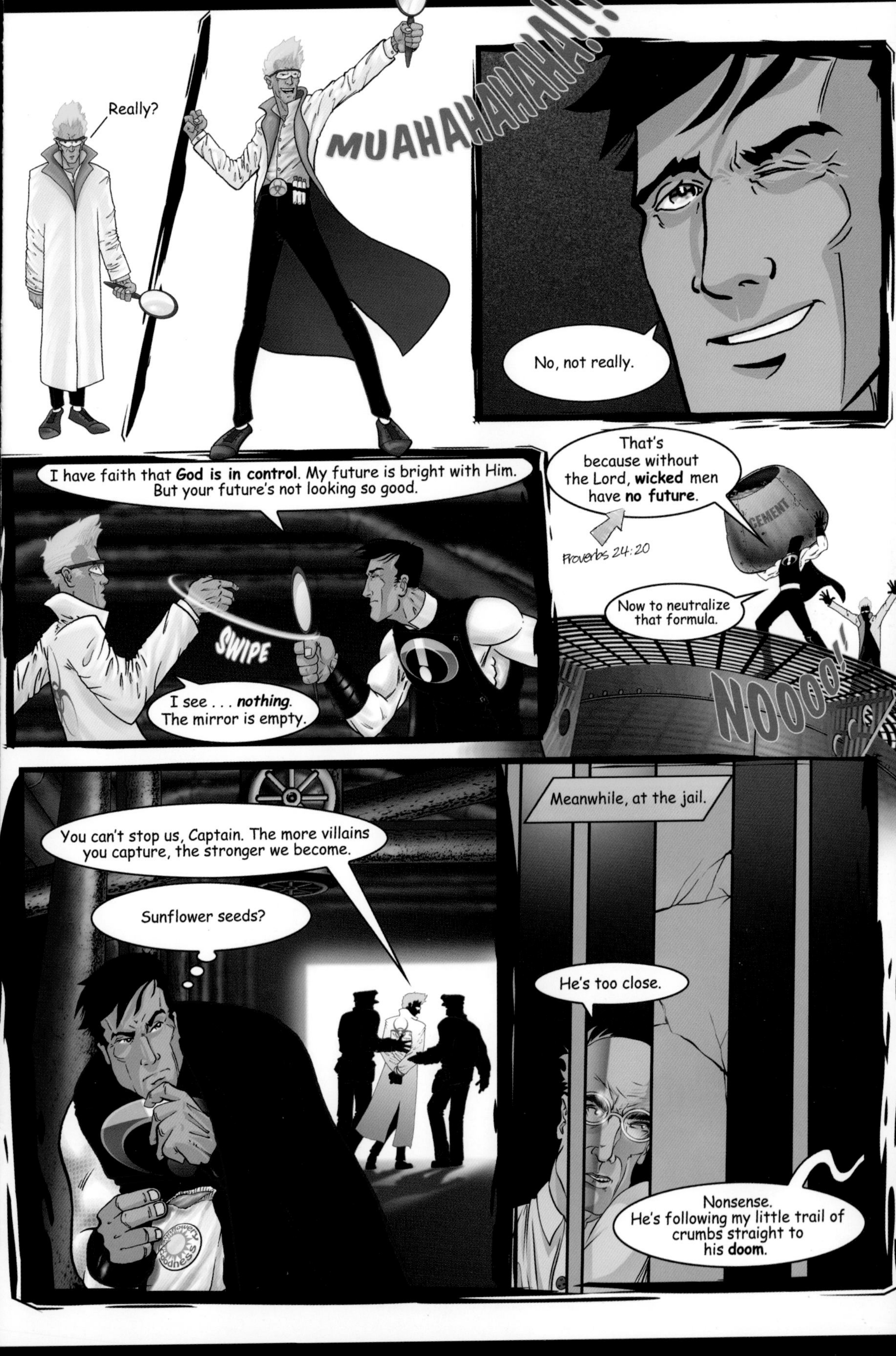

Really?
MUAHAHAHAHA!!!
No, not really.
I have faith that **God is in control**. My future is bright with Him. But your future's not looking so good.
SWIPE
I see . . . ***nothing***. The mirror is empty.
That's because without the Lord, **wicked** men have **no future**.
Proverbs 24:20
CEMENT
Now to neutralize that formula.
NOOOO!
You can't stop us, Captain. The more villains you capture, the stronger we become.
Sunflower seeds?
Meanwhile, at the jail.
He's too close.
Nonsense. He's following my little trail of crumbs straight to his **doom**.

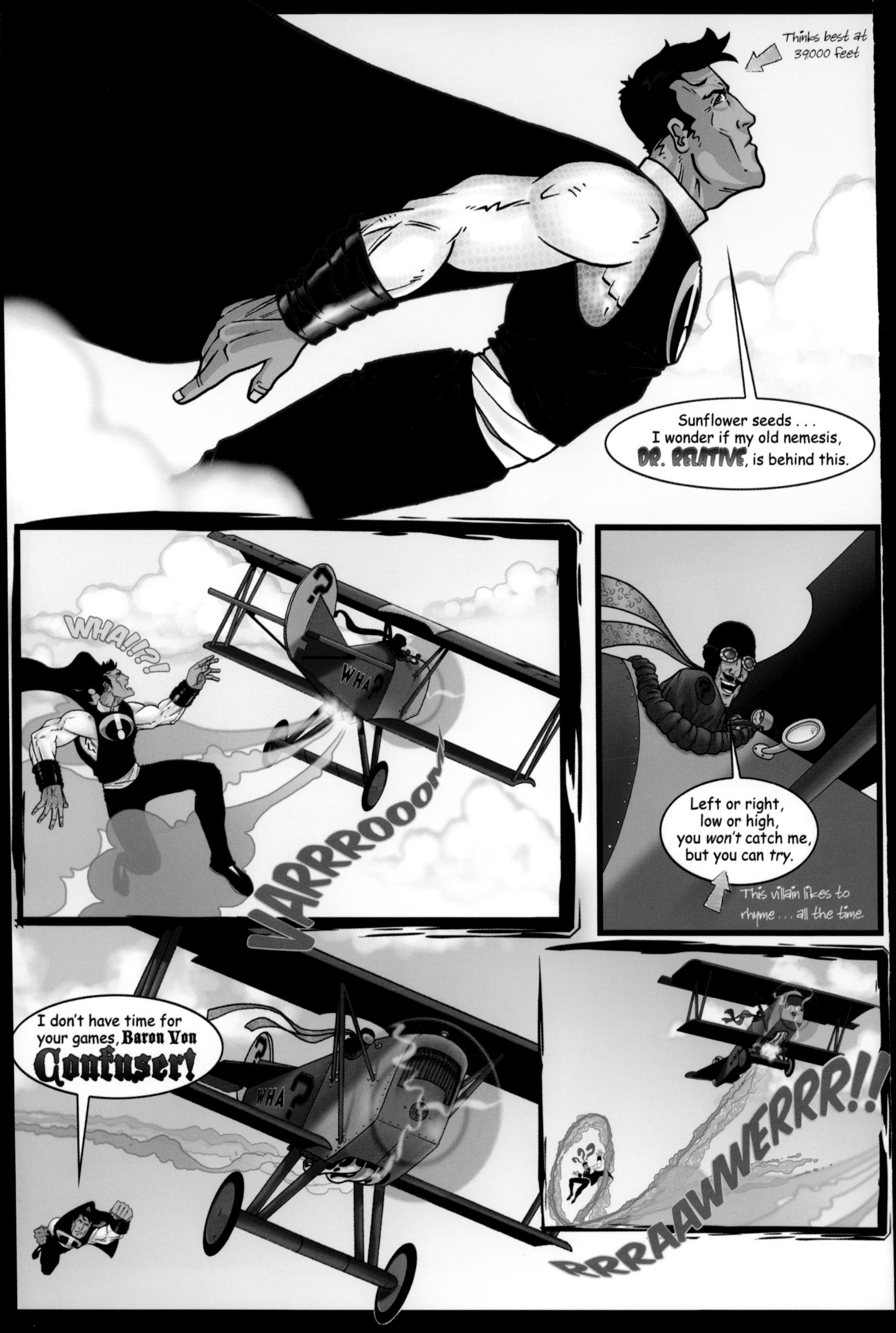
Thinks best at 39,000 feet
Sunflower seeds . . . I wonder if my old nemesis, DR. RELATIVE, is behind this.
WHA!!?!
WHA?
VARROOOOM
Left or right, low or high, you *won't* catch me, but you can *try*.
This villain likes to rhyme . . . all the time.
I don't have time for your games, Baron Von Confuser!
WHA?
RRRAAWWERRR!!

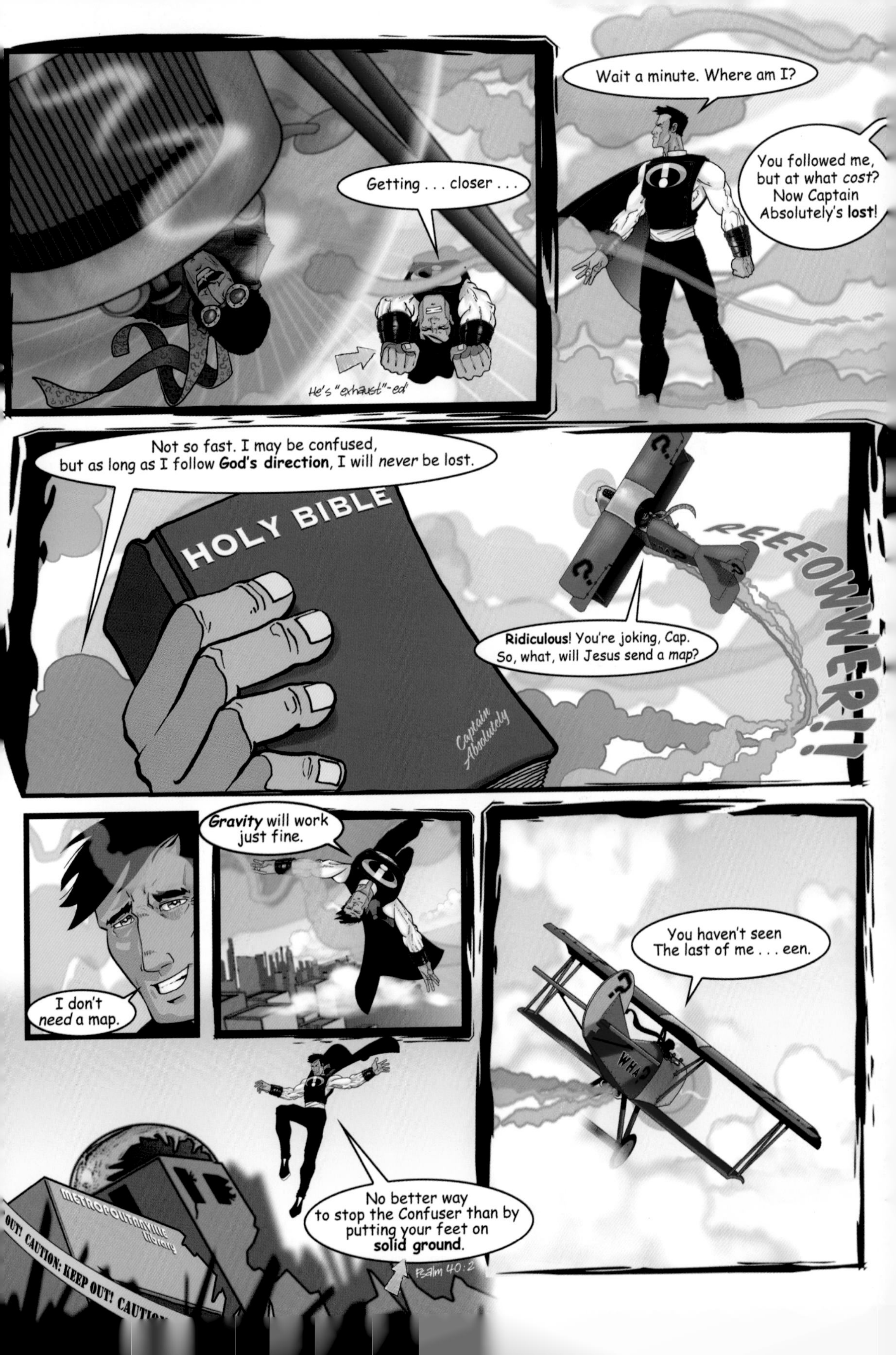
Getting . . . closer . . .
He's "exhaust"-ed
Wait a minute. Where am I?
You followed me, but at what *cost*? Now Captain Absolutely's **lost**!
Not so fast. I may be confused, but as long as I follow **God's direction**, I will *never* be lost.
HOLY BIBLE
Captain Absolutely
REEEOWWER!!
Ridiculous! You're joking, Cap. So, what, will Jesus send a *map*?
I don't *need* a map.
Gravity will work just fine.
You haven't seen The last of me . . . een.
WHA?
No better way to stop the Confuser than by putting your feet on **solid ground**.
Psalm 40:2
METROPOLITANVILLE library
OUT! CAUTION: KEEP OUT! CAUTION

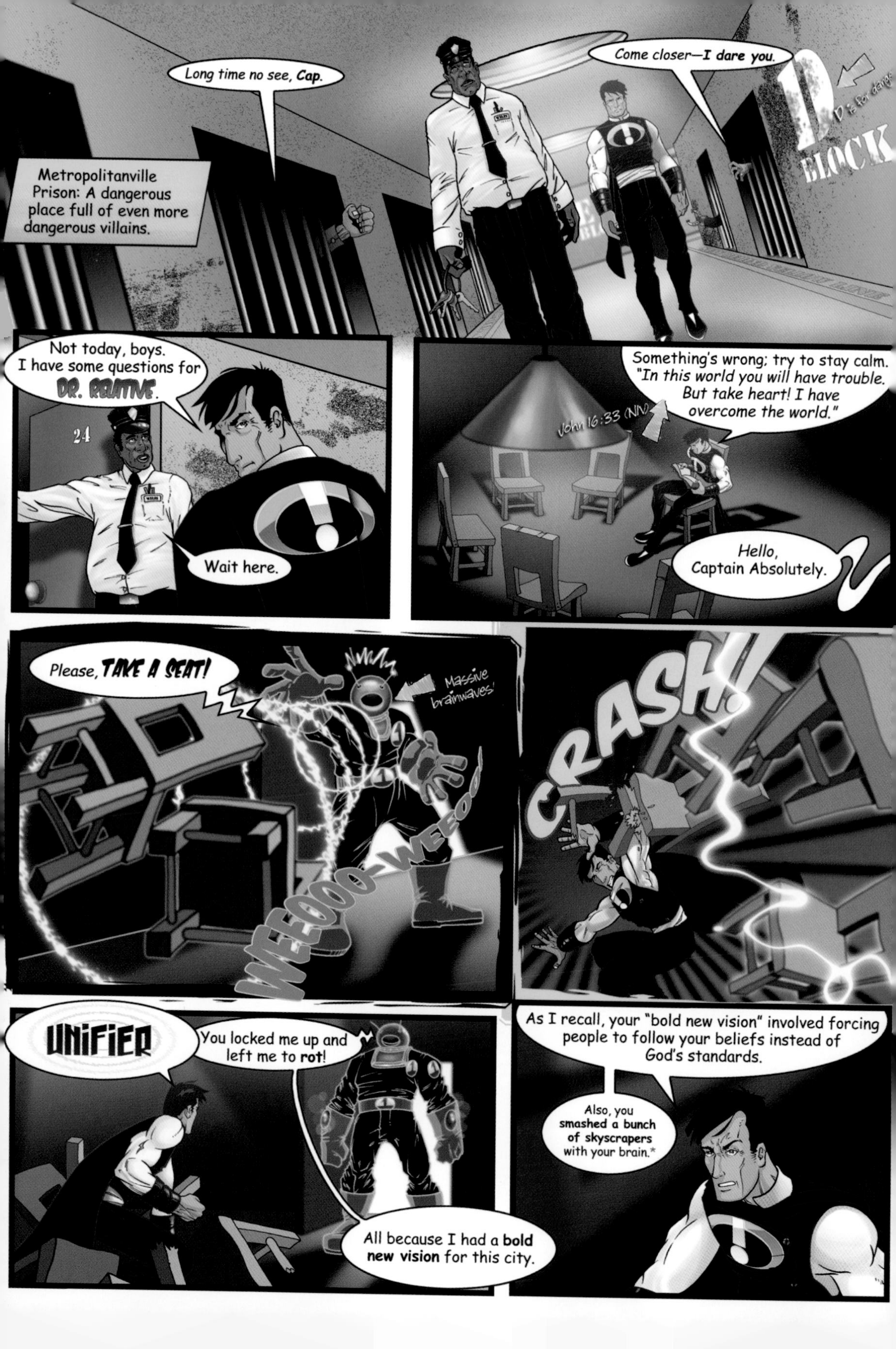

Metropolitanville Prison: A dangerous place full of even more dangerous villains.
Long time no see, **Cap.**
Come closer—**I dare you.**
D
D is for dange
BLOCK
Not today, boys. I have some questions for **DR. RELATIVE.**
24
Wait here.
Something's wrong; try to stay calm. *"In this world you will have trouble. But take heart! I have overcome the world."*
John 16:33 (NIV)
Hello, Captain Absolutely.
Please, **TAKE A SEAT!**
Massive brainwaves!
WEEOOO-WEEOOO!
CRASH!
UNIFIER
You locked me up and left me to **rot!**
All because I had a **bold new vision** for this city.
As I recall, your "bold new vision" involved forcing people to follow your beliefs instead of God's standards.
Also, you **smashed a bunch of skyscrapers** with your brain.*

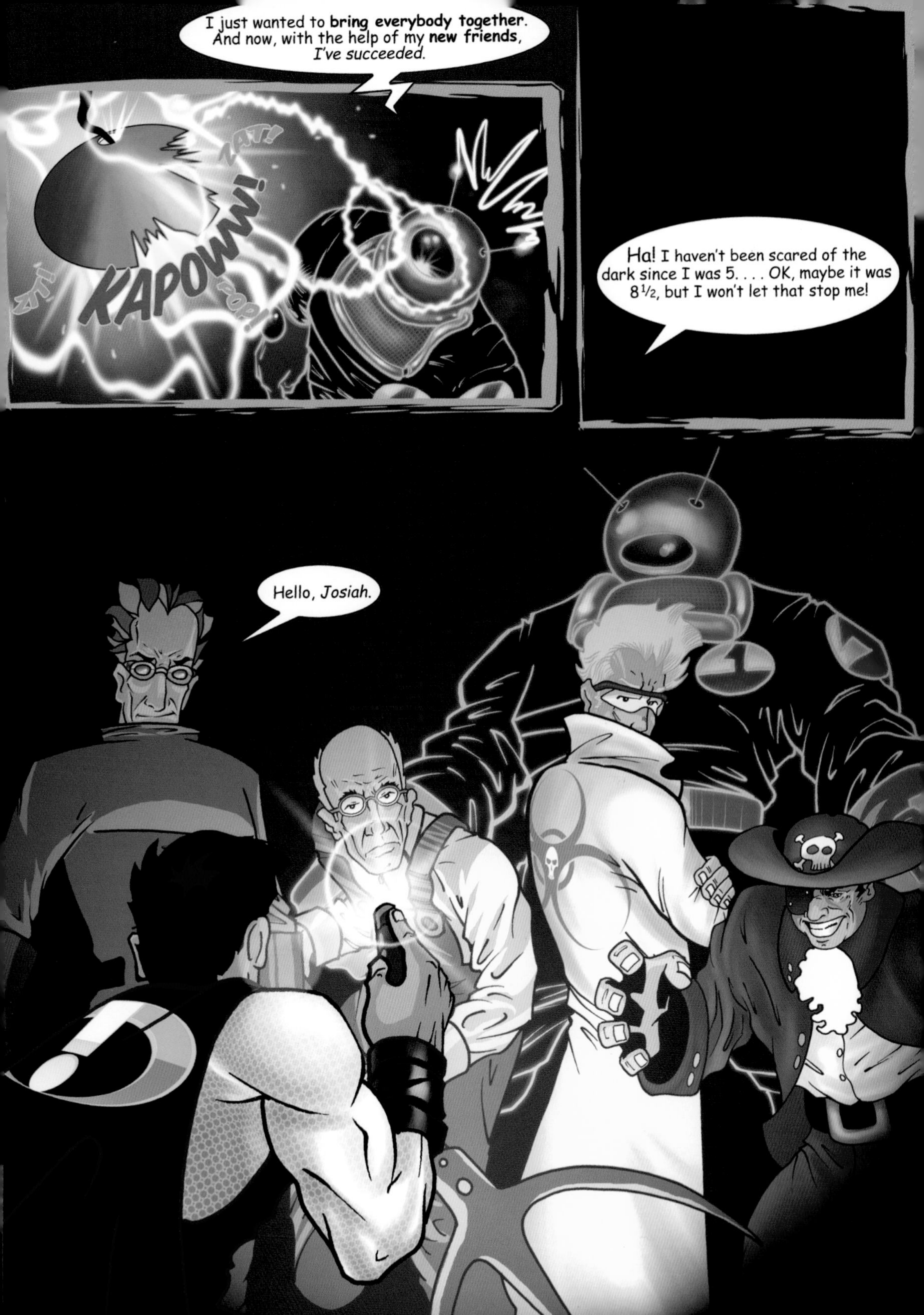
I just wanted to **bring everybody together**. And now, with the help of my **new friends**, *I've succeeded.*
ZAT!
KAPOWW!
POP!
Ha! I haven't been scared of the dark since I was 5. . . . OK, maybe it was 8½, but I won't let that stop me!
Hello, *Josiah*.

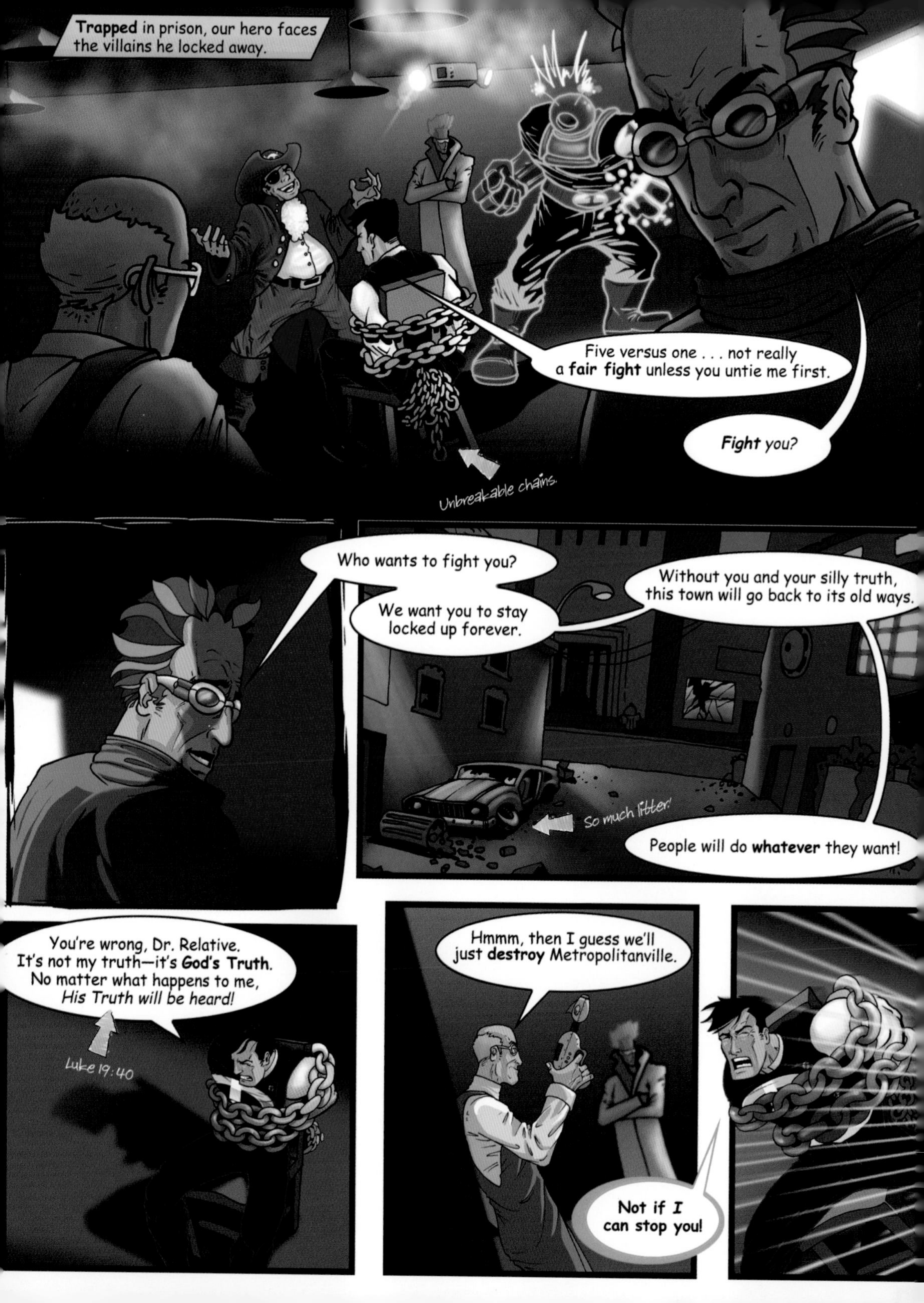

Trapped in prison, our hero faces the villains he locked away.
Five versus one . . . not really a **fair fight** unless you untie me first.
Fight *you?*
Unbreakable chains.
Who wants to fight you?
We want you to stay locked up forever.
Without you and your silly truth, this town will go back to its old ways.
So much litter!
People will do **whatever** they want!
You're wrong, Dr. Relative. It's not my truth—it's **God's Truth**. No matter what happens to me, *His Truth will be heard!*
Luke 19:40
Hmmm, then I guess we'll just **destroy** Metropolitanville.
Not if *I* can stop you!

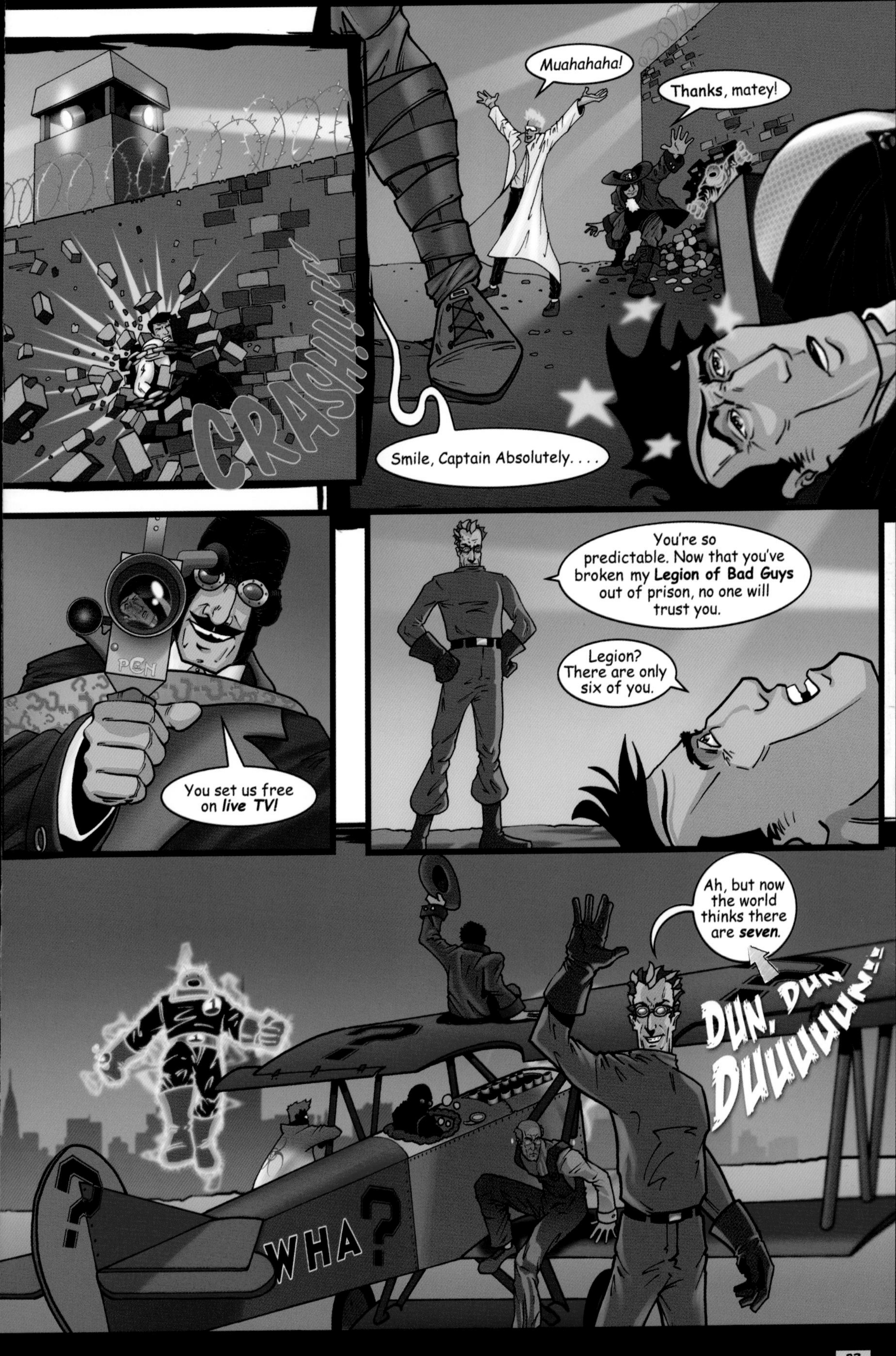

CRASH!!!!
Muahahaha!
Thanks, matey!
Smile, Captain Absolutely. . . .
You set us free on *live TV!*
You're so predictable. Now that you've broken my **Legion of Bad Guys** out of prison, no one will trust you.
Legion? There are only six of you.
Ah, but now the world thinks there are *seven*.
DUN, DUN DUUUUUN!!
WHA?

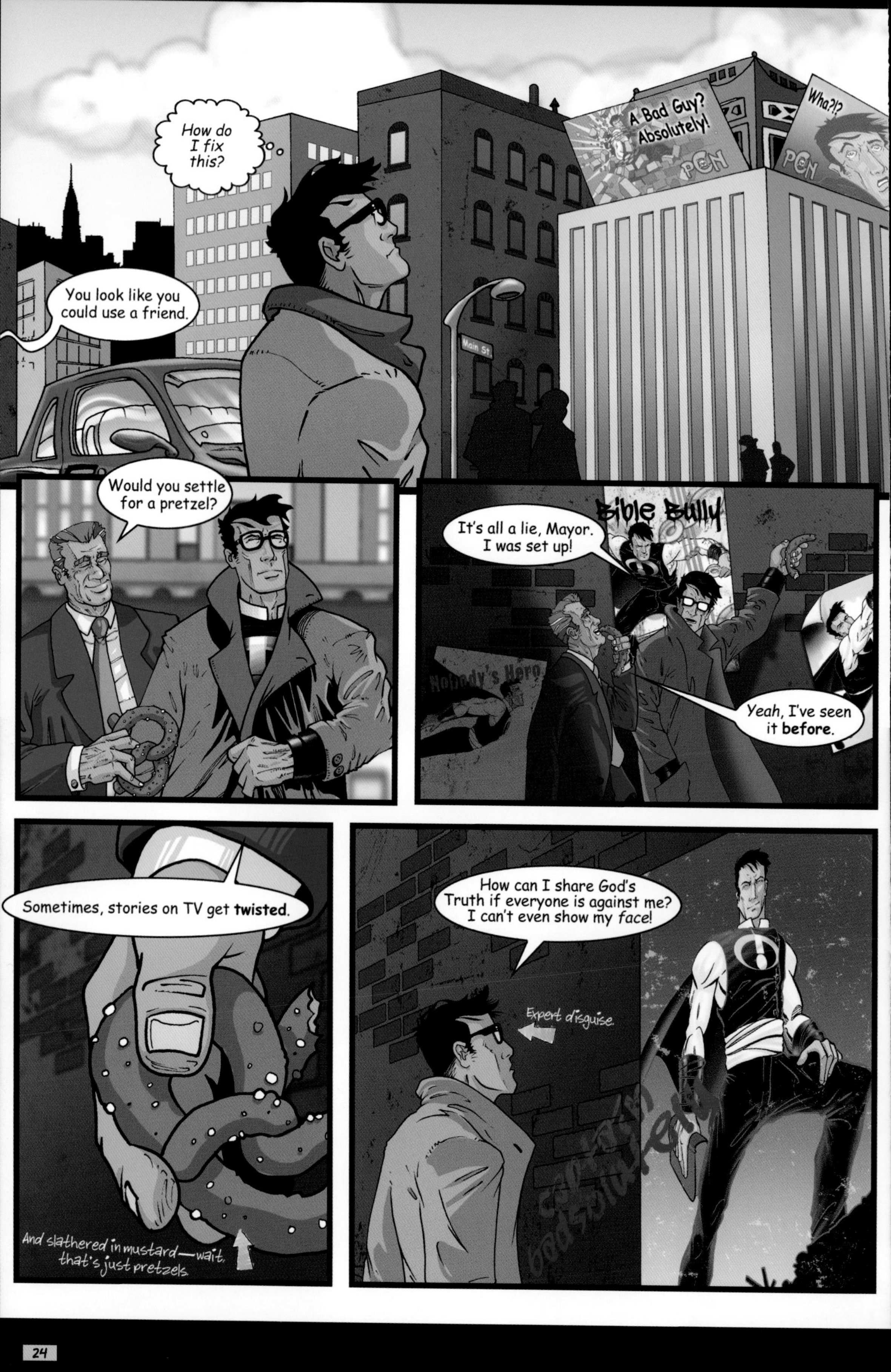
How do I fix this?
A Bad Guy? Absolutely!
PCN
Wha?!?
PCN
Main St.
You look like you could use a friend.
Would you settle for a pretzel?
Bible Bully
It's all a lie, Mayor. I was set up!
Nobody's Hero
Yeah, I've seen it **before**.
Sometimes, stories on TV get **twisted**.
And slathered in mustard—wait, that's just pretzels.
How can I share God's Truth if everyone is against me? I can't even show my *face*!
Expert disguise.

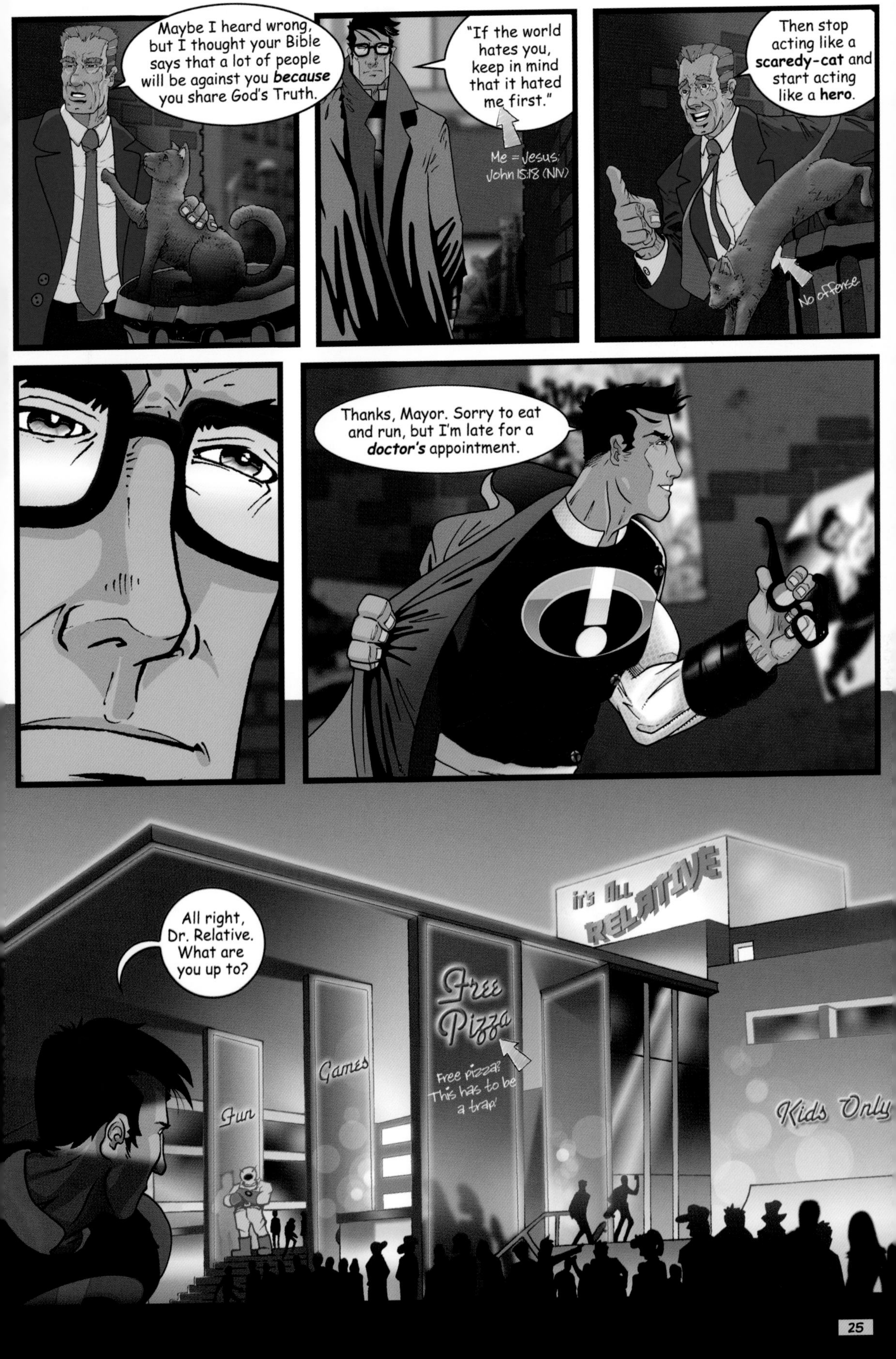
Maybe I heard wrong, but I thought your Bible says that a lot of people will be against you **because** you share God's Truth.
"If the world hates you, keep in mind that it hated me first."
Me = Jesus; John 15:18 (NIV)
Then stop acting like a **scaredy-cat** and start acting like a **hero**.
No offense
Thanks, Mayor. Sorry to eat and run, but I'm late for a ***doctor's*** appointment.
It's All Relative
All right, Dr. Relative. What are you up to?
Free Pizza
Free pizza? This has to be a trap!
Games
Fun
Kids Only

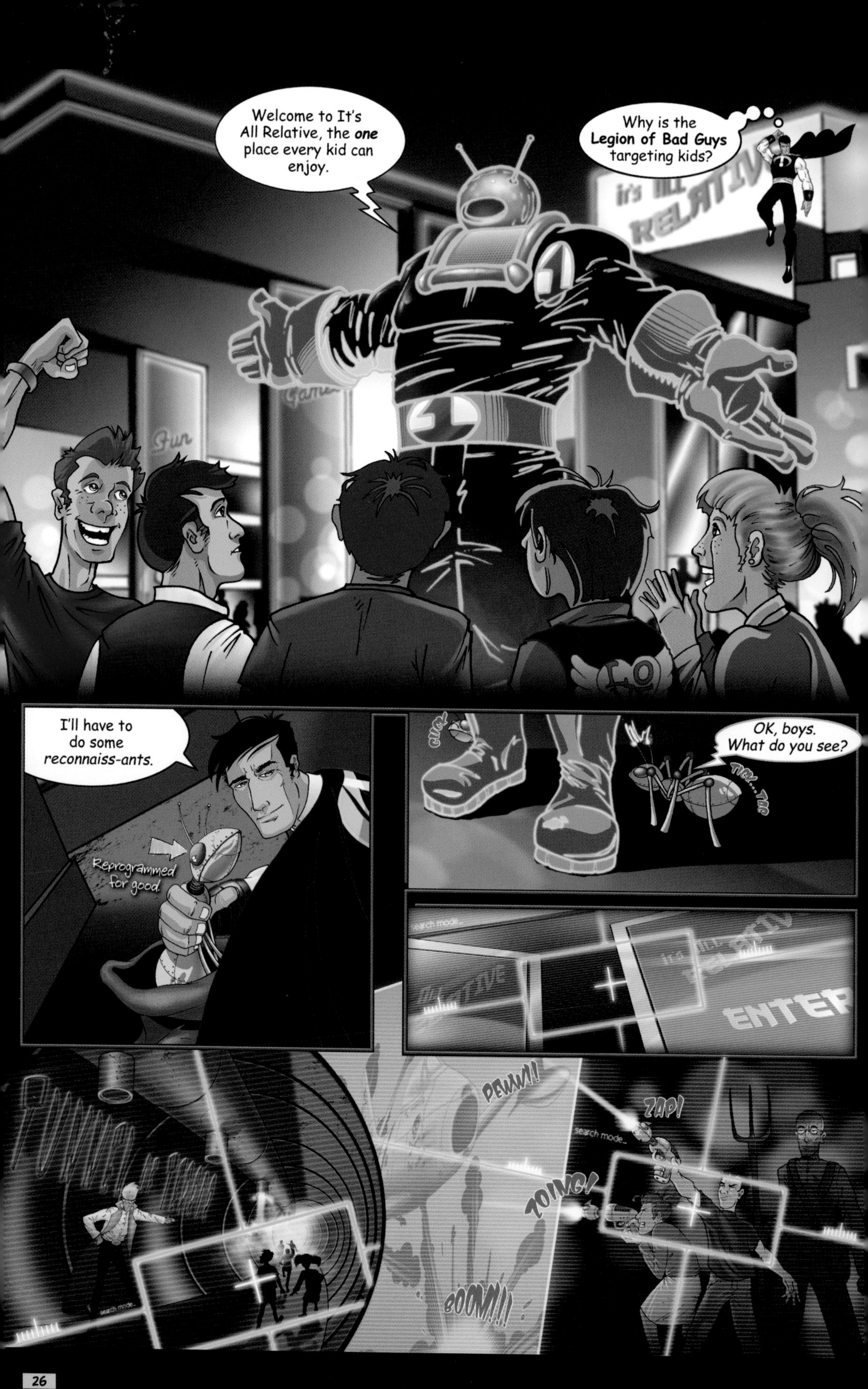
Welcome to It's All Relative, the **one** place every kid can enjoy.
Why is the **Legion of Bad Guys** targeting kids?
It's All Relative
I'll have to do some reconnaiss-ants.
Reprogrammed for good.
CLICK
OK, boys. What do you see?
TICK...TAC
search mode_
ENTER
PEWW!!
ZAP!
search mode_
ZOING!
BOOM!!!
search mode_

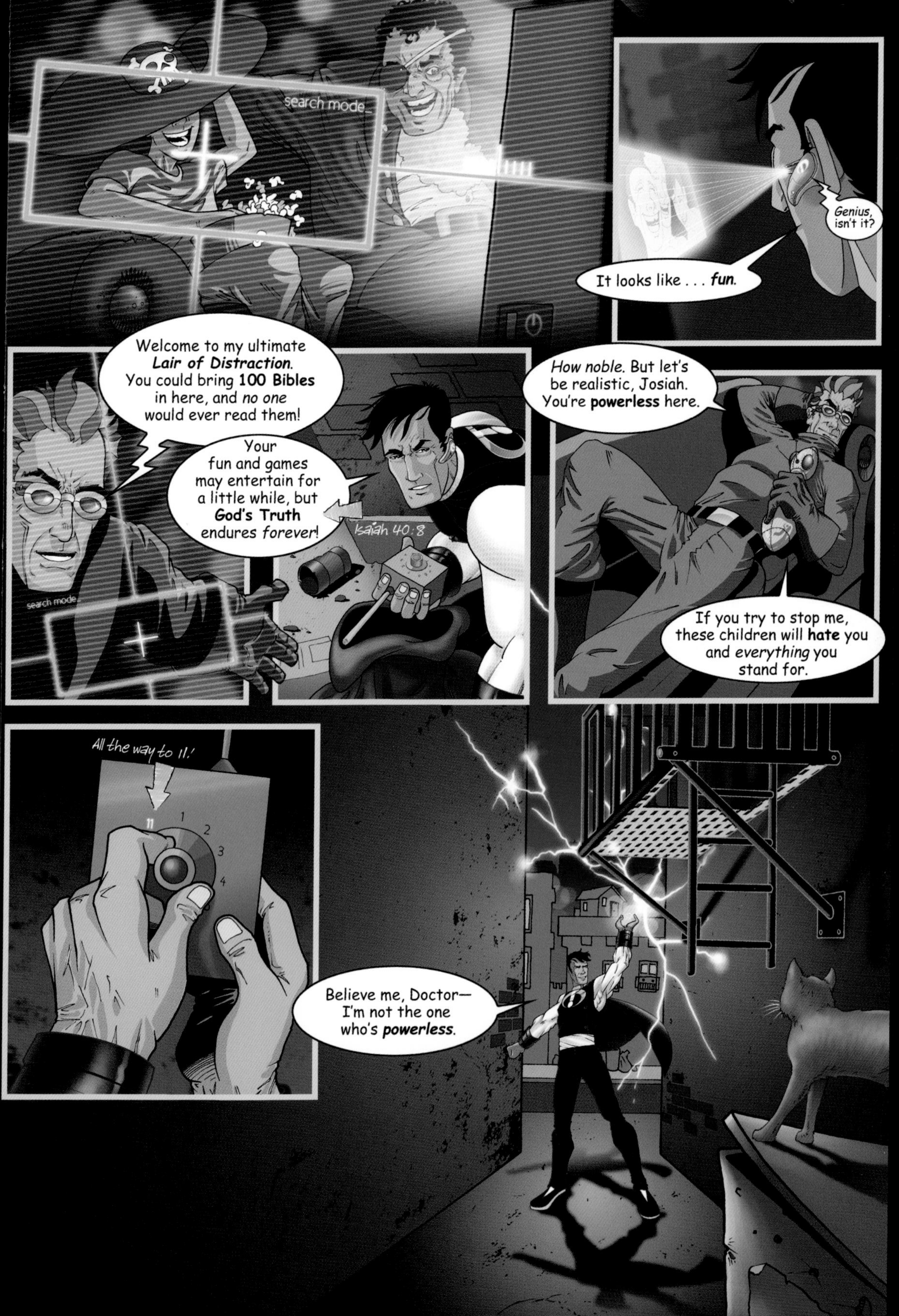
search mode_
Genius, isn't it?
It looks like . . . *fun*.
Welcome to my ultimate ***Lair of Distraction***. You could bring **100 Bibles** in here, and *no one* would ever read them!
search mode_
Your fun and games may entertain for a little while, but **God's Truth** endures *forever*!
Isaiah 40:8
How noble. But let's be realistic, Josiah. You're **powerless** here.
If you try to stop me, these children will **hate** you and *everything* you stand for.
All the way to 11!
11
1
2
3
4
Believe me, Doctor— I'm not the one who's ***powerless***.

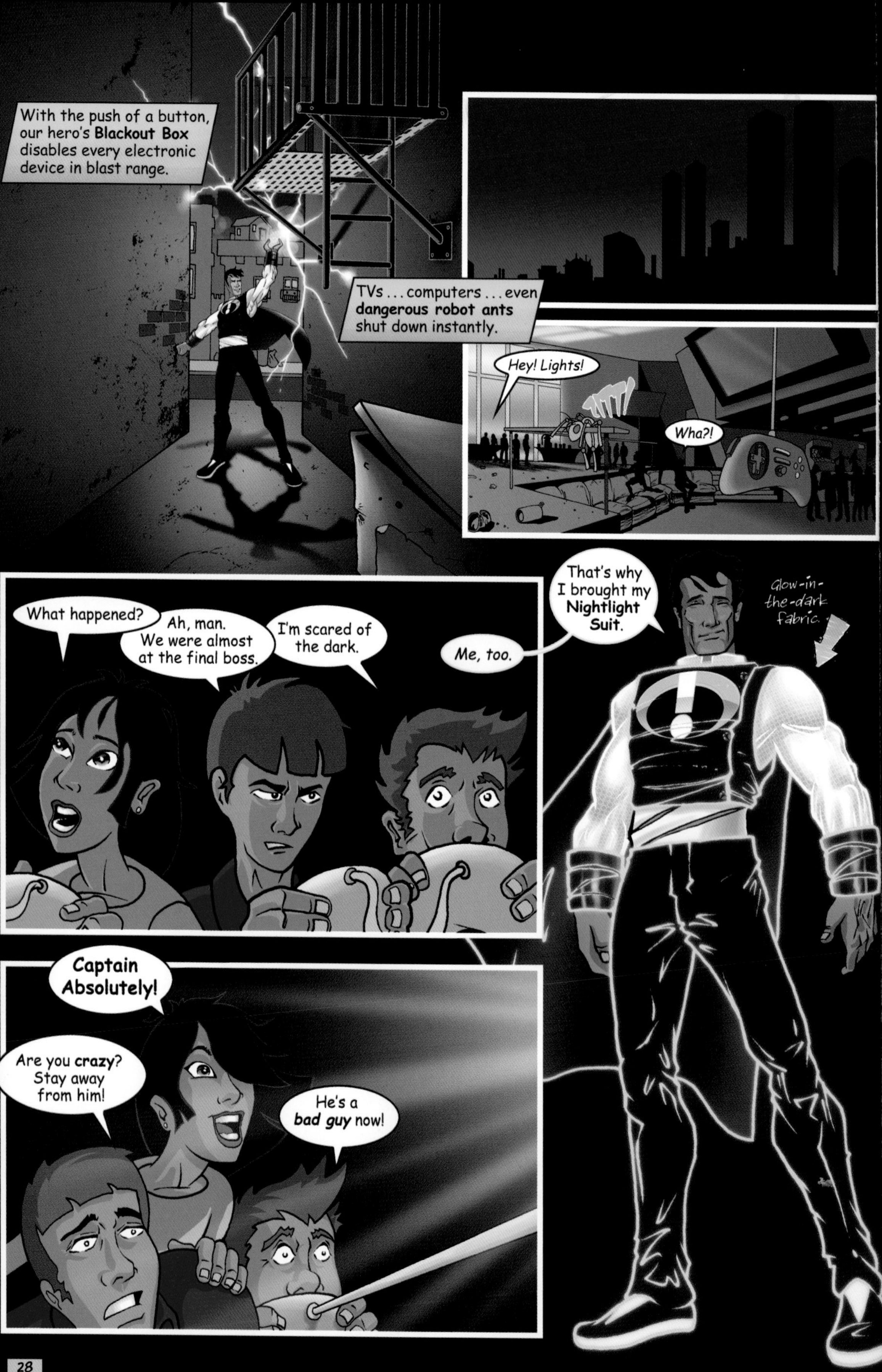

With the push of a button, our hero's **Blackout Box** disables every electronic device in blast range.
TVs . . . computers . . . even **dangerous robot ants** shut down instantly.
Hey! Lights!
Wha?!
What happened?
Ah, man. We were almost at the final boss.
I'm scared of the dark.
Me, too.
That's why I brought my **Nightlight Suit**.
Glow-in-the-dark fabric.
Captain Absolutely!
Are you **crazy**? Stay away from him!
He's a ***bad guy*** now!

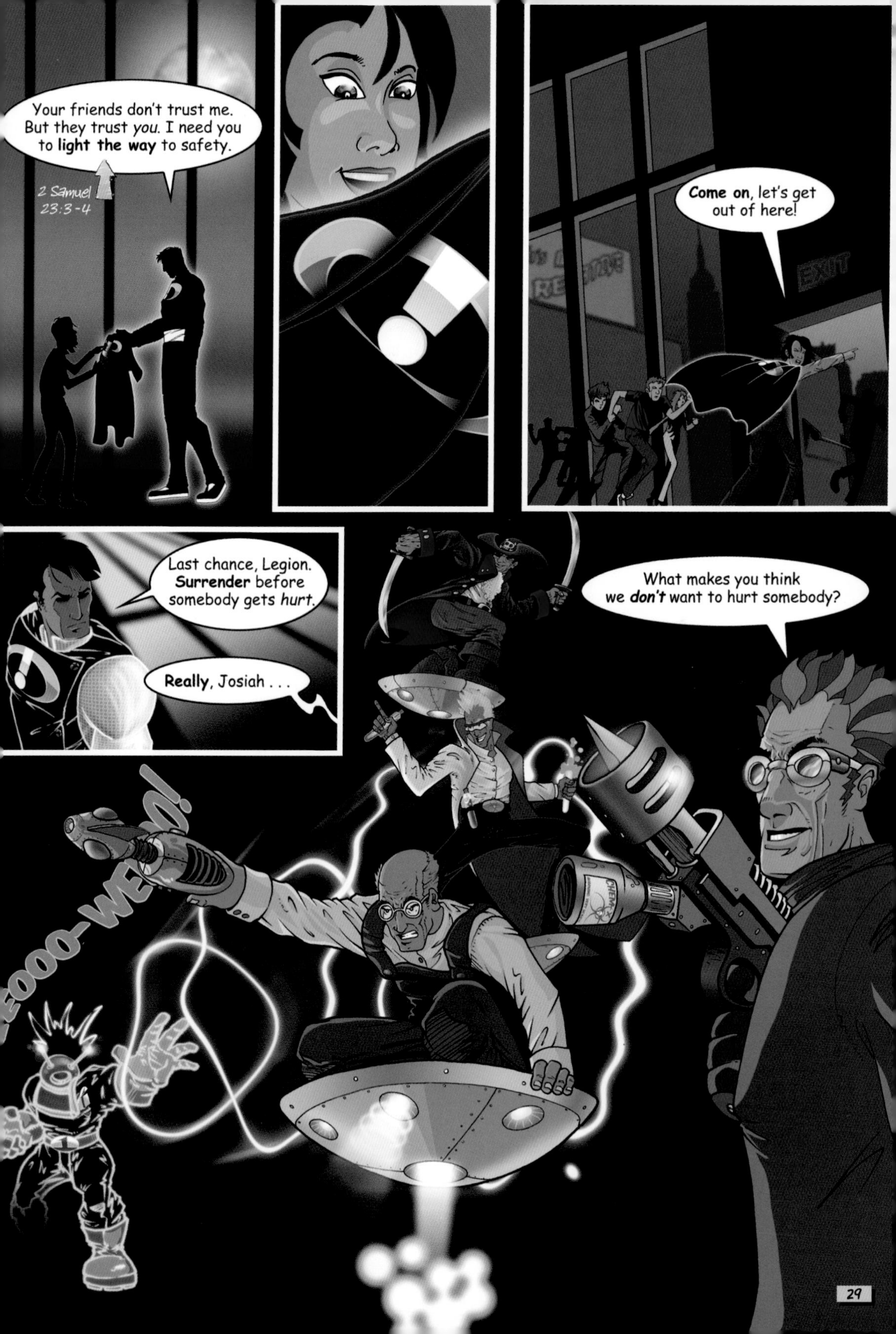
Your friends don't trust me. But they trust *you*. I need you to **light the way** to safety.
2 Samuel 23:3-4
Come on, let's get out of here!
EXIT
Last chance, Legion. **Surrender** before somebody gets *hurt*.
Really, Josiah . . .
What makes you think we ***don't*** want to hurt somebody?

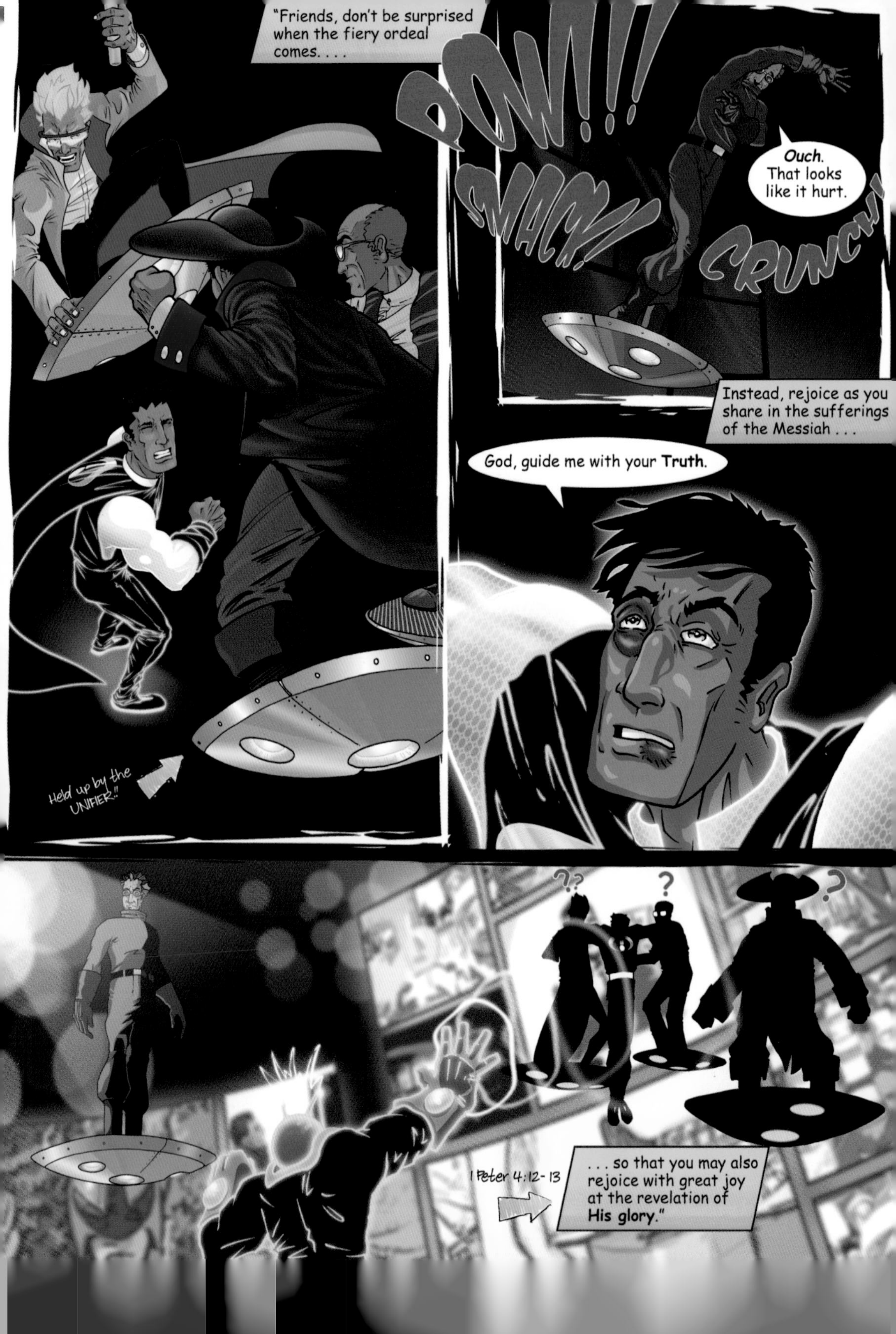
"Friends, don't be surprised when the fiery ordeal comes. . . .
POW!!!
SMACK!!
CRUNCH!
Ouch. That looks like it hurt.
Held up by the UNIFIER!!
Instead, rejoice as you share in the sufferings of the Messiah . . .
God, guide me with your **Truth**.
??
?
?
1 Peter 4:12-13
. . . so that you may also rejoice with great joy at the revelation of **His glory**."

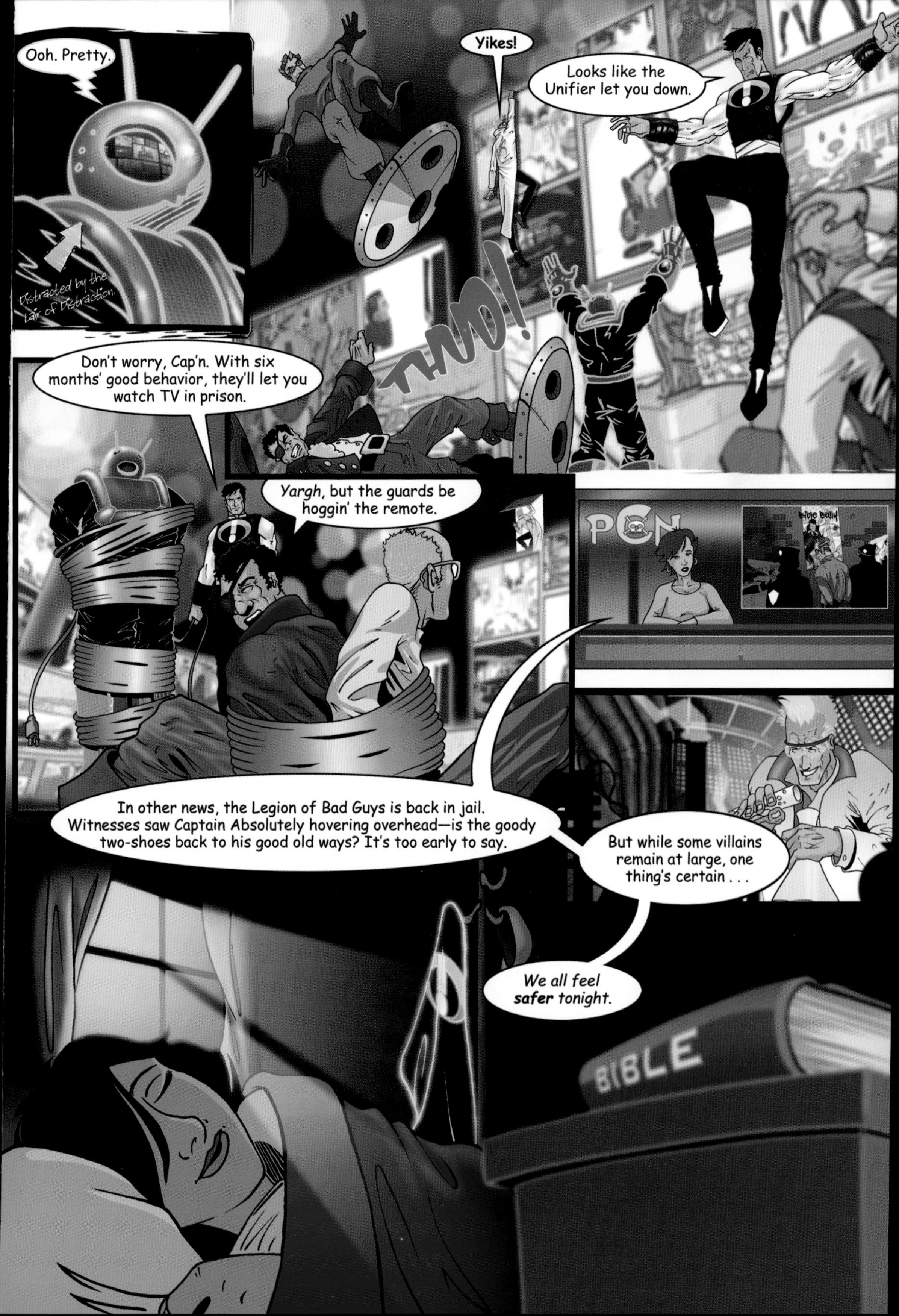
Ooh. Pretty.
Distracted by the Lair of Distraction.
Yikes!
Looks like the Unifier let you down.
THUD!
Don't worry, Cap'n. With six months' good behavior, they'll let you watch TV in prison.
Yargh, but the guards be hoggin' the remote.
PCN
In other news, the Legion of Bad Guys is back in jail. Witnesses saw Captain Absolutely hovering overhead—is the goody two-shoes back to his good old ways? It's too early to say.
But while some villains remain at large, one thing's certain . . .
We all feel ***safer*** *tonight.*
BIBLE

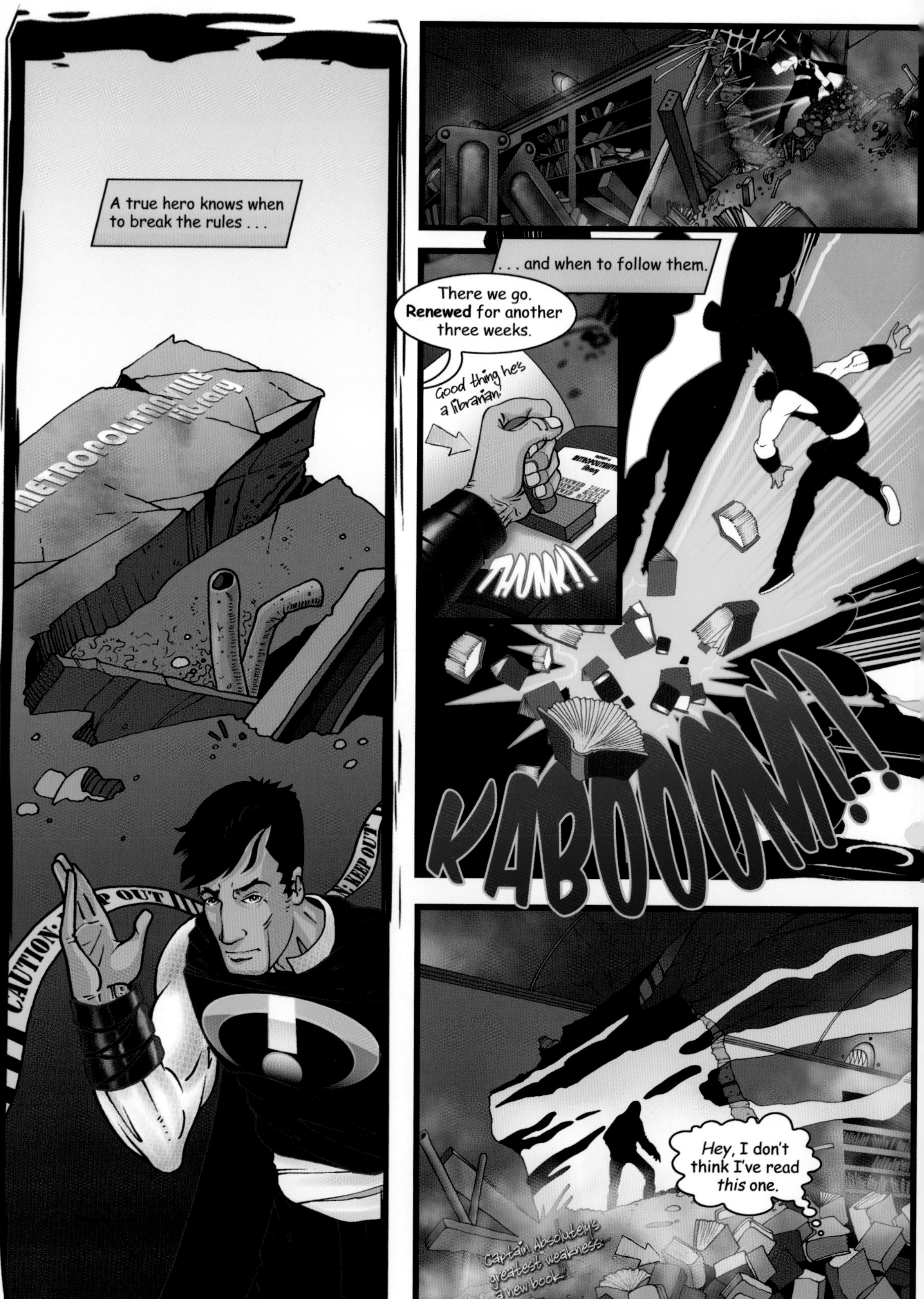

A true hero knows when to break the rules . . .
METROPOLITANVILLE library
CAUTION:
OUT
KEEP OUT
. . . and when to follow them.
There we go. **Renewed** for another three weeks.
Good thing he's a librarian!
THUNK!!
KABOOOM!!
Hey, I don't think I've read *this* one.
Captain Absolutely's greatest weakness... a new book!

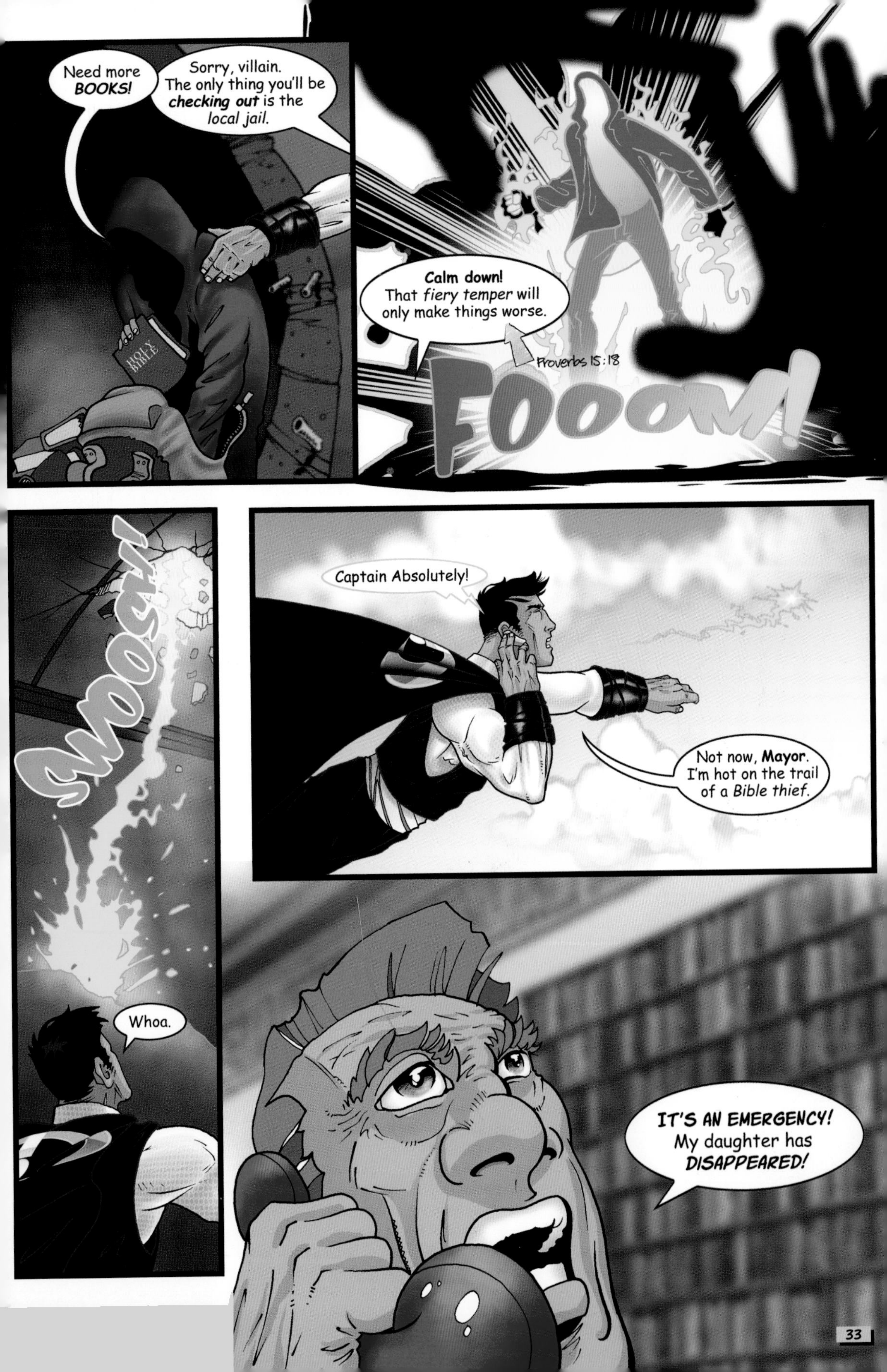
Need more BOOKS!
Sorry, villain. The only thing you'll be checking out is the local jail.
Calm down! That fiery temper will only make things worse.
Proverbs 15:18
FOOOM!
SWOOSH!
Whoa.
Captain Absolutely!
Not now, Mayor. I'm hot on the trail of a Bible thief.
IT'S AN EMERGENCY! My daughter has DISAPPEARED!

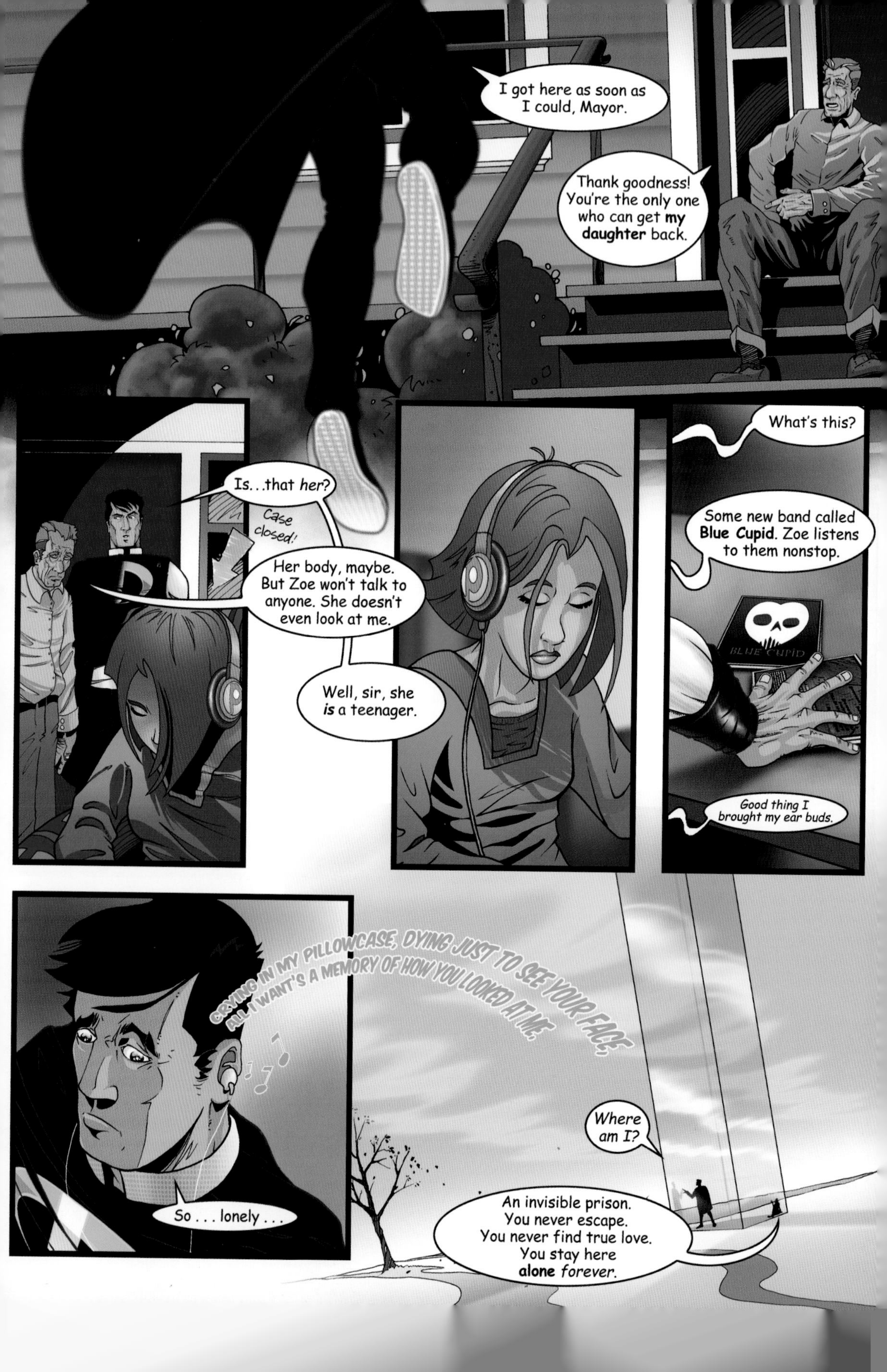
I got here as soon as I could, Mayor.
Thank goodness! You're the only one who can get **my daughter** back.
Is...that *her*?
Case closed!
Her body, maybe. But Zoe won't talk to anyone. She doesn't even look at me.
Well, sir, she *is* a teenager.
What's this?
Some new band called **Blue Cupid**. Zoe listens to them nonstop.
BLUE CUPID
Good thing I brought my ear buds.
CRYING IN MY PILLOWCASE, DYING JUST TO SEE YOUR FACE.
ALL I WANT'S A MEMORY OF HOW YOU LOOKED AT ME.
So . . . lonely . . .
Where am I?
An invisible prison. You never escape. You never find true love. You stay here **alone** *forever*.

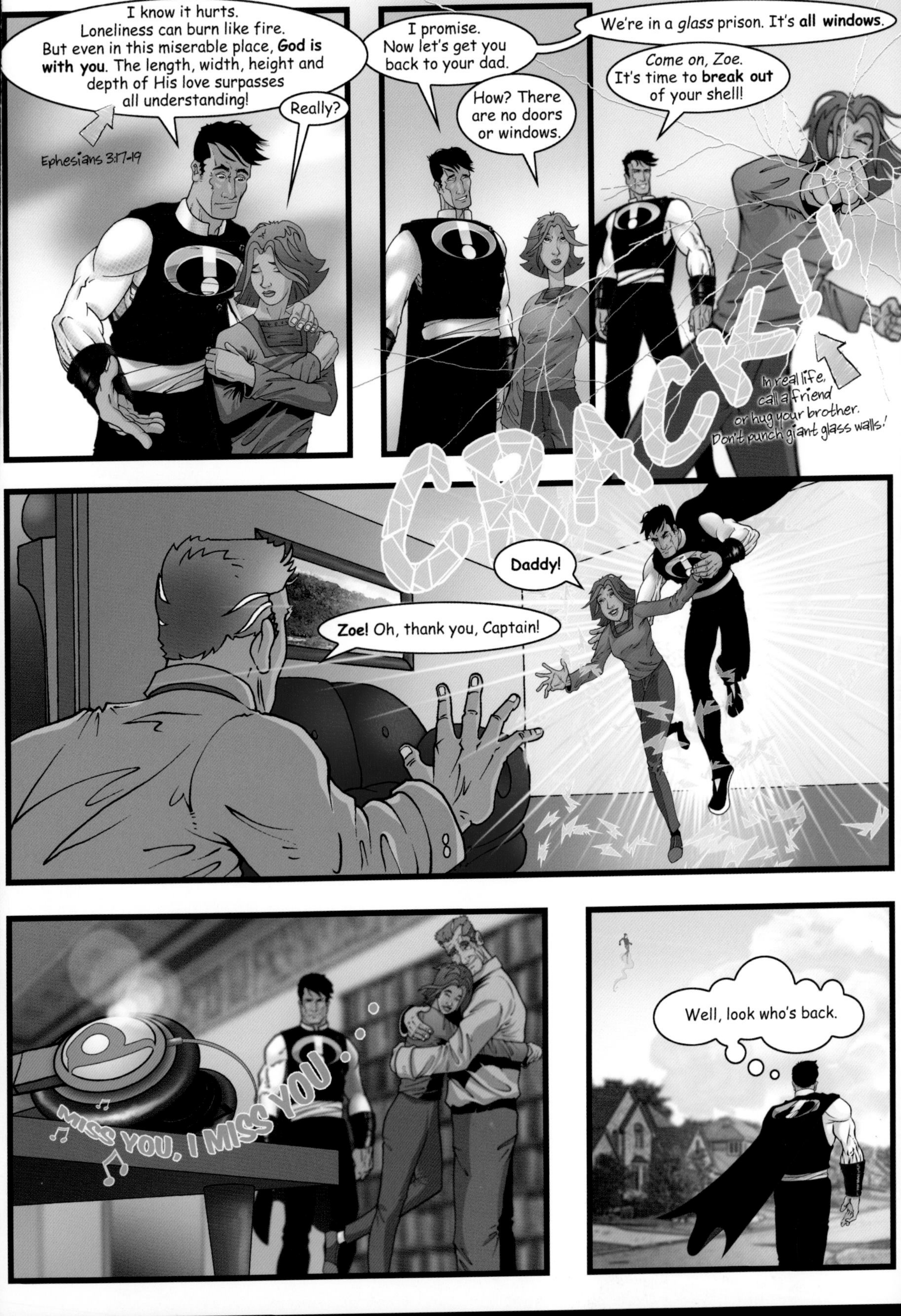
I know it hurts. Loneliness can burn like fire. But even in this miserable place, **God is with you**. The length, width, height and depth of His love surpasses all understanding!
Ephesians 3:17-19
Really?
I promise. Now let's get you back to your dad.
How? There are no doors or windows.
We're in a *glass* prison. It's **all windows**.
Come on, Zoe. It's time to **break out** of your shell!
CRACK!!
In real life, call a friend or hug your brother. Don't punch giant glass walls!
Daddy!
Zoe! Oh, thank you, Captain!
MISS YOU, I MISS YOU...
Well, look who's back.

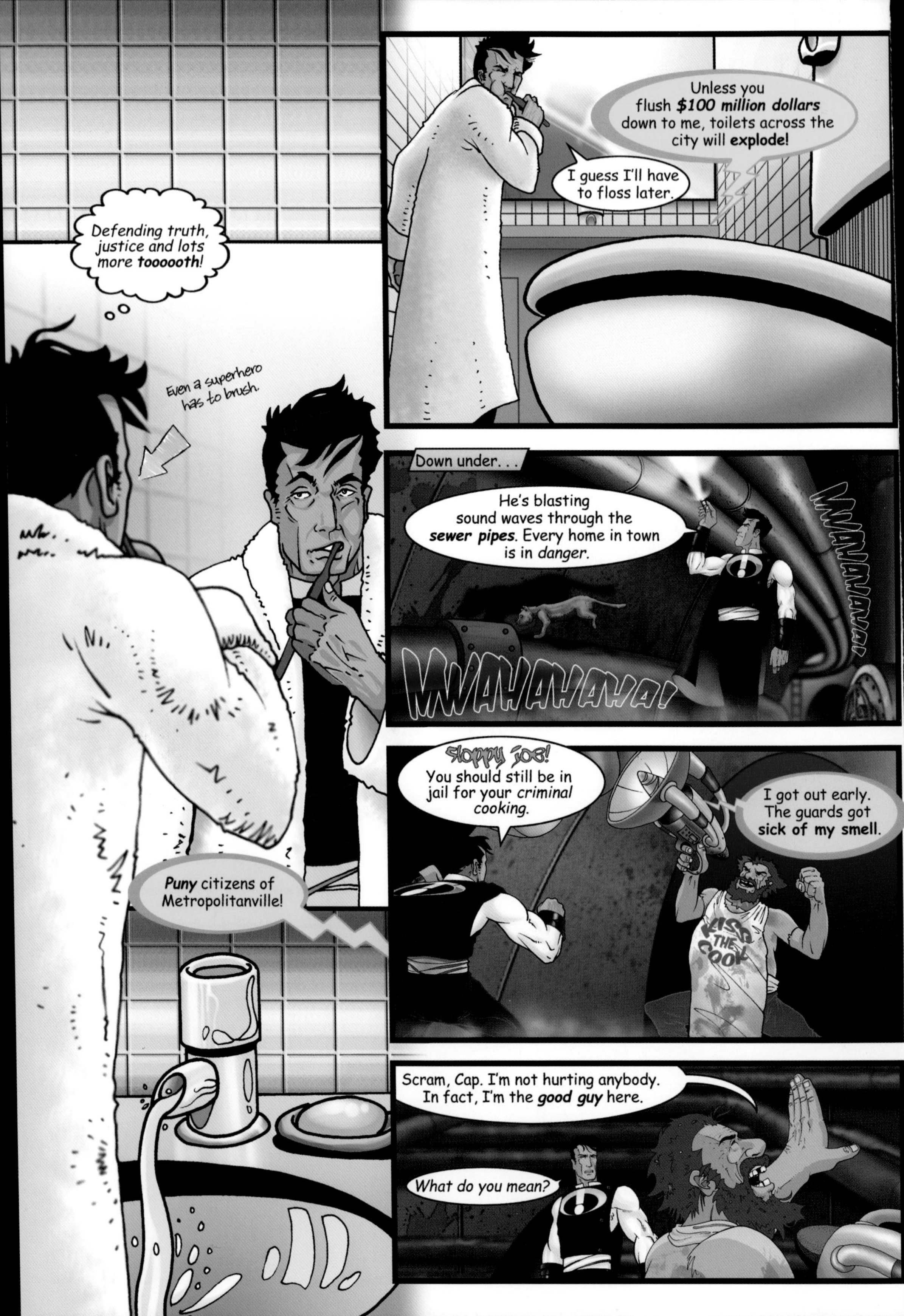
Defending truth, justice and lots more tooooth!
Even a superhero has to brush.
Puny citizens of Metropolitanville!
Unless you flush $100 million dollars down to me, toilets across the city will explode!
I guess I'll have to floss later.
Down under...
He's blasting sound waves through the sewer pipes. Every home in town is in danger.
MWAHAHAHAHA!
MWAHAHAHAHA!
Sloppy Joe! You should still be in jail for your criminal cooking.
I got out early. The guards got sick of my smell.
KISS THE COOK
Scram, Cap. I'm not hurting anybody. In fact, I'm the good guy here.
What do you mean?

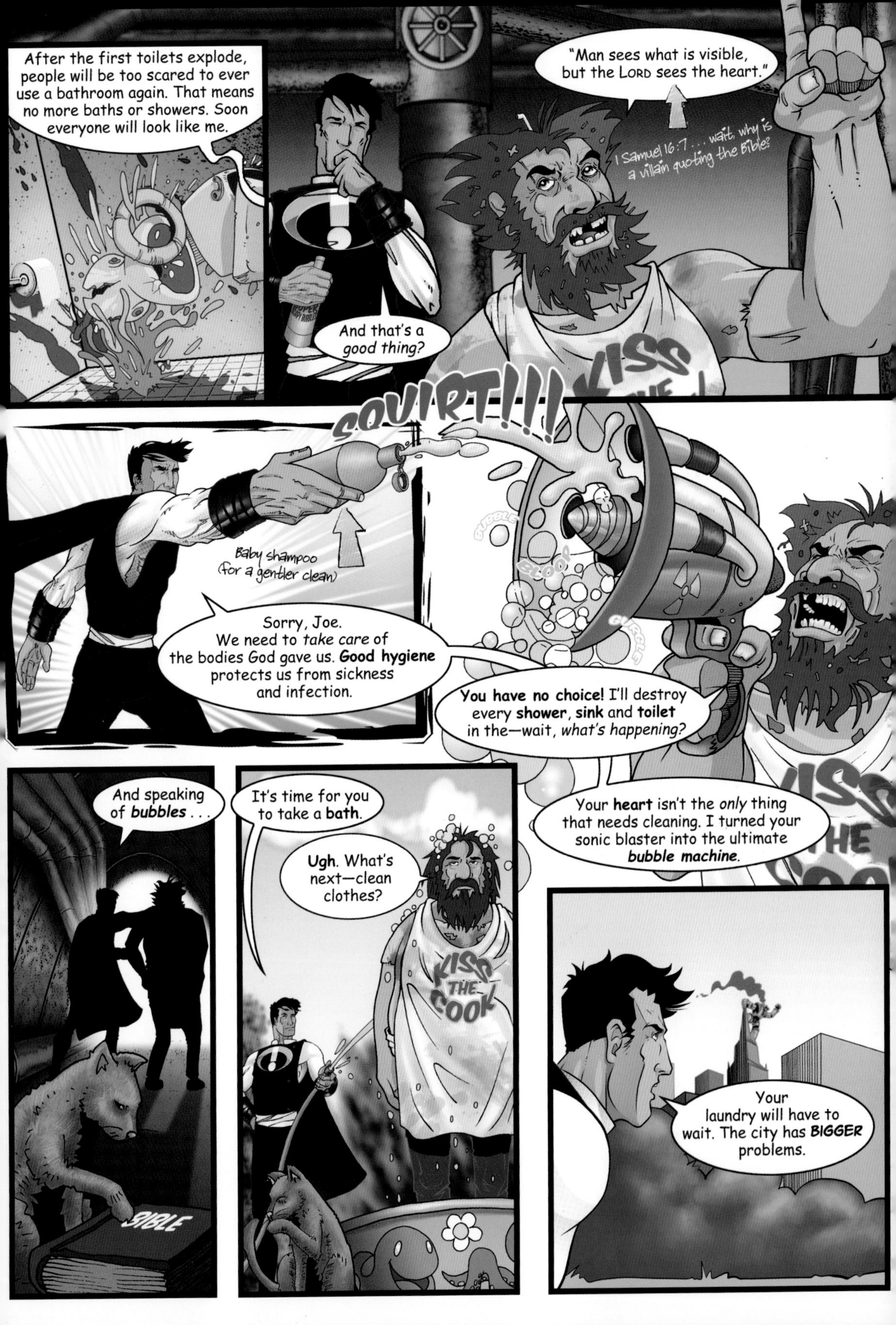
After the first toilets explode, people will be too scared to ever use a bathroom again. That means no more baths or showers. Soon everyone will look like me.
And that's a *good thing?*
"Man sees what is visible, but the LORD sees the heart."
I Samuel 16:7 . . . wait, why is a villain quoting the Bible?
KISS
SQUIRT!!!
Baby shampoo (for a gentler clean)
Sorry, Joe. We need to *take care* of the bodies God gave us. **Good hygiene** protects us from sickness and infection.
BUBBLE
BLOOP
GURGLE
You have no choice! I'll destroy every **shower**, **sink** and **toilet** in the—wait, *what's happening?*
Your **heart** isn't the *only* thing that needs cleaning. I turned your sonic blaster into the ultimate ***bubble machine***.
And speaking of ***bubbles*** . . .
It's time for you to take a **bath**.
Ugh. What's next—clean clothes?
KISS THE COOK
BIBLE
Your laundry will have to wait. The city has **BIGGER** problems.

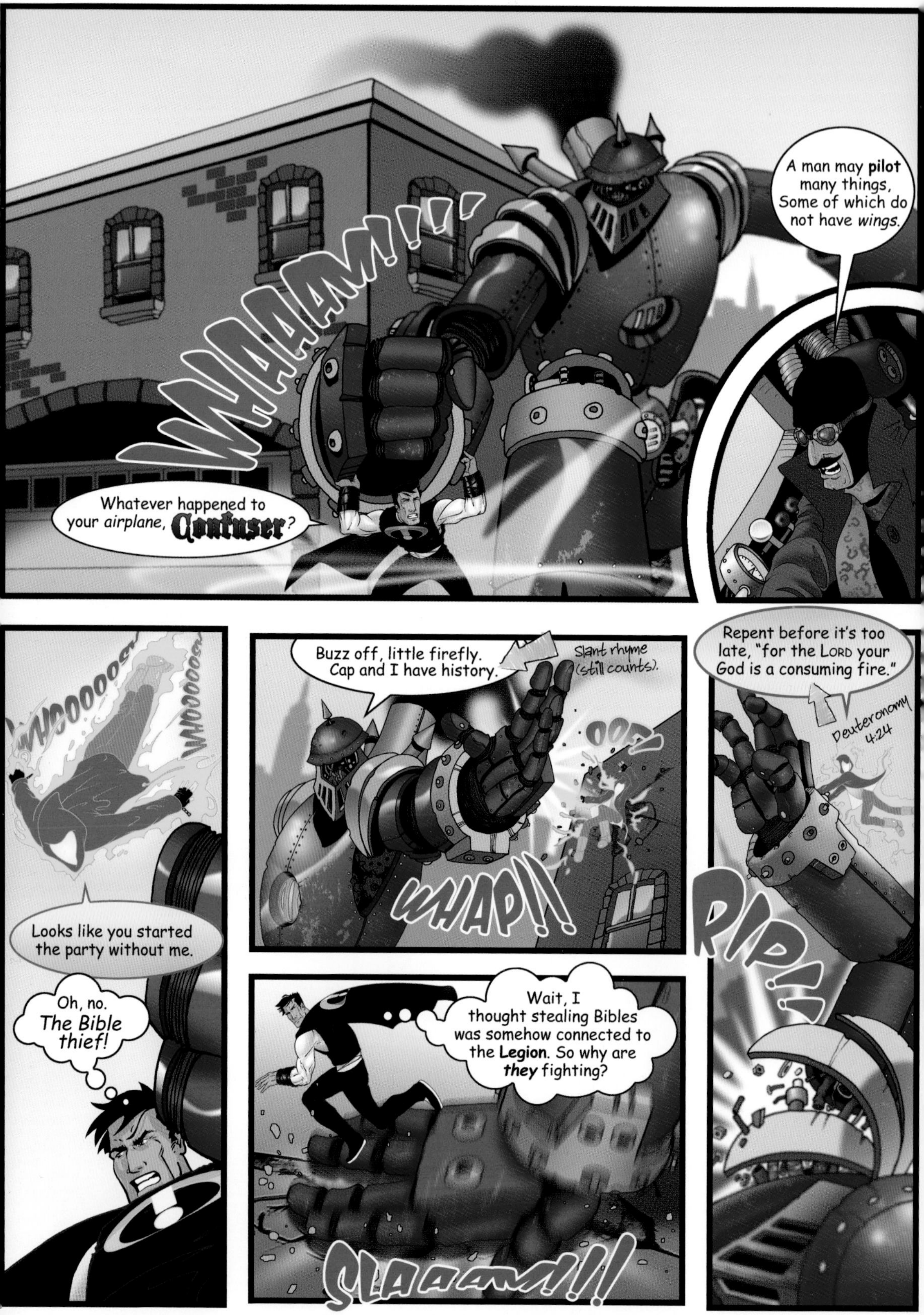
WHAAAM!!!
Whatever happened to your airplane, Confuser?
A man may pilot many things, Some of which do not have wings.
WHOOOOOSH
WHOOOOOSH
Looks like you started the party without me.
Oh, no. The Bible thief!
Buzz off, little firefly. Cap and I have history.
Slant rhyme (still counts).
OOF!
WHAP!!
Wait, I thought stealing Bibles was somehow connected to the Legion. So why are they fighting?
SLAaaAM!!
Repent before it's too late, "for the LORD your God is a consuming fire."
Deuteronomy 4:24
RIP!!

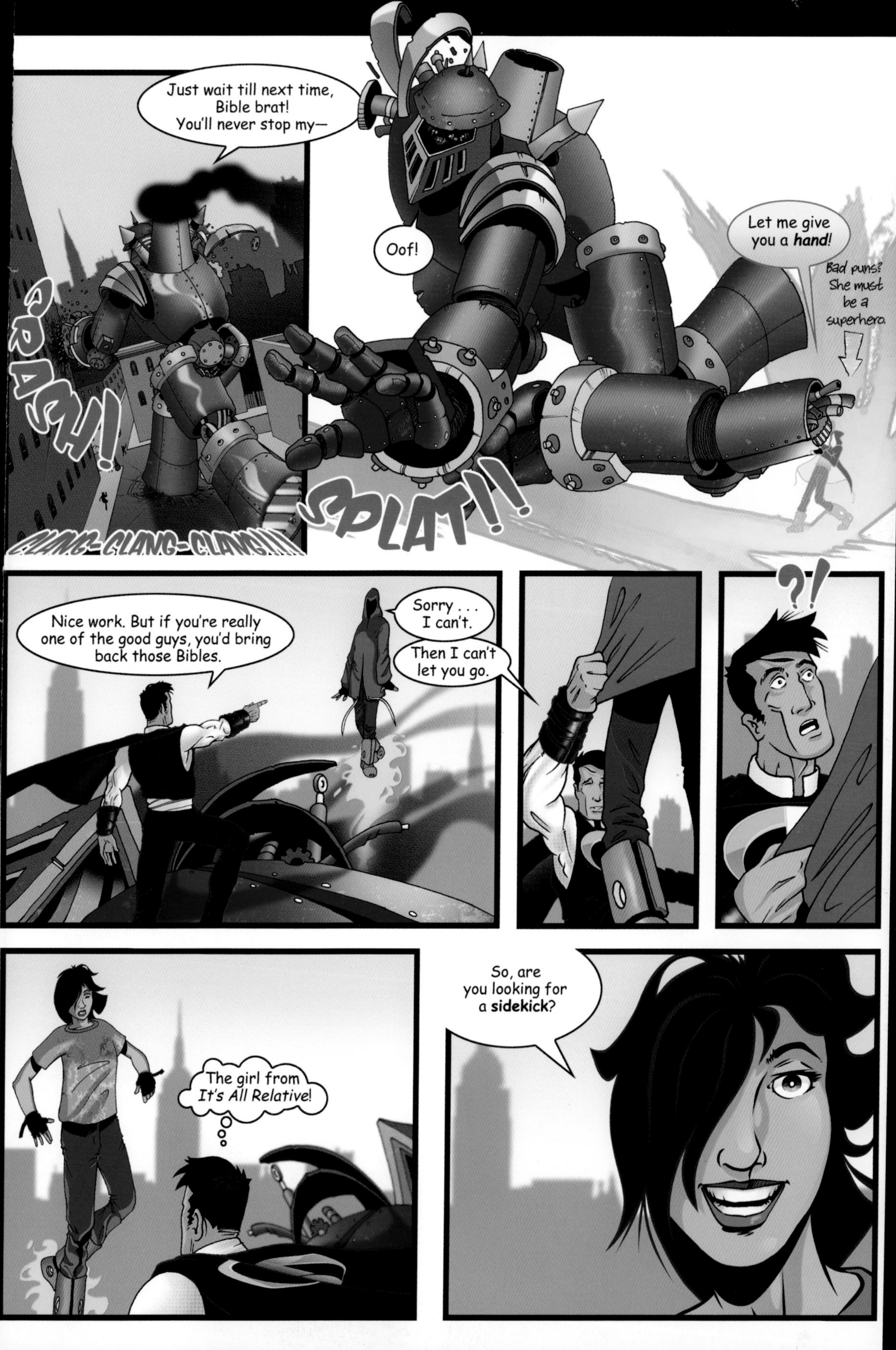

Just wait till next time, Bible brat! You'll never stop my—
CRASH!
CLANG-CLANG-CLANG!!!
Oof!
SPLAT!!
Let me give you a **hand**!
Bad puns? She must be a superhero.
Nice work. But if you're really one of the good guys, you'd bring back those Bibles.
Sorry . . . I can't.
Then I can't let you go.
?!
The girl from *It's All Relative*!
So, are you looking for a **sidekick**?

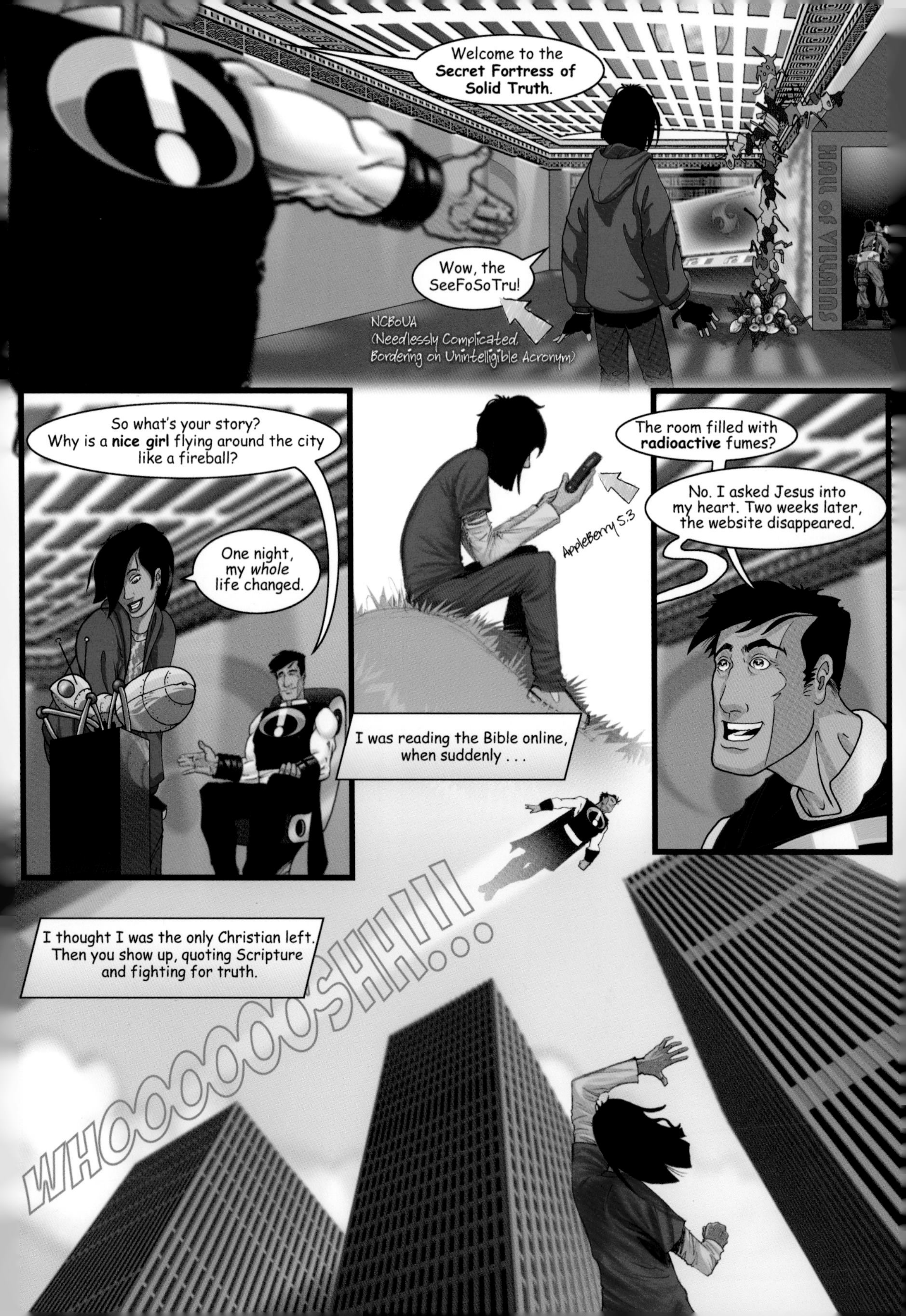
Welcome to the Secret Fortress of Solid Truth.
HALL of VILLAINS
Wow, the SeeFoSoTru!
NCBoUA (Needlessly Complicated, Bordering on Unintelligible Acronym)
So what's your story? Why is a nice girl flying around the city like a fireball?
One night, my whole life changed.
AppleBerry S.3
I was reading the Bible online, when suddenly . . .
The room filled with radioactive fumes?
No. I asked Jesus into my heart. Two weeks later, the website disappeared.
I thought I was the only Christian left. Then you show up, quoting Scripture and fighting for truth.
WHOOOOOOSHH!!!...

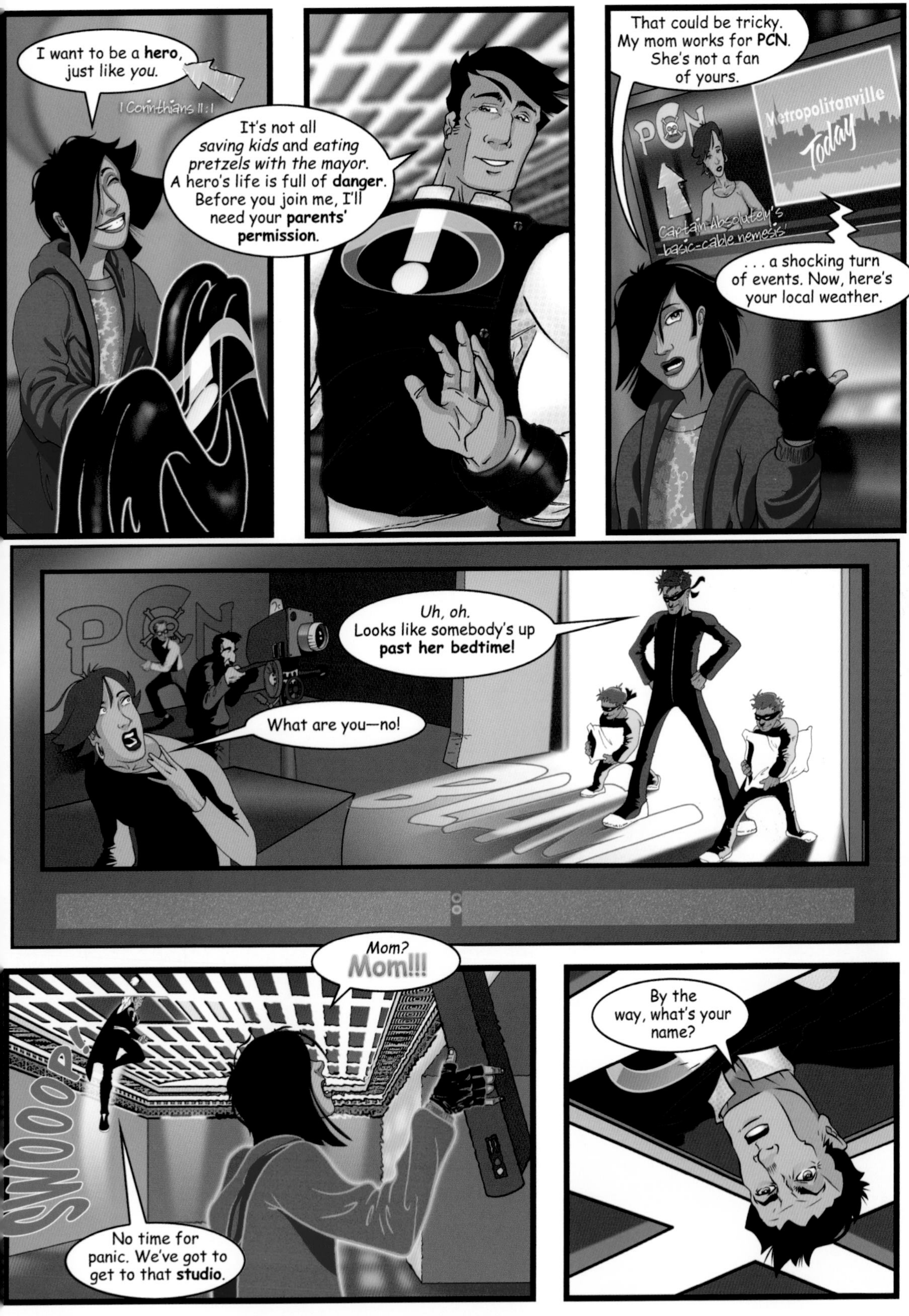

I want to be a **hero**, just like *you*.
I Corinthians 11:1
It's not all *saving kids* and *eating pretzels with the mayor*. A hero's life is full of **danger**. Before you join me, I'll need your **parents' permission**.
That could be tricky. My mom works for **PCN**. She's not a fan of yours.
PCN
Metropolitanville Today
Captain Absolutely's basic-cable nemesis
. . . a shocking turn of events. Now, here's your local weather.
PCN
Uh, oh. Looks like somebody's up **past her bedtime!**
What are you—no!
Mom? **Mom!!!**
SWOOP!
No time for panic. We've got to get to that **studio**.
By the way, what's your name?

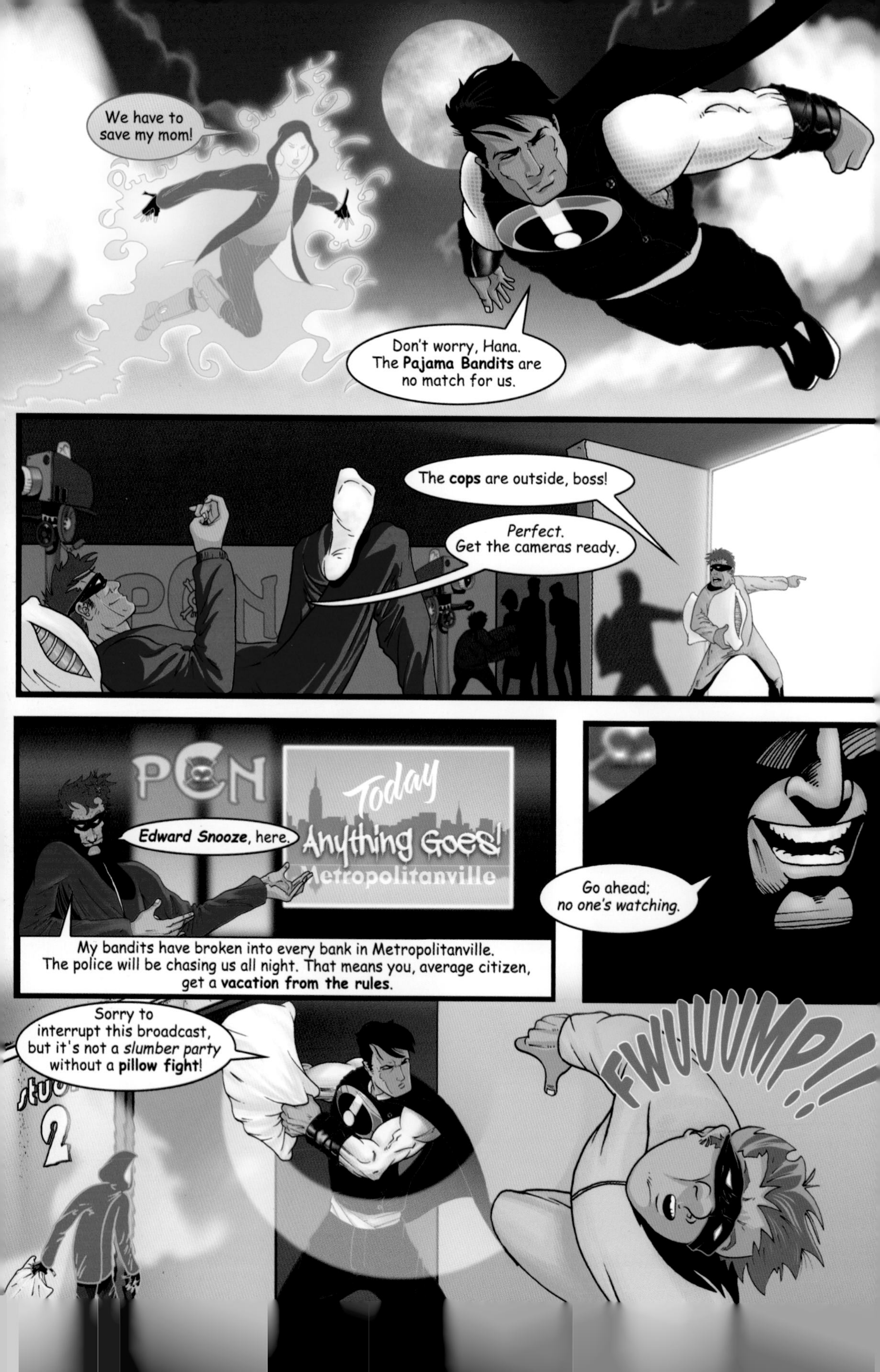
We have to save my mom!
Don't worry, Hana. The **Pajama Bandits** are no match for us.
The **cops** are outside, boss!
Perfect. Get the cameras ready.
PCN
Today
Anything Goes!
Metropolitanville
Edward Snooze, here.
My bandits have broken into every bank in Metropolitanville. The police will be chasing us all night. That means you, average citizen, get a **vacation from the rules**.
Go ahead; no one's watching.
Sorry to interrupt this broadcast, but it's not a *slumber party* without a **pillow fight**!
2
FWUUUMP!!

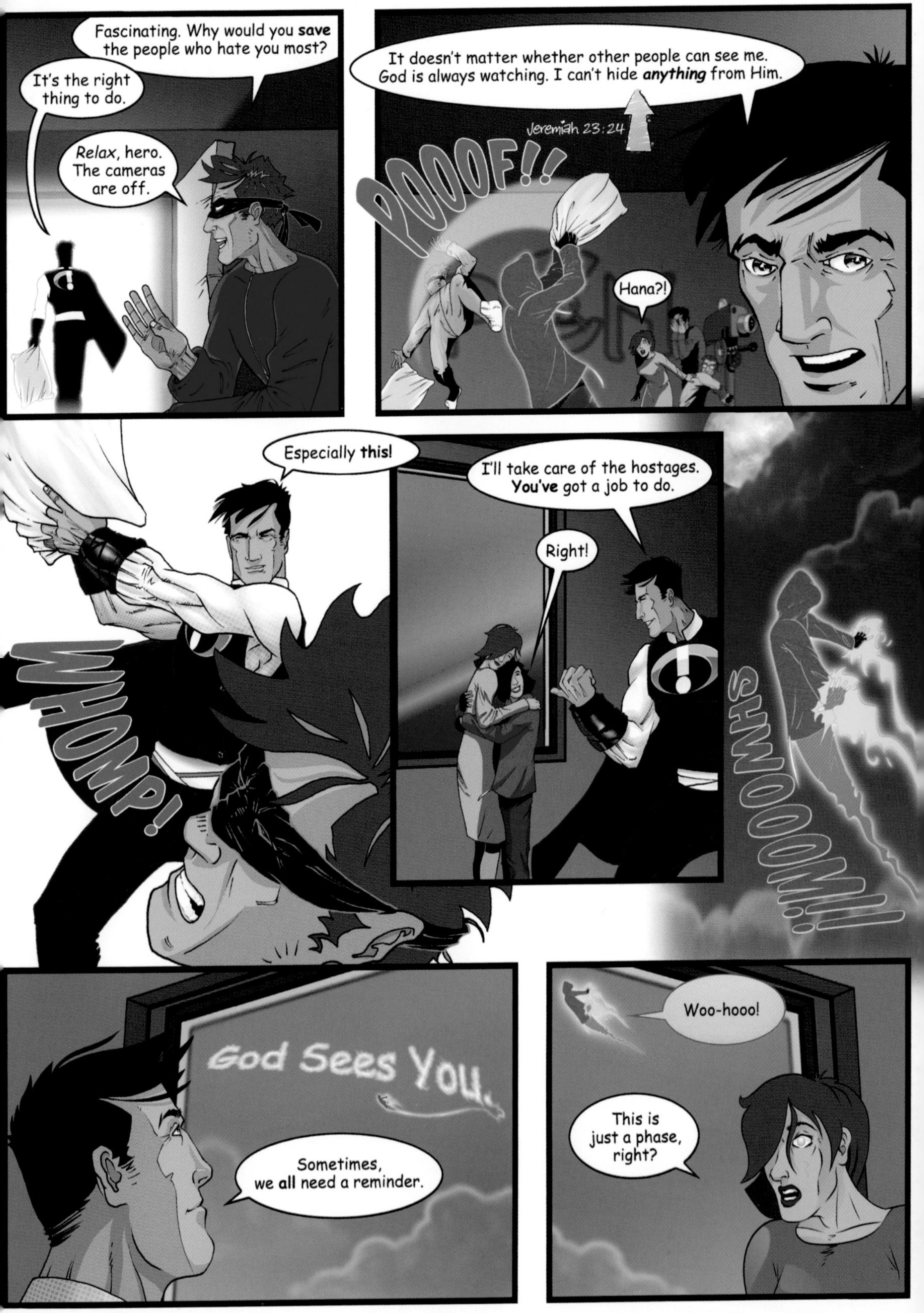
Fascinating. Why would you **save** the people who hate you most?
It's the right thing to do.
Relax, hero. The cameras are off.
It doesn't matter whether other people can see me. God is always watching. I can't hide ***anything*** from Him.
Jeremiah 23:24
POOOF!!
Hana?!
Especially **this**!
WHOMP!
I'll take care of the hostages. **You've** got a job to do.
Right!
SHWOOOM!!
God Sees You.
Sometimes, we **all** need a reminder.
Woo-hooo!
This is just a phase, right?

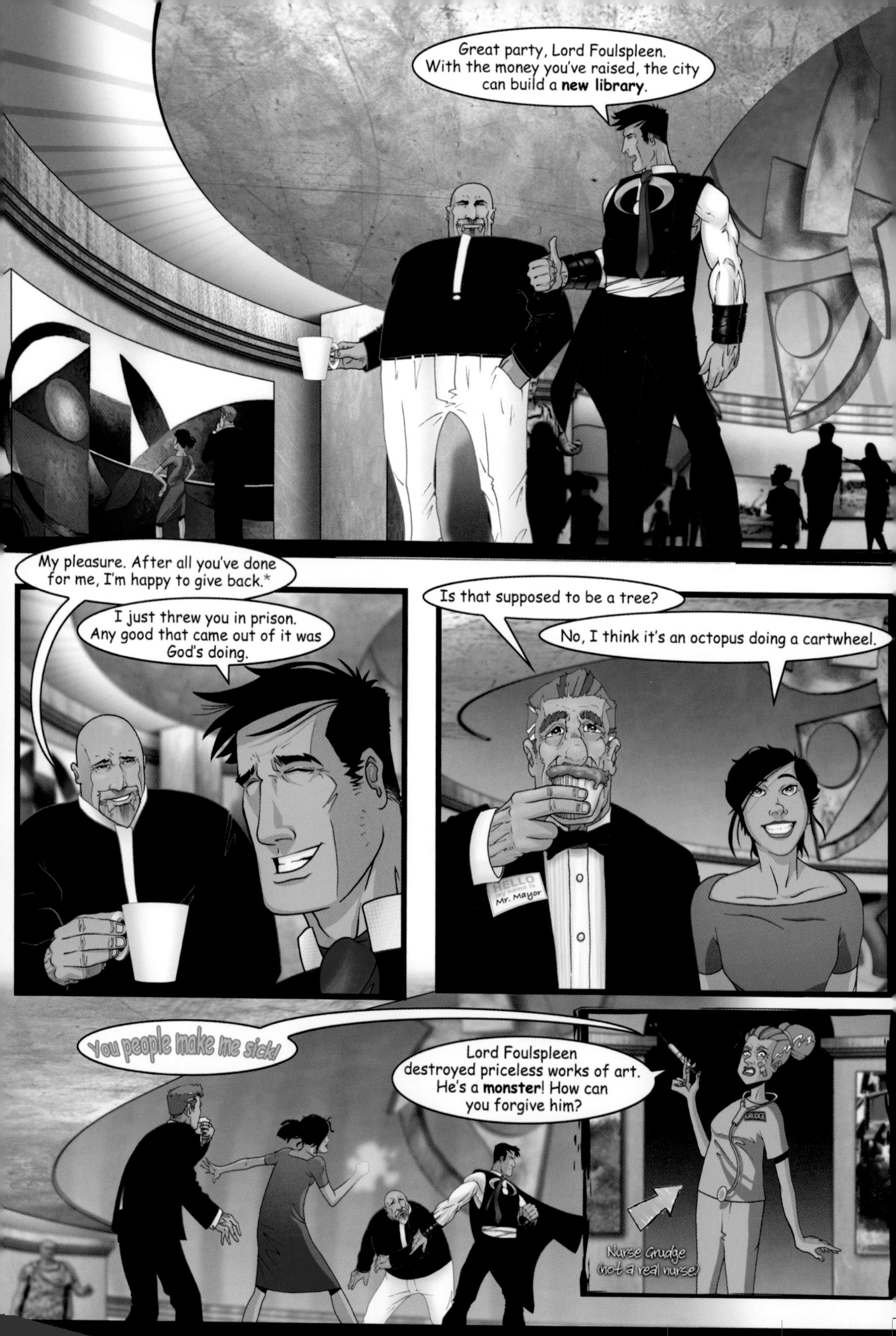

Great party, Lord Foulspleen. With the money you've raised, the city can build a new library.
My pleasure. After all you've done for me, I'm happy to give back.*
I just threw you in prison. Any good that came out of it was God's doing.
Is that supposed to be a tree?
No, I think it's an octopus doing a cartwheel.
HELLO my name is Mr. Mayor
You people make me sick!
Lord Foulspleen destroyed priceless works of art. He's a monster! How can you forgive him?
GRUDGE
Nurse Grudge (not a real nurse)

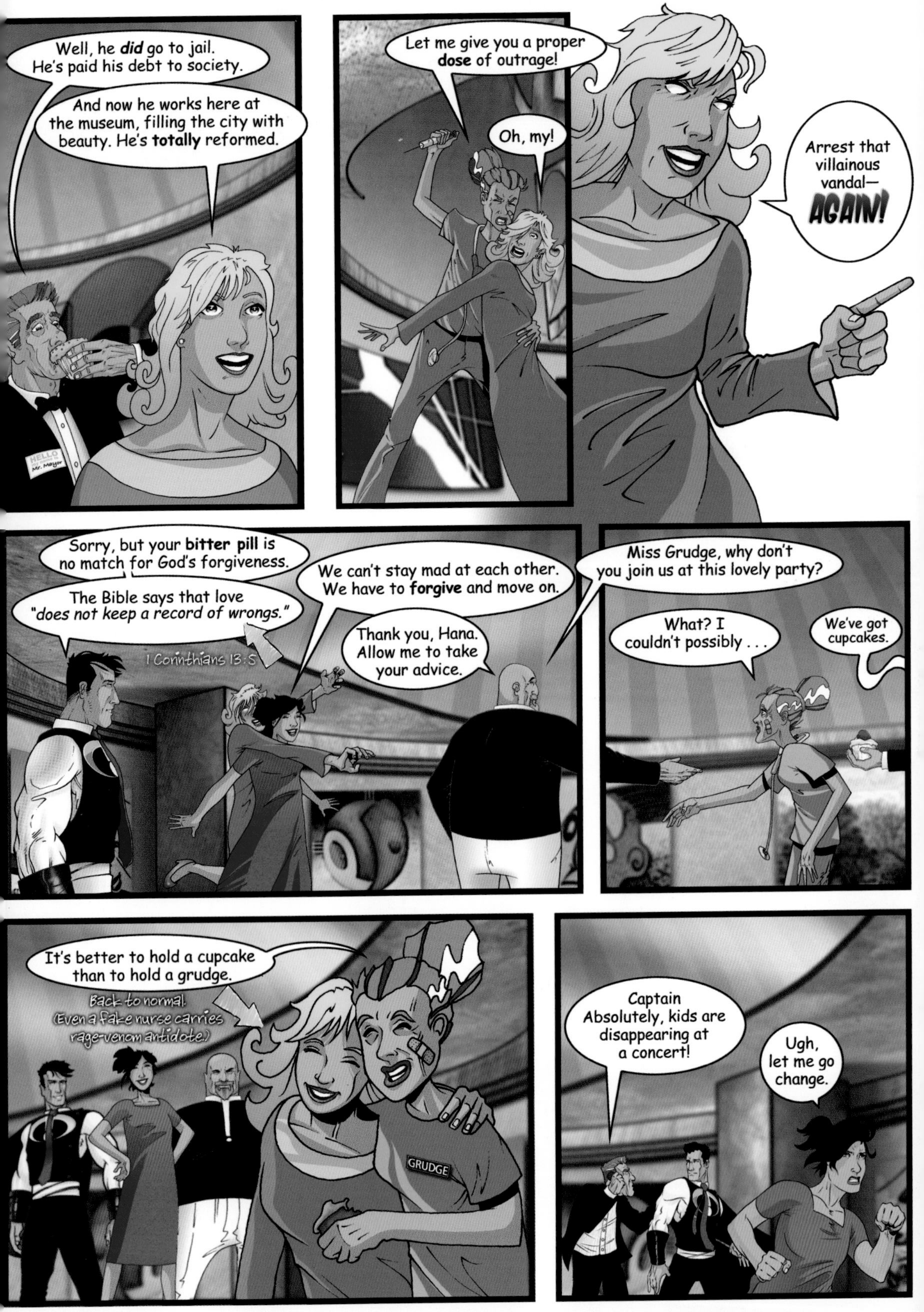
Well, he **did** go to jail. He's paid his debt to society.
And now he works here at the museum, filling the city with beauty. He's **totally** reformed.
HELLO Mr. Mayor
Let me give you a proper **dose** of outrage!
Oh, my!
Arrest that villainous vandal—AGAIN!
Sorry, but your **bitter pill** is no match for God's forgiveness.
The Bible says that love *"does not keep a record of wrongs."*
1 Corinthians 13:5
We can't stay mad at each other. We have to **forgive** and move on.
Thank you, Hana. Allow me to take your advice.
Miss Grudge, why don't you join us at this lovely party?
What? I couldn't possibly . . .
We've got cupcakes.
It's better to hold a cupcake than to hold a grudge.
Back to normal. (Even a fake nurse carries rage-venom antidote.)
GRUDGE
Captain Absolutely, kids are disappearing at a concert!
Ugh, let me go change.

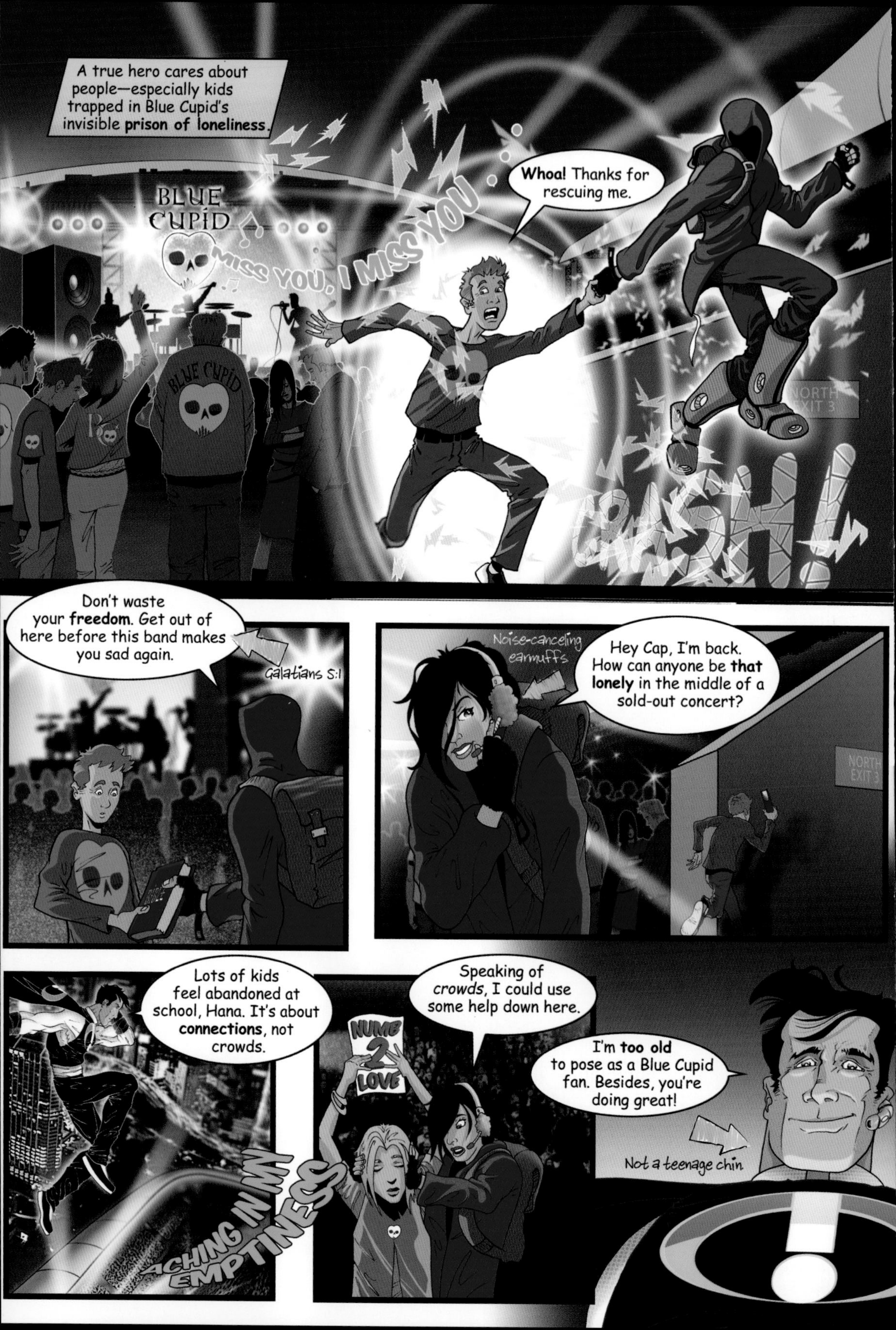

A true hero cares about people—especially kids trapped in Blue Cupid's invisible **prison of loneliness**.
BLUE CUPID
MISS YOU, I MISS YOU
BLUE CUPID
Whoa! Thanks for rescuing me.
NORTH EXIT 3
CRASH!
Don't waste your **freedom**. Get out of here before this band makes you sad again.
Galatians 5:1
BIBLE
Noise-canceling earmuffs
Hey Cap, I'm back. How can anyone be **that lonely** in the middle of a sold-out concert?
NORTH EXIT 3
Lots of kids feel abandoned at school, Hana. It's about **connections**, not crowds.
ACHING IN MY EMPTINESS
NUMB 2 LOVE
Speaking of *crowds*, I could use some help down here.
I'm **too old** to pose as a Blue Cupid fan. Besides, you're doing great!
Not a teenage chin.

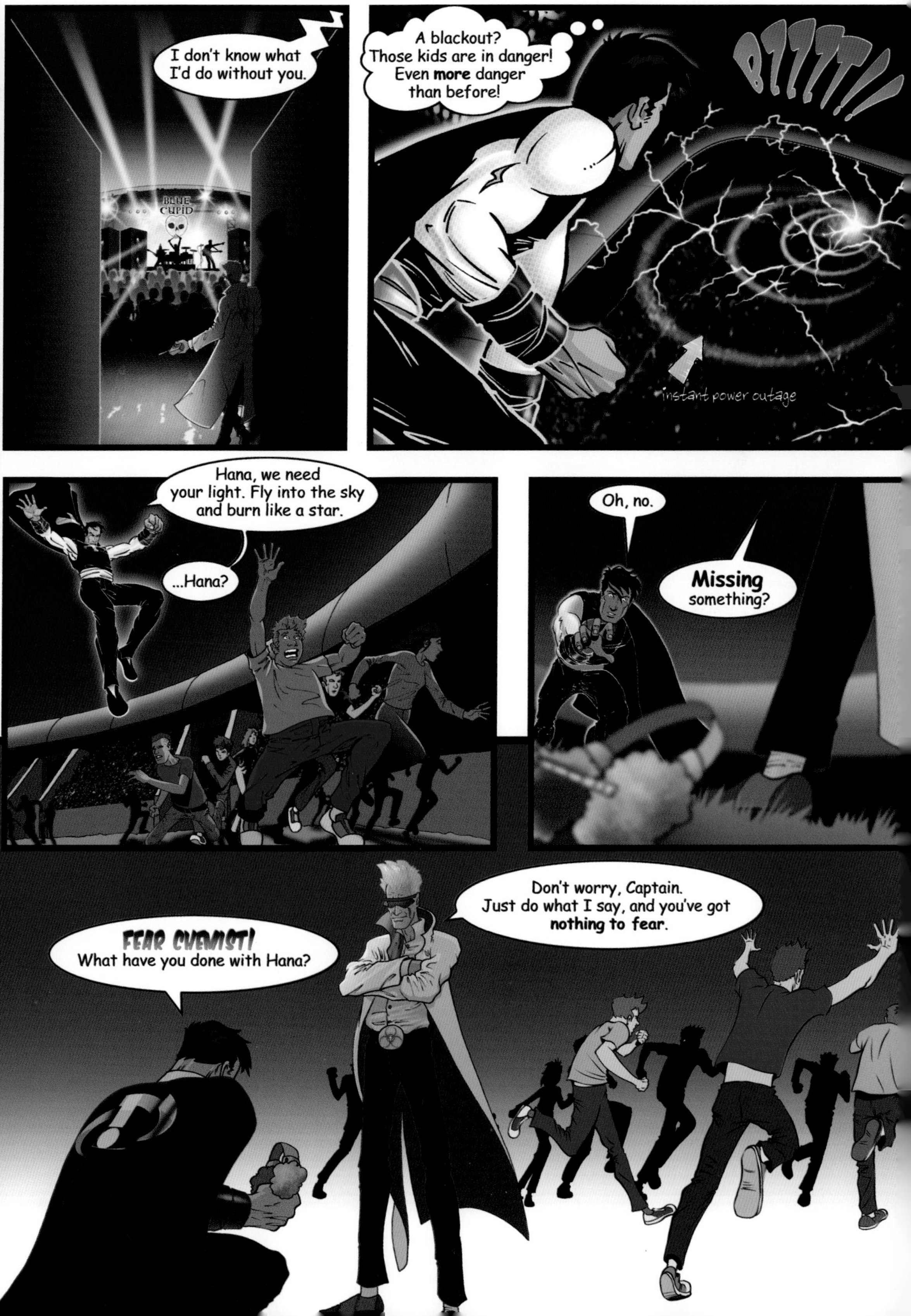
I don't know what I'd do without you.
A blackout? Those kids are in danger! Even more danger than before!
BZZZT!!
instant power outage
Hana, we need your light. Fly into the sky and burn like a star.
...Hana?
Oh, no.
Missing something?
FEAR CHEMIST! What have you done with Hana?
Don't worry, Captain. Just do what I say, and you've got nothing to fear.

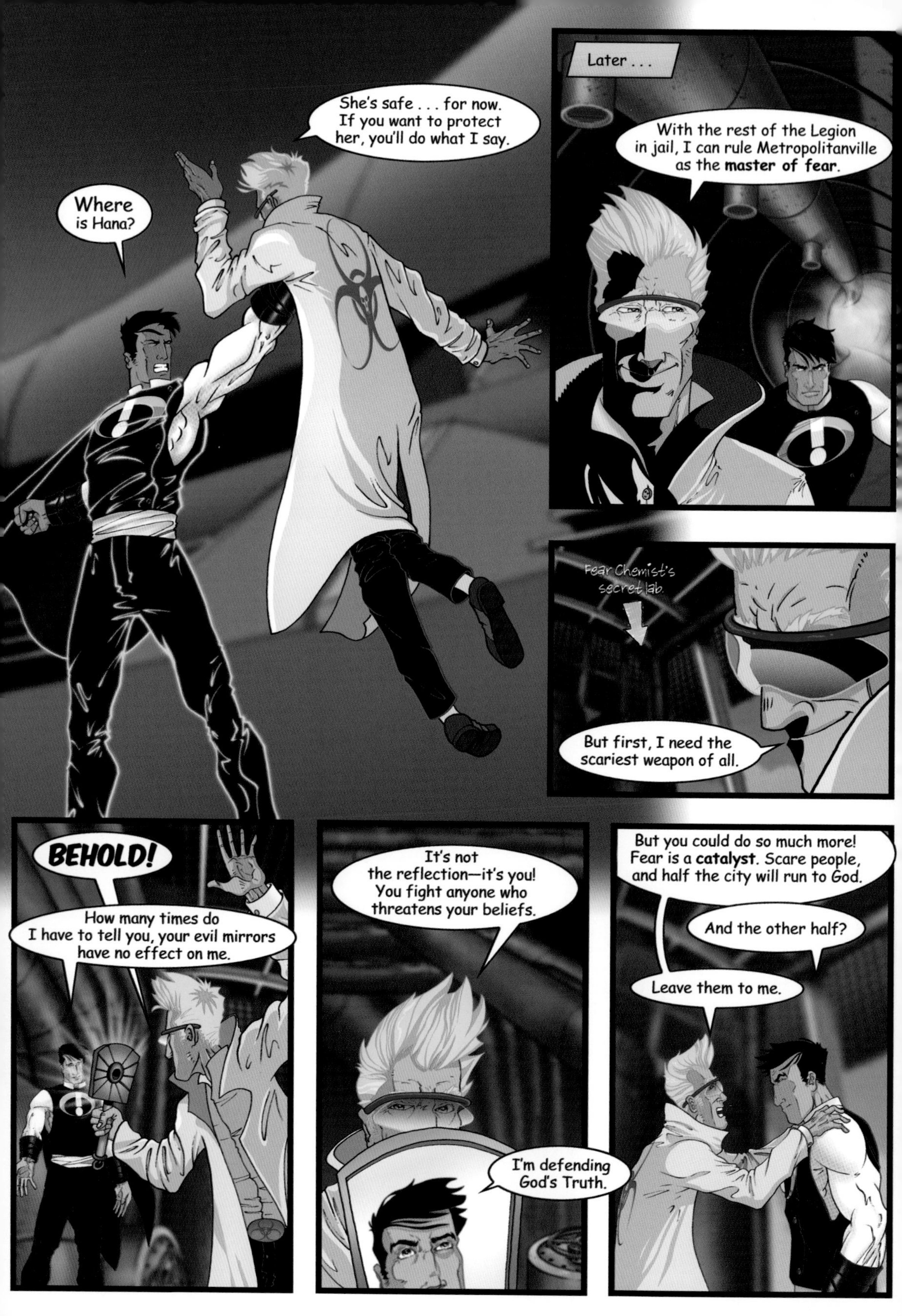
Where is Hana?
She's safe . . . for now. If you want to protect her, you'll do what I say.
Later . . .
With the rest of the Legion in jail, I can rule Metropolitanville as the master of fear.
Fear Chemist's secret lab.
But first, I need the scariest weapon of all.
BEHOLD!
How many times do I have to tell you, your evil mirrors have no effect on me.
It's not the reflection—it's you! You fight anyone who threatens your beliefs.
I'm defending God's Truth.
But you could do so much more! Fear is a catalyst. Scare people, and half the city will run to God.
And the other half?
Leave them to me.

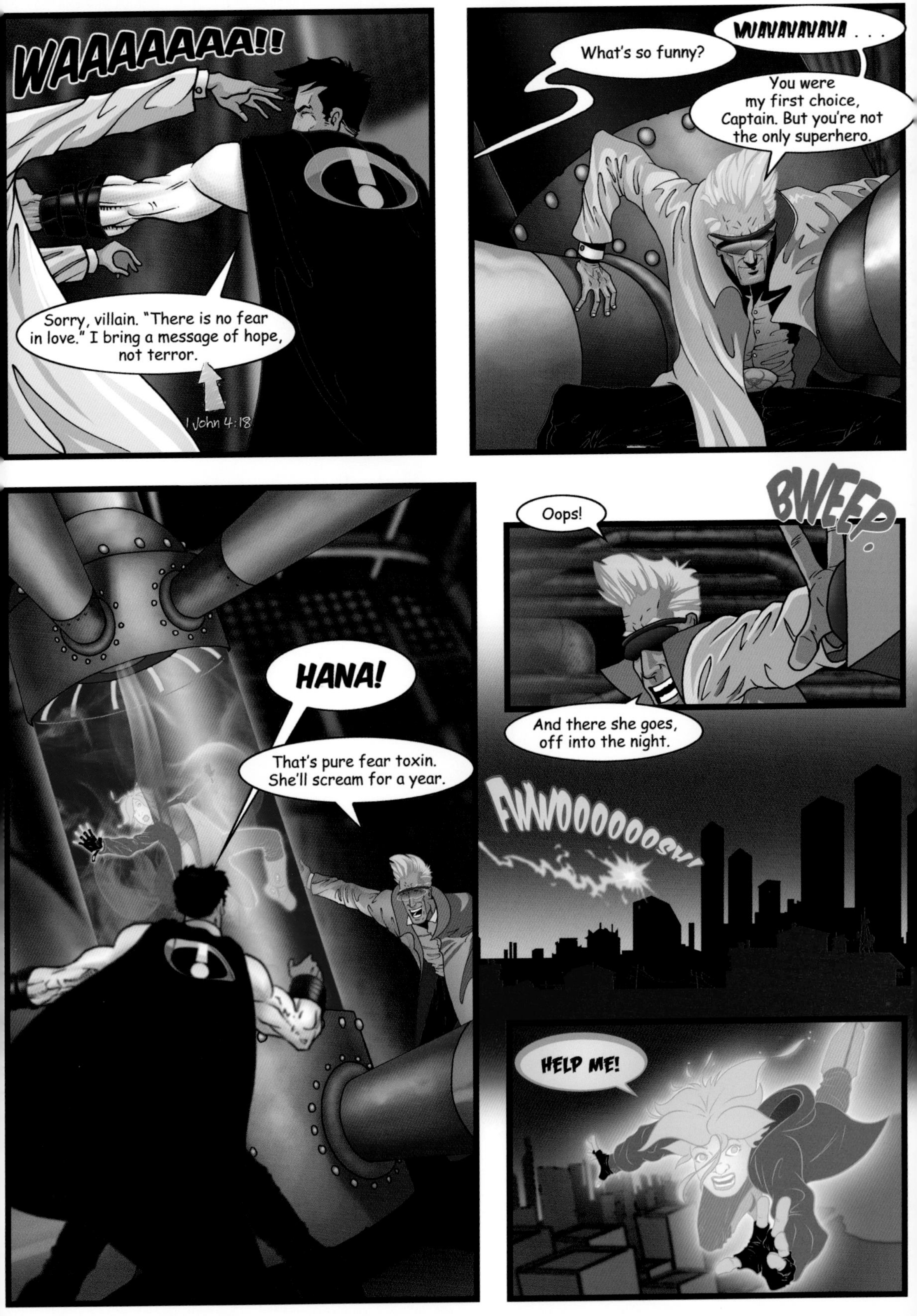
WAAAAAAA!!
Sorry, villain. "There is no fear in love." I bring a message of hope, not terror.
1 John 4:18
What's so funny?
MWAHAHAHAHA . . .
You were my first choice, Captain. But you're not the only superhero.
HANA!
That's pure fear toxin. She'll scream for a year.
Oops!
BWEEP.
And there she goes, off into the night.
FWWOOOOOOOSH!
HELP ME!

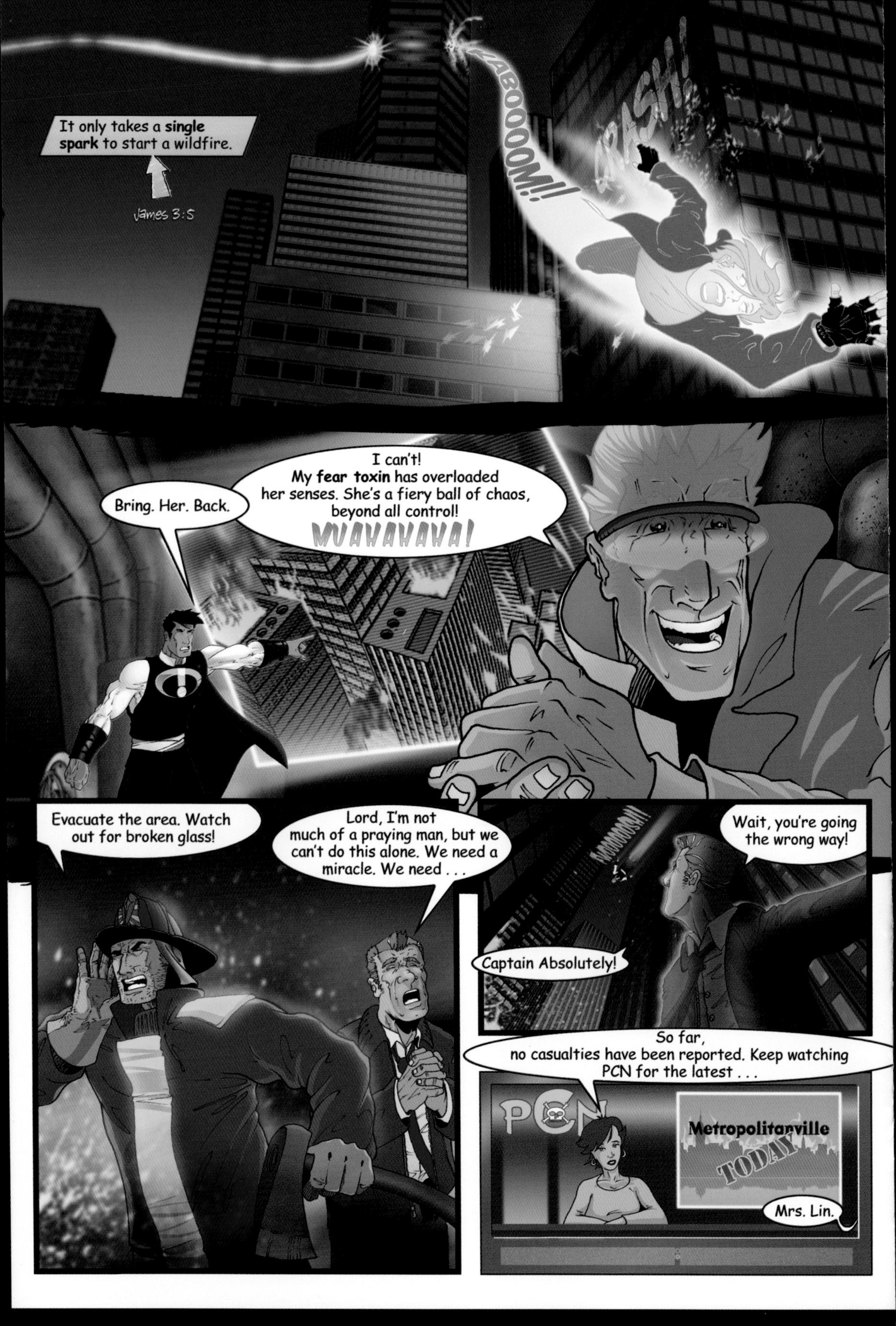
It only takes a **single spark** to start a wildfire.
James 3:5
KABOOOOM!!!
CRASH!
Bring. Her. Back.
I can't!
My **fear toxin** has overloaded her senses. She's a fiery ball of chaos, beyond all control!
MUAHAHAHA!
Evacuate the area. Watch out for broken glass!
Lord, I'm not much of a praying man, but we can't do this alone. We need a miracle. We need . . .
Wait, you're going the wrong way!
Captain Absolutely!
So far, no casualties have been reported. Keep watching PCN for the latest . . .
PCN
Metropolitanville
TODAY
Mrs. Lin.

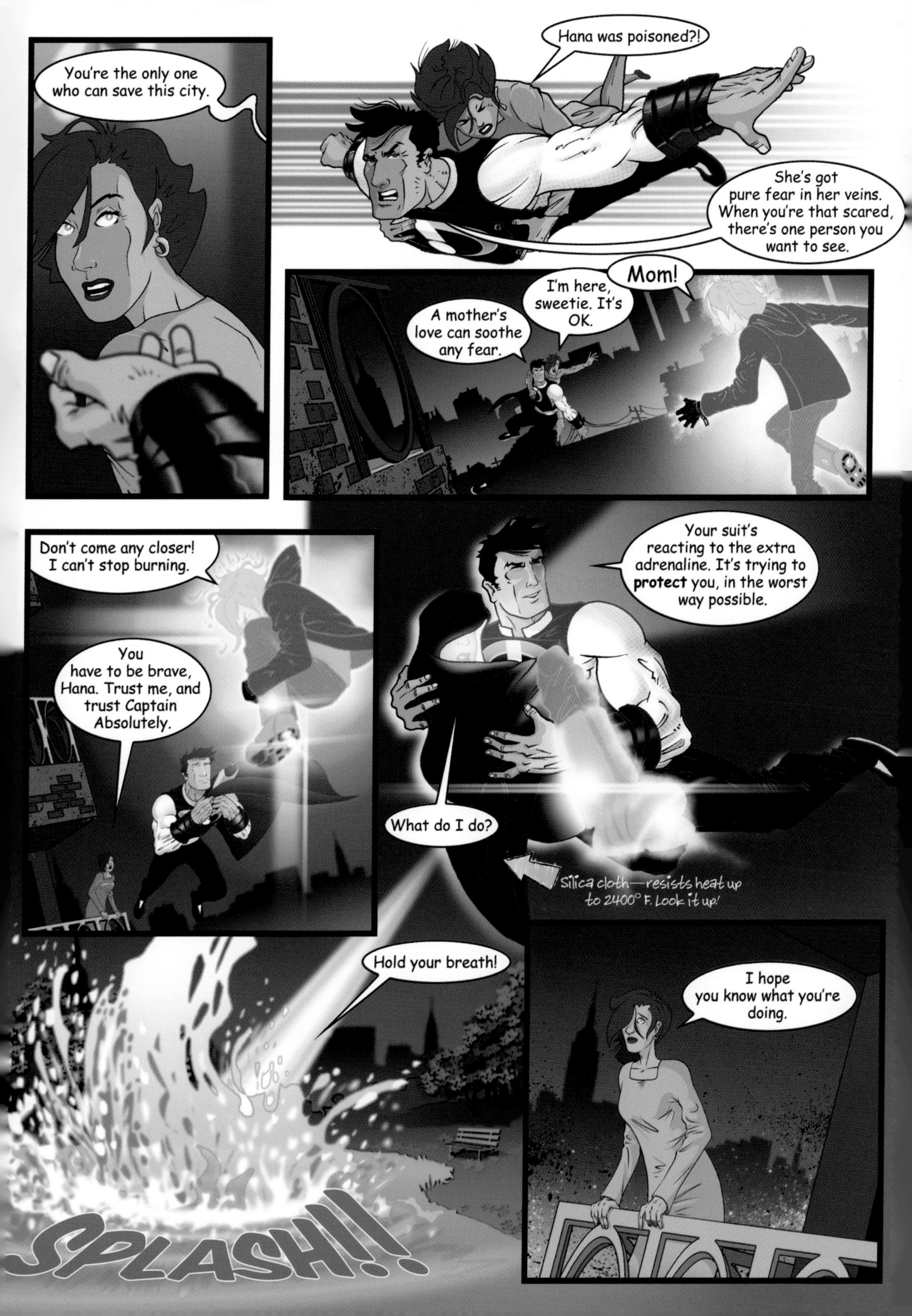

You're the only one who can save this city.
Hana was poisoned?!
She's got pure fear in her veins. When you're that scared, there's one person you want to see.
A mother's love can soothe any fear.
I'm here, sweetie. It's OK.
Mom!
Don't come any closer! I can't stop burning.
You have to be brave, Hana. Trust me, and trust Captain Absolutely.
Your suit's reacting to the extra adrenaline. It's trying to **protect** you, in the worst way possible.
What do I do?
Silica cloth—resists heat up to 2400° F. Look it up!
Hold your breath!
I hope you know what you're doing.
SPLASH!!

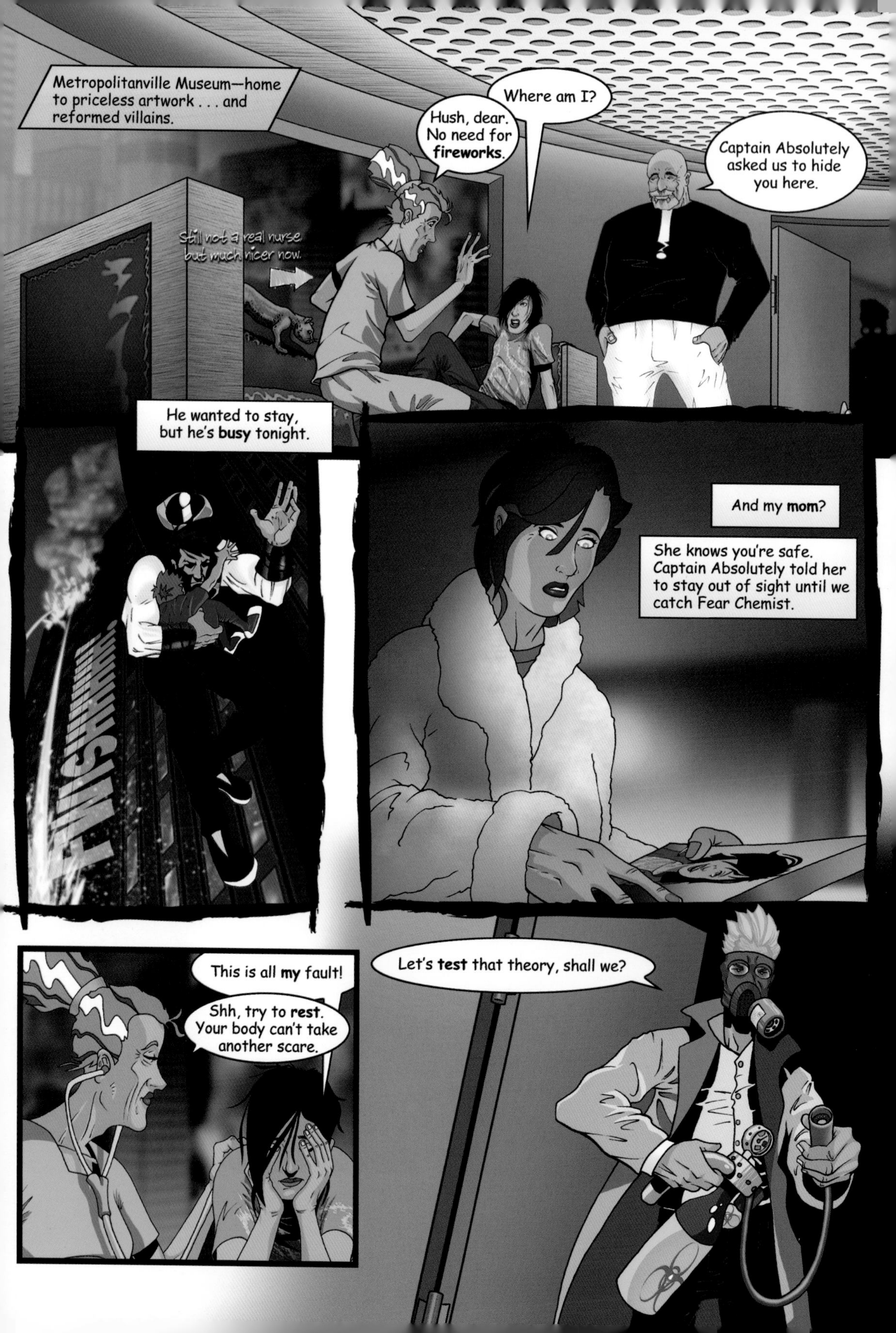

Metropolitanville Museum—home to priceless artwork . . . and reformed villains.
Where am I?
Hush, dear. No need for **fireworks**.
Captain Absolutely asked us to hide you here.
Still not a real nurse but much nicer now.
He wanted to stay, but he's **busy** tonight.
FWASHHHHH
And my **mom**?
She knows you're safe. Captain Absolutely told her to stay out of sight until we catch Fear Chemist.
This is all **my** fault!
Shh, try to **rest**. Your body can't take another scare.
Let's **test** that theory, shall we?

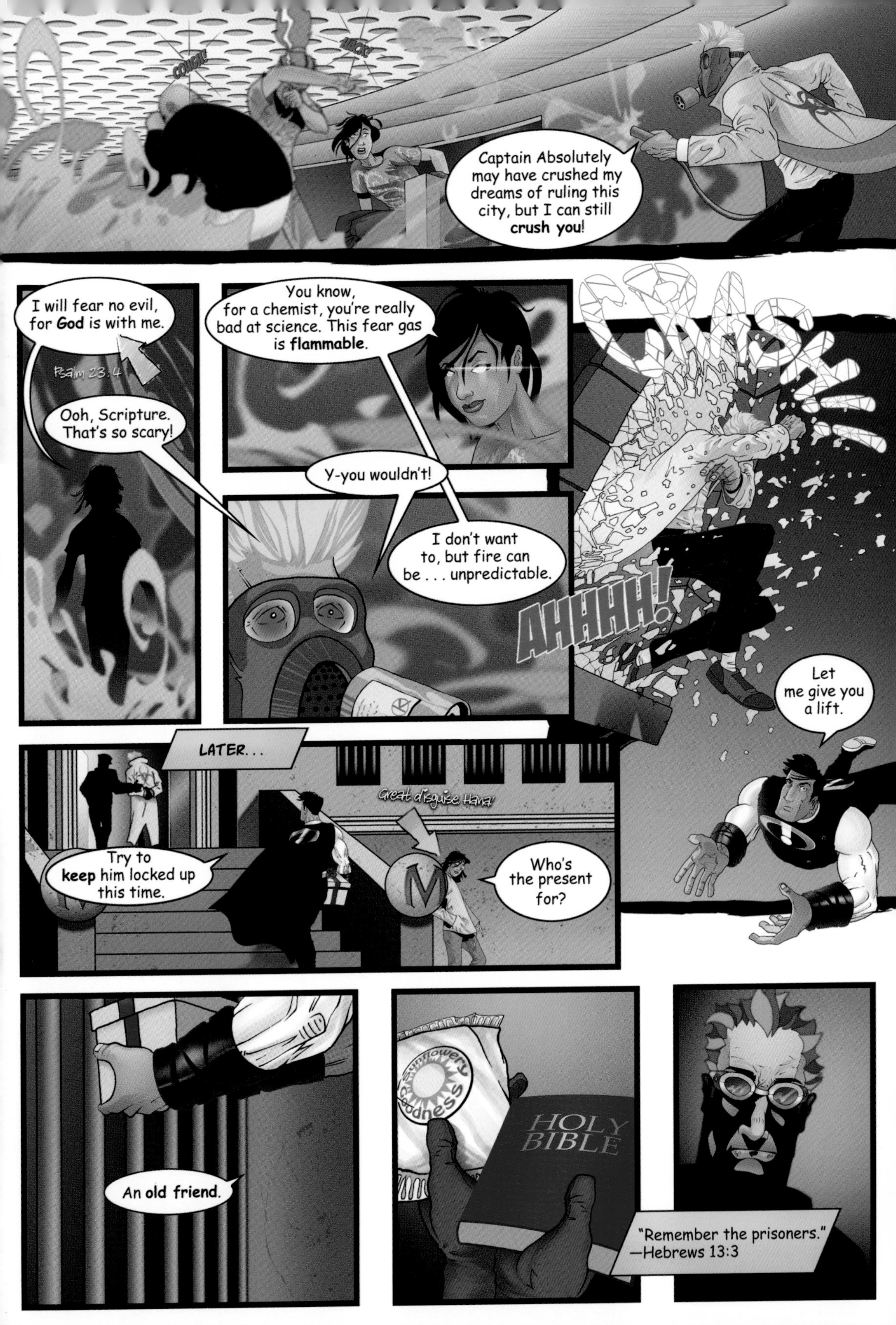

COUGH!
HACK!
Captain Absolutely may have crushed my dreams of ruling this city, but I can still **crush you**!
I will fear no evil, for **God** is with me.
Psalm 23:4
Ooh, Scripture. That's so scary!
You know, for a chemist, you're really bad at science. This fear gas is **flammable**.
Y-you wouldn't!
I don't want to, but fire can be . . . unpredictable.
CRASH!
AHHHH!
Let me give you a lift.
LATER . . .
Try to **keep** him locked up this time.
Great disguise, Hana!
Who's the present for?
An **old friend**.
Sunflowery Goodness
HOLY BIBLE
"Remember the prisoners."
—Hebrews 13:3

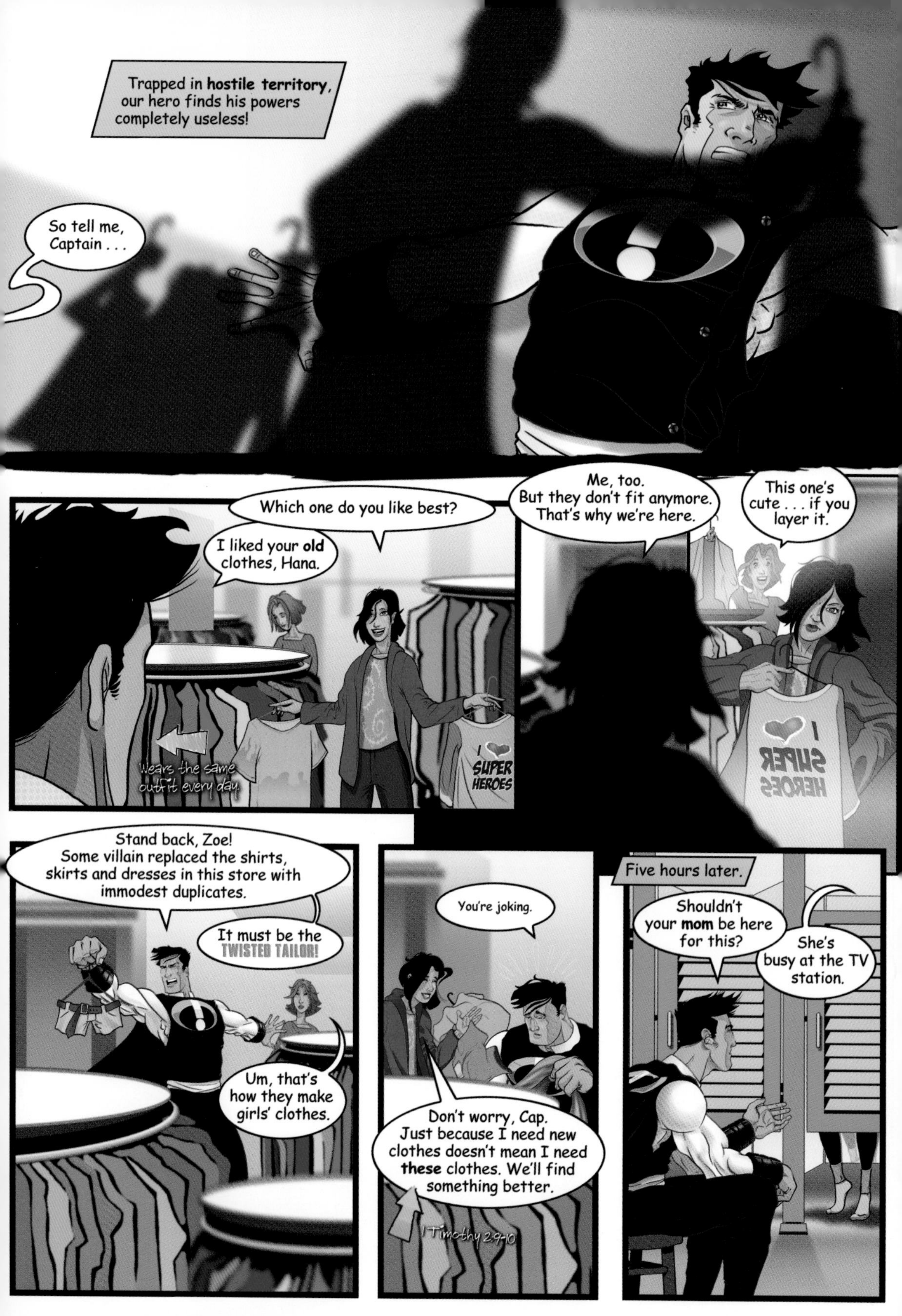

Trapped in **hostile territory**, our hero finds his powers completely useless!
So tell me, Captain . . .
Which one do you like best?
I liked your **old** clothes, Hana.
Wears the same outfit every day.
I ♥ SUPER HEROES
Me, too. But they don't fit anymore. That's why we're here.
This one's cute . . . if you layer it.
Stand back, Zoe! Some villain replaced the shirts, skirts and dresses in this store with immodest duplicates.
It must be the TWISTED TAILOR!
Um, that's how they make girls' clothes.
You're joking.
Don't worry, Cap. Just because I need new clothes doesn't mean I need **these** clothes. We'll find something better.
1 Timothy 2:9-10
Five hours later.
Shouldn't your **mom** be here for this?
She's busy at the TV station.

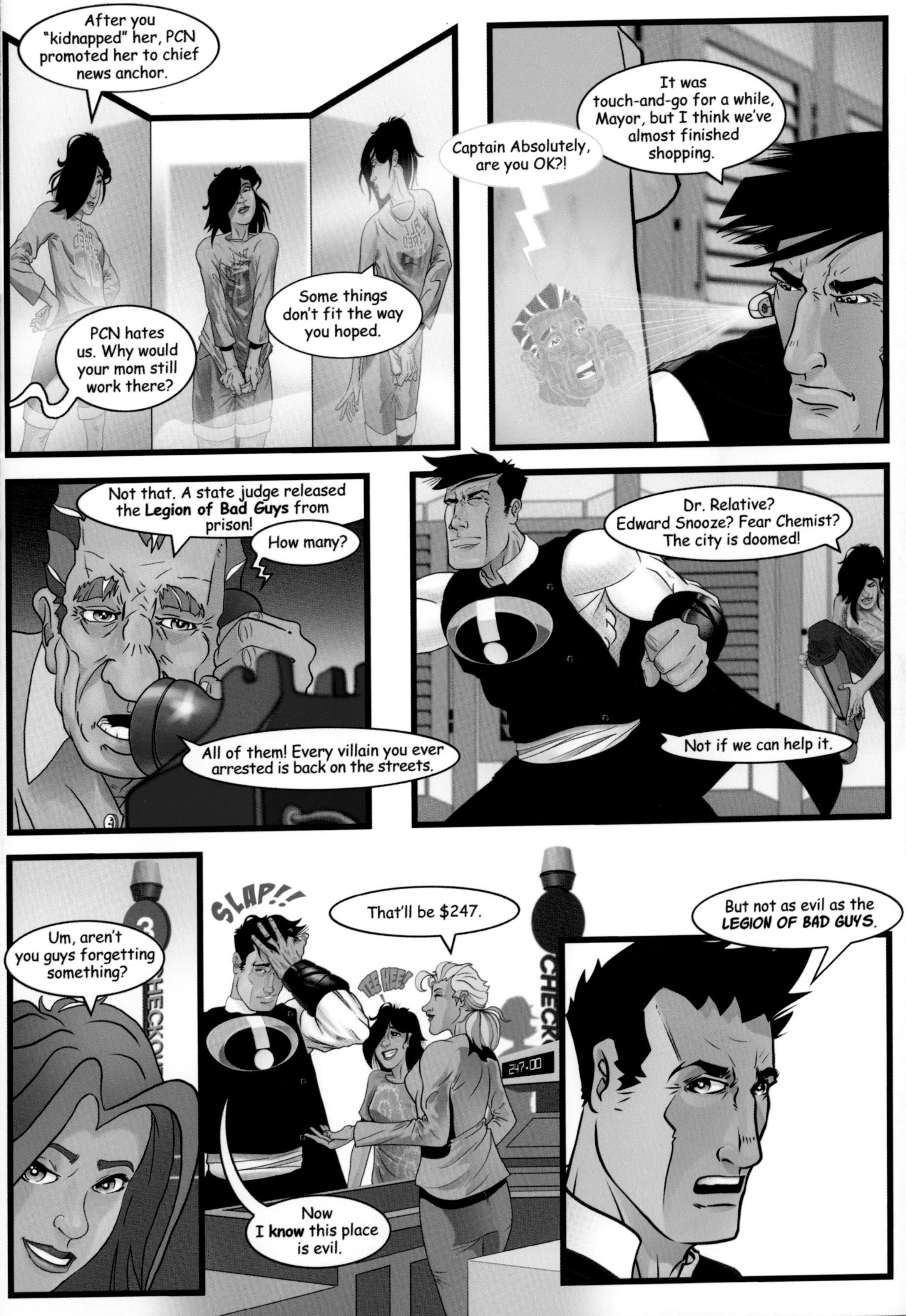
After you "kidnapped" her, PCN promoted her to chief news anchor.
PCN hates us. Why would your mom still work there?
Some things don't fit the way you hoped.
Captain Absolutely, are you OK?!
It was touch-and-go for a while, Mayor, but I think we've almost finished shopping.
Not that. A state judge released the **Legion of Bad Guys** from prison!
How many?
All of them! Every villain you ever arrested is back on the streets.
Dr. Relative? Edward Snooze? Fear Chemist? The city is doomed!
Not if we can help it.
Um, aren't you guys forgetting something?
SLAP!!
That'll be $247.
TEE HEE!
247.00
Now I **know** this place is evil.
But not as evil as the **LEGION OF BAD GUYS**.

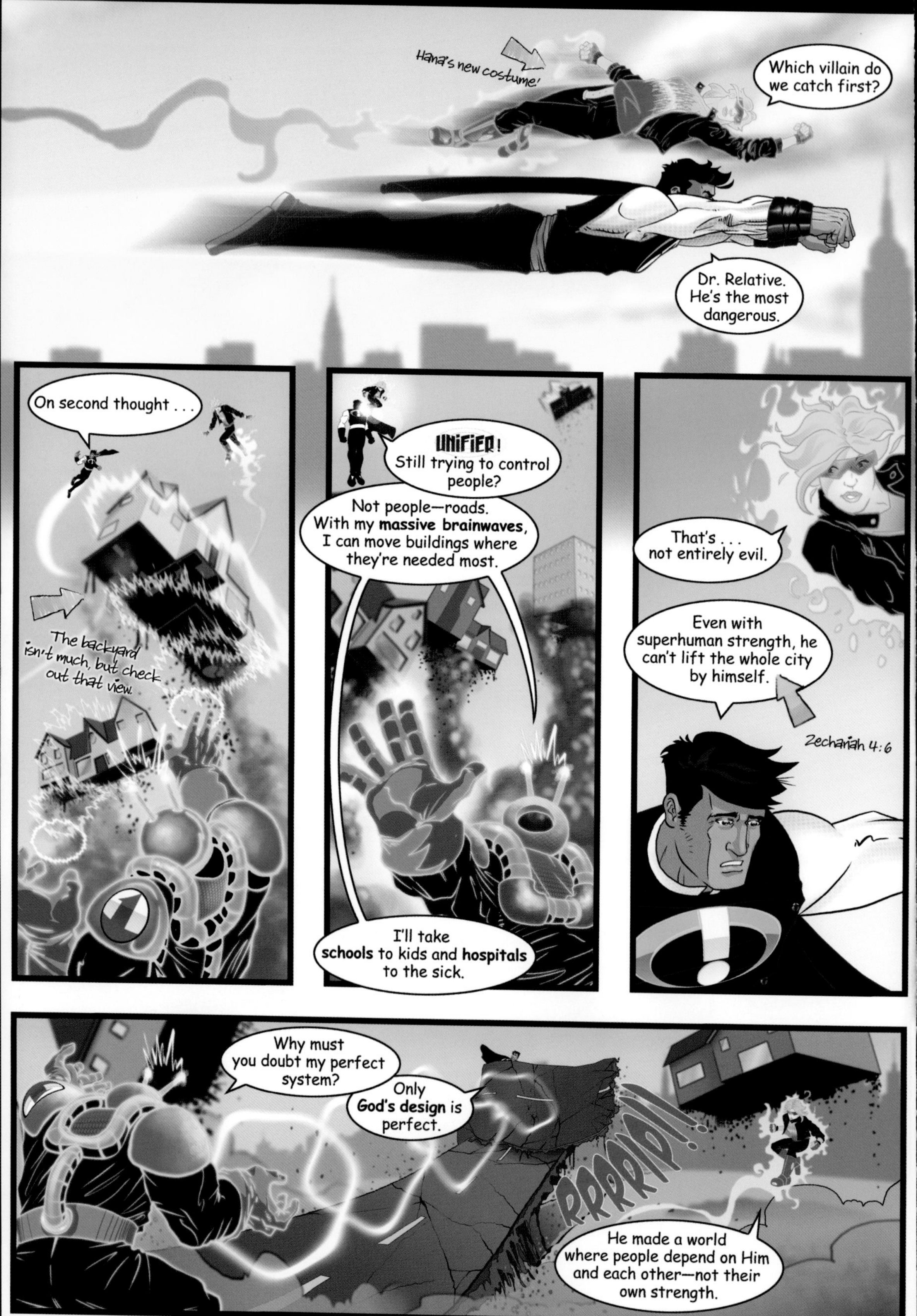
Hana's new costume!
Which villain do we catch first?
Dr. Relative. He's the most dangerous.
On second thought . . .
The backyard isn't much, but check out that view.
UNIFIER! Still trying to control people?
Not people—roads. With my **massive brainwaves**, I can move buildings where they're needed most.
I'll take **schools** to kids and **hospitals** to the sick.
That's . . . not entirely evil.
Even with superhuman strength, he can't lift the whole city by himself.
Zechariah 4:6
Why must you doubt my perfect system?
Only **God's design** is perfect.
RRRIP!!
He made a world where people depend on Him and each other—not their own strength.

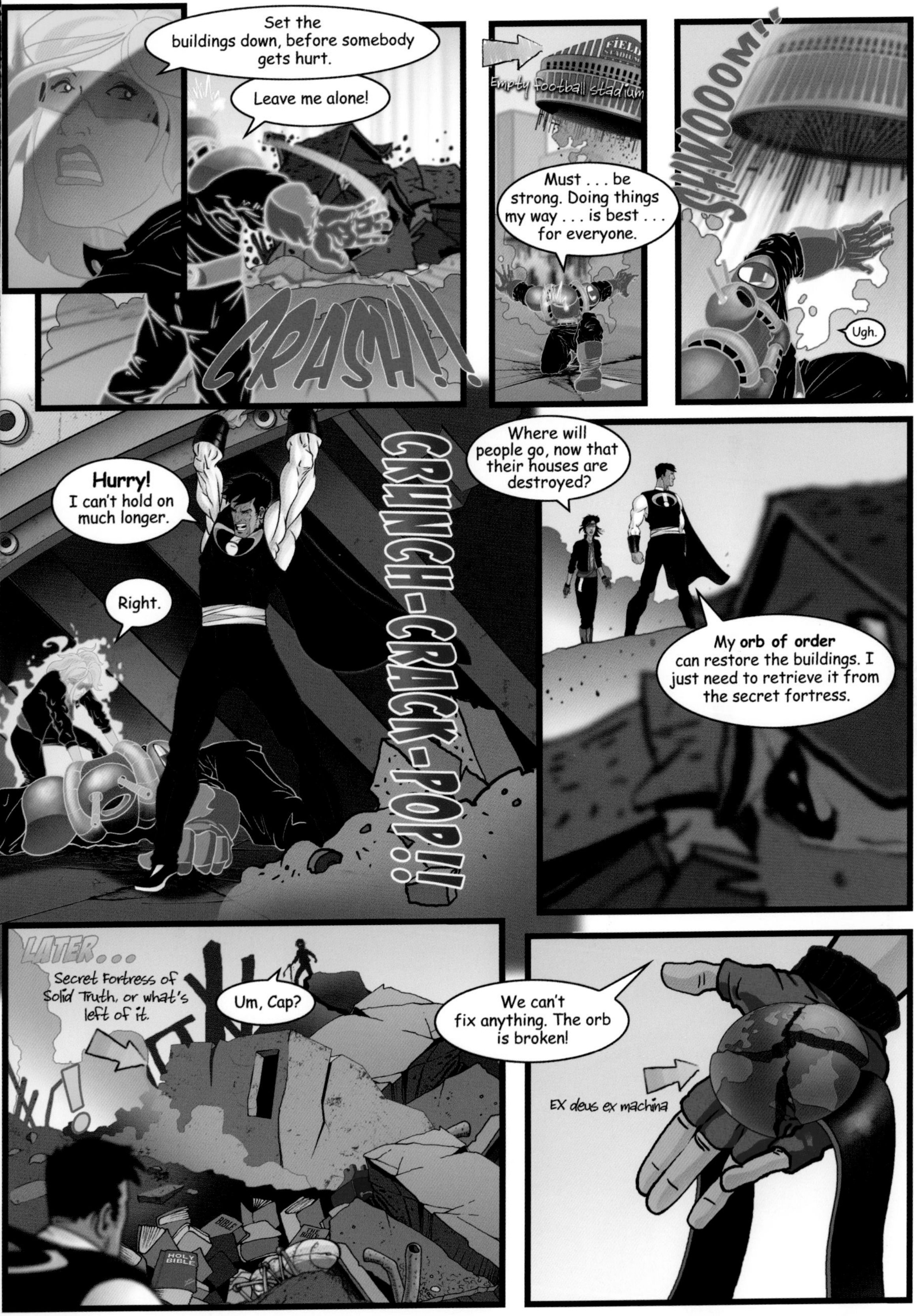

Set the buildings down, before somebody gets hurt.
Leave me alone!
CRASH!!
Empty football stadium
Must . . . be strong. Doing things my way . . . is best . . . for everyone.
SHWOOOM!!
Ugh.
Hurry! I can't hold on much longer.
Right.
CRUNCH-CRACK-POP!!!
Where will people go, now that their houses are destroyed?
My orb of order can restore the buildings. I just need to retrieve it from the secret fortress.
LATER . . .
Secret Fortress of Solid Truth, or what's left of it.
Um, Cap?
HOLY BIBLE
BIBLE
We can't fix anything. The orb is broken!
EX deus ex machina

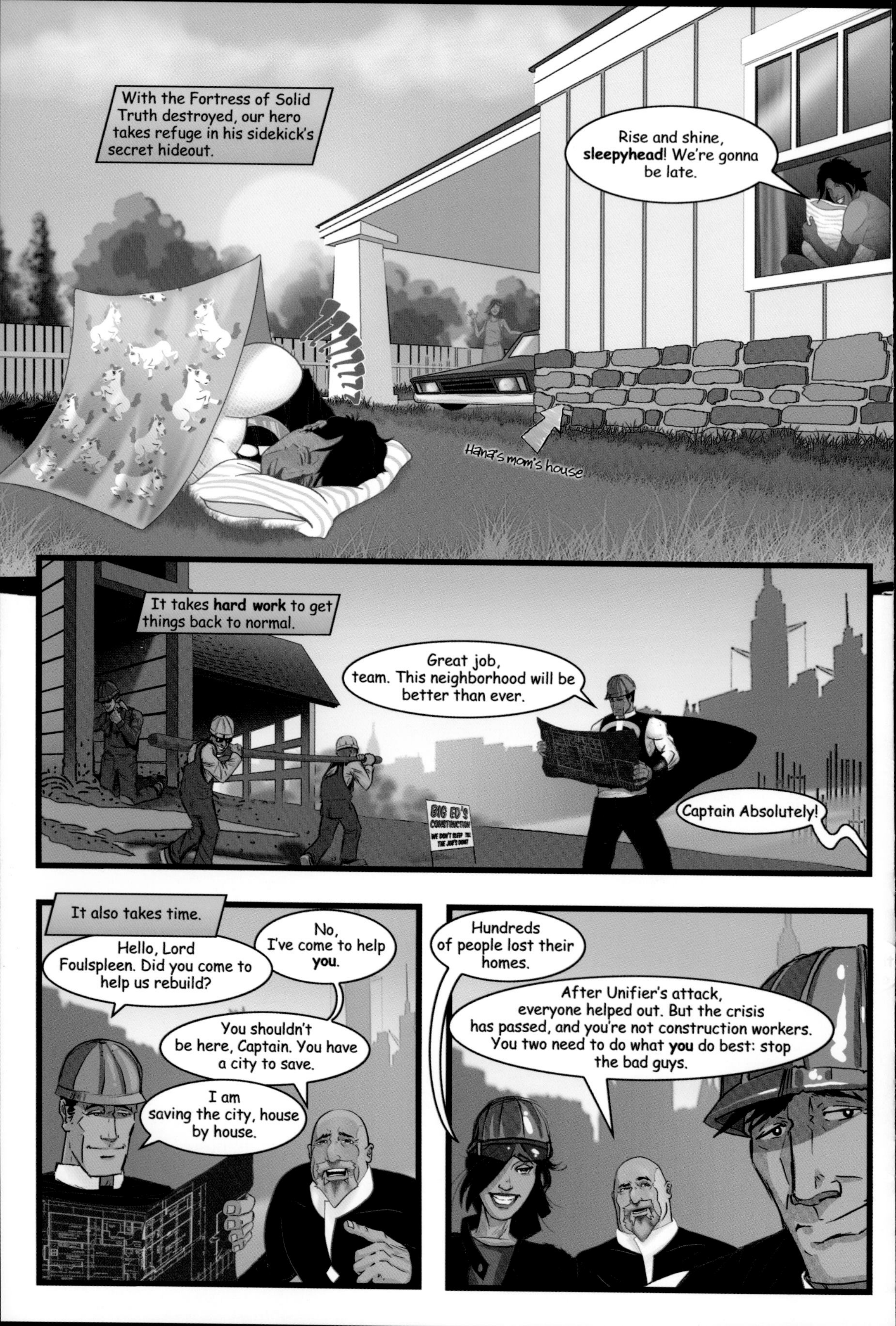

With the Fortress of Solid Truth destroyed, our hero takes refuge in his sidekick's secret hideout.
Rise and shine, **sleepyhead**! We're gonna be late.
Hana's mom's house
It takes **hard work** to get things back to normal.
Great job, team. This neighborhood will be better than ever.
BIG ED'S CONSTRUCTION
Captain Absolutely!
It also takes time.
Hello, Lord Foulspleen. Did you come to help us rebuild?
No, I've come to help **you**.
You shouldn't be here, Captain. You have a city to save.
I am saving the city, house by house.
Hundreds of people lost their homes.
After Unifier's attack, everyone helped out. But the crisis has passed, and you're not construction workers. You two need to do what **you** do best: stop the bad guys.

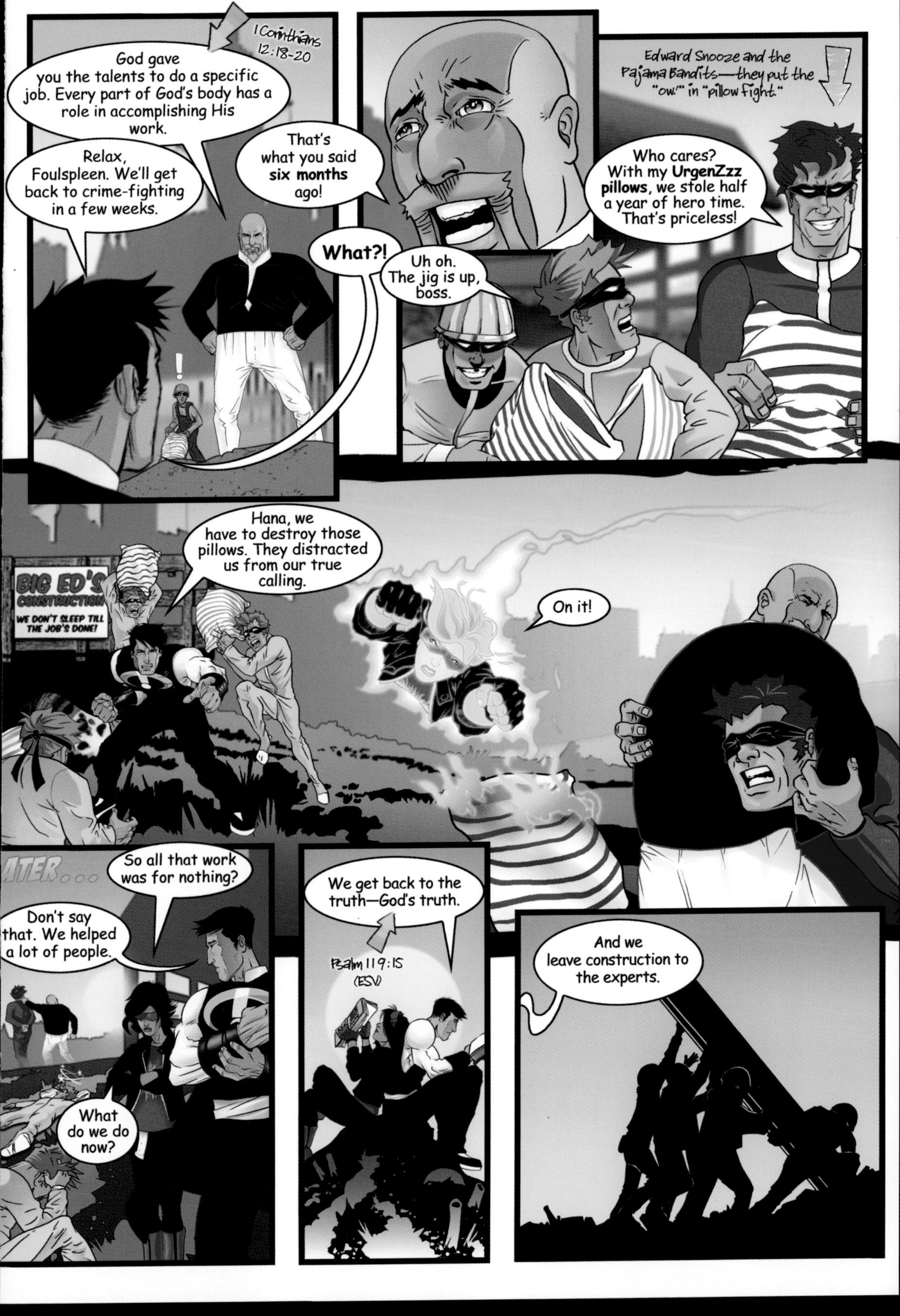
1 Corinthians 12:18-20
God gave you the talents to do a specific job. Every part of God's body has a role in accomplishing His work.
Relax, Foulspleen. We'll get back to crime-fighting in a few weeks.
That's what you said **six months** ago!
What?!
Edward Snooze and the Pajama Bandits—they put the "ow!" in "pillow fight."
Who cares? With my **UrgenZzz pillows**, we stole half a year of hero time. That's priceless!
Uh oh. The jig is up, boss.
BIG ED'S CONSTRUCTION
WE DON'T SLEEP TILL THE JOB'S DONE!
Hana, we have to destroy those pillows. They distracted us from our true calling.
On it!
So all that work was for nothing?
Don't say that. We helped a lot of people.
What do we do now?
We get back to the truth—God's truth.
Psalm 119:15 (ESV)
And we leave construction to the experts.

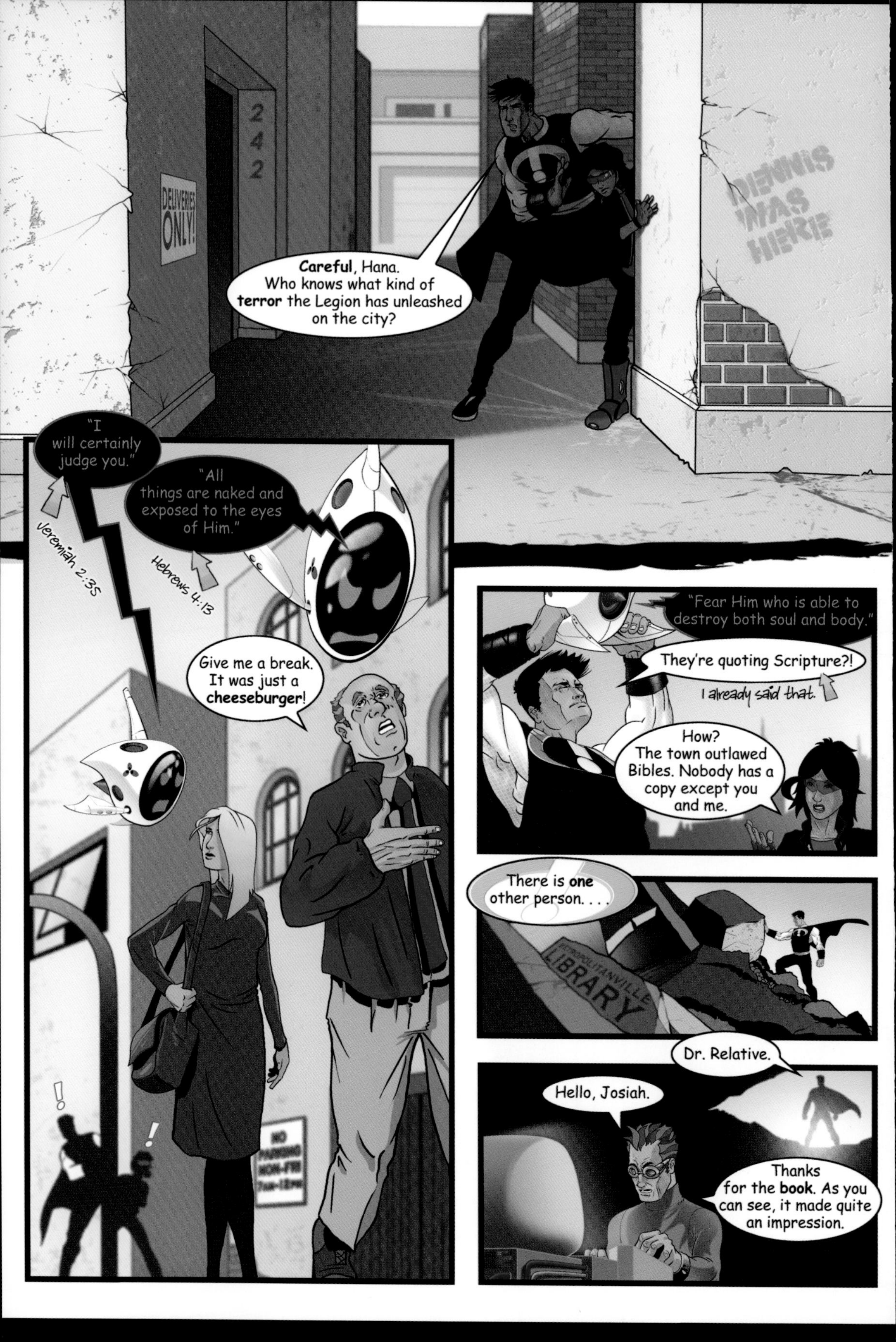
242
DELIVERIES ONLY!
DENNIS WAS HERE
Careful, Hana. Who knows what kind of terror the Legion has unleashed on the city?
"I will certainly judge you."
Jeremiah 2:35
"All things are naked and exposed to the eyes of Him."
Hebrews 4:13
Give me a break. It was just a cheeseburger!
!
!
NO PARKING MON-FRI 7AM-12PM
"Fear Him who is able to destroy both soul and body."
They're quoting Scripture?!
I already said that.
How? The town outlawed Bibles. Nobody has a copy except you and me.
There is one other person. . . .
METROPOLITANVILLE LIBRARY
Dr. Relative.
Hello, Josiah.
Thanks for the book. As you can see, it made quite an impression.

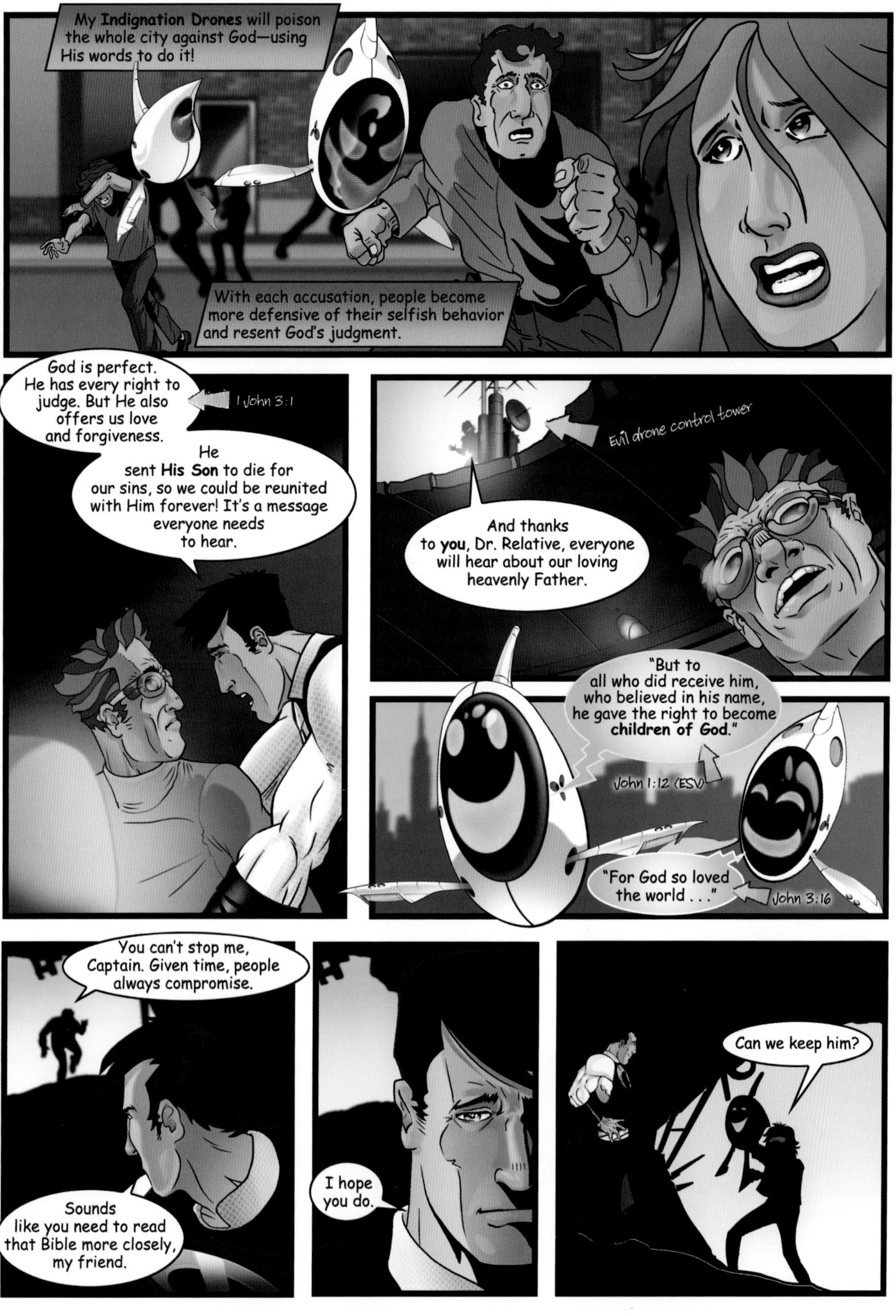

My Indignation Drones will poison the whole city against God—using His words to do it!
With each accusation, people become more defensive of their selfish behavior and resent God's judgment.
God is perfect. He has every right to judge. But He also offers us love and forgiveness.
1 John 3:1
He sent His Son to die for our sins, so we could be reunited with Him forever! It's a message everyone needs to hear.
Evil drone control tower
And thanks to you, Dr. Relative, everyone will hear about our loving heavenly Father.
"But to all who did receive him, who believed in his name, he gave the right to become children of God."
John 1:12 (ESV)
"For God so loved the world . . ."
John 3:16
You can't stop me, Captain. Given time, people always compromise.
Sounds like you need to read that Bible more closely, my friend.
I hope you do.
Can we keep him?

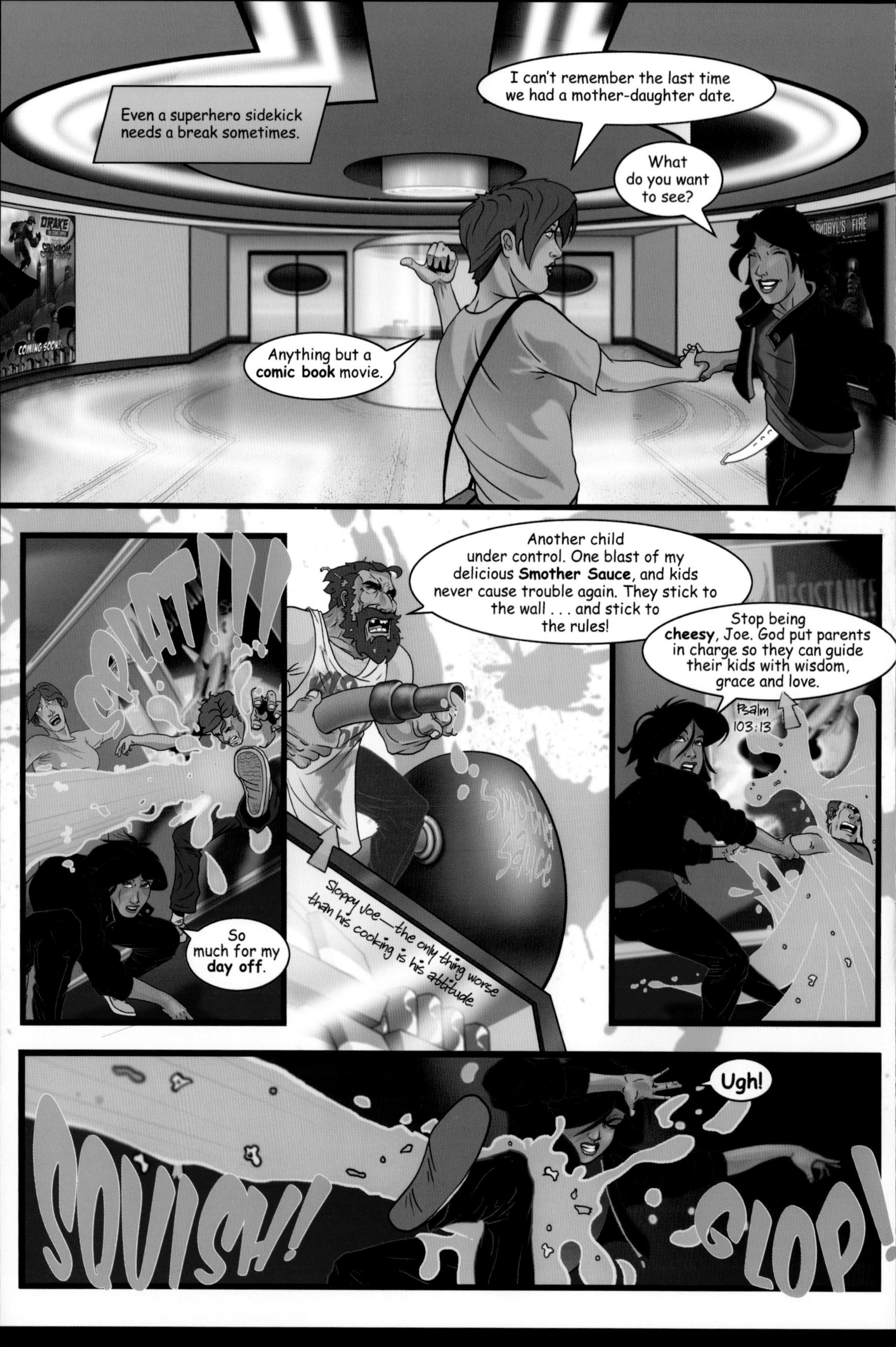
Even a superhero sidekick needs a break sometimes.
I can't remember the last time we had a mother-daughter date.
What do you want to see?
Anything but a **comic book** movie.
DRAKE
COMING SOON!
SPLAT!!!
Another child under control. One blast of my delicious **Smother Sauce**, and kids never cause trouble again. They stick to the wall . . . and stick to the rules!
Stop being **cheesy**, Joe. God put parents in charge so they can guide their kids with wisdom, grace and love.
Psalm 103:13
Smother Sauce
Sloppy Joe—the only thing worse than his cooking is his attitude.
So much for my **day off**.
Ugh!
SQUISH!
SLOP!

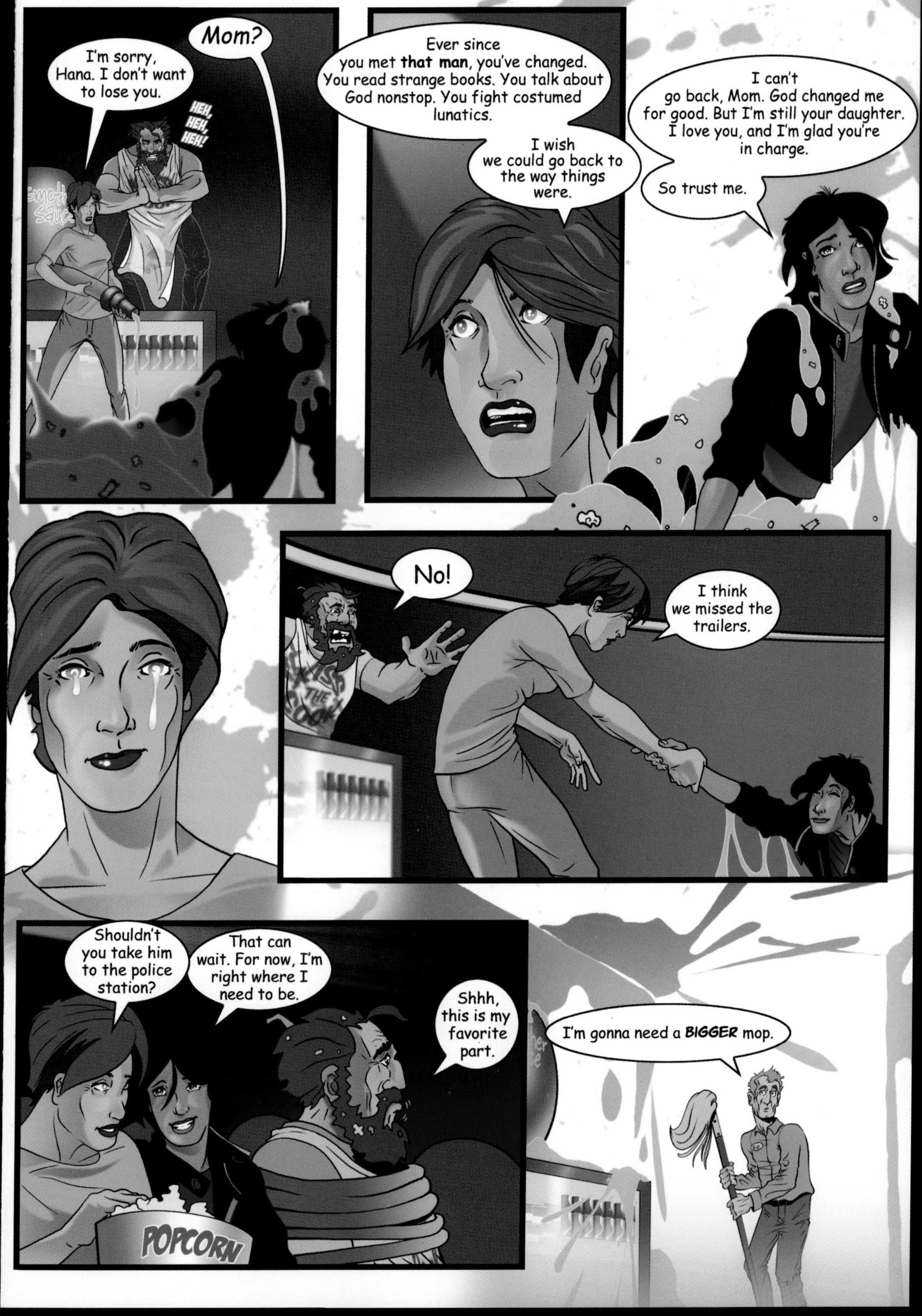
I'm sorry, Hana. I don't want to lose you.
Mom?
HEH, HEH, HEH!
Ever since you met **that man**, you've changed. You read strange books. You talk about God nonstop. You fight costumed lunatics.
I wish we could go back to the way things were.
I can't go back, Mom. God changed me for good. But I'm still your daughter. I love you, and I'm glad you're in charge.
So trust me.
No!
I think we missed the trailers.
Shouldn't you take him to the police station?
That can wait. For now, I'm right where I need to be.
Shhh, this is my favorite part.
I'm gonna need a **BIGGER** mop.
POPCORN

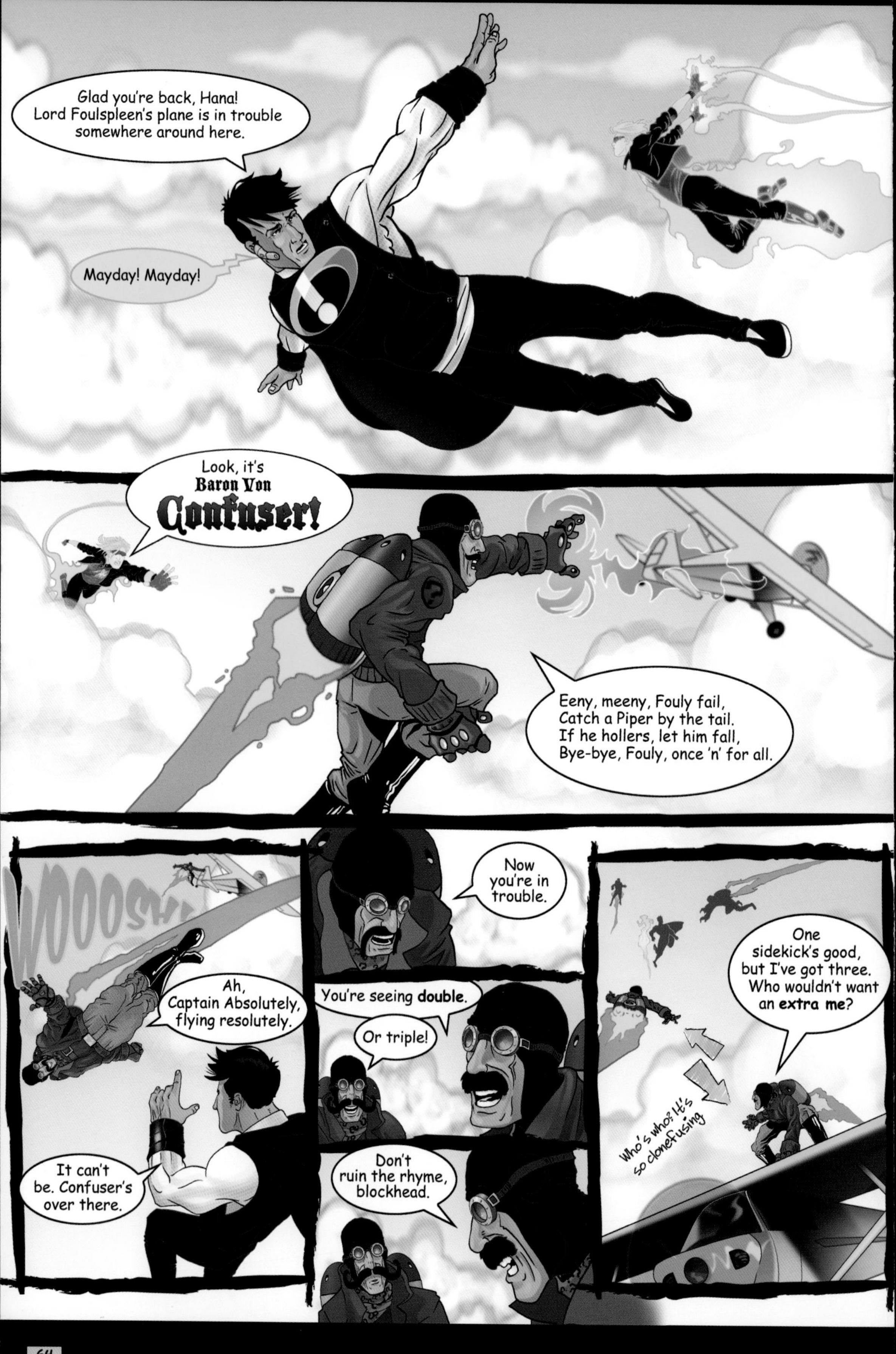
Glad you're back, Hana! Lord Foulspleen's plane is in trouble somewhere around here.
Mayday! Mayday!
Look, it's Baron Von Confuser!
Eeny, meeny, Fouly fail, Catch a Piper by the tail. If he hollers, let him fall, Bye-bye, Fouly, once 'n' for all.
Ah, Captain Absolutely, flying resolutely.
It can't be. Confuser's over there.
Now you're in trouble.
You're seeing **double**.
Or triple!
Don't ruin the rhyme, blockhead.
One sidekick's good, but I've got three. Who wouldn't want an **extra me**?
Who's who? It's so clonefusing

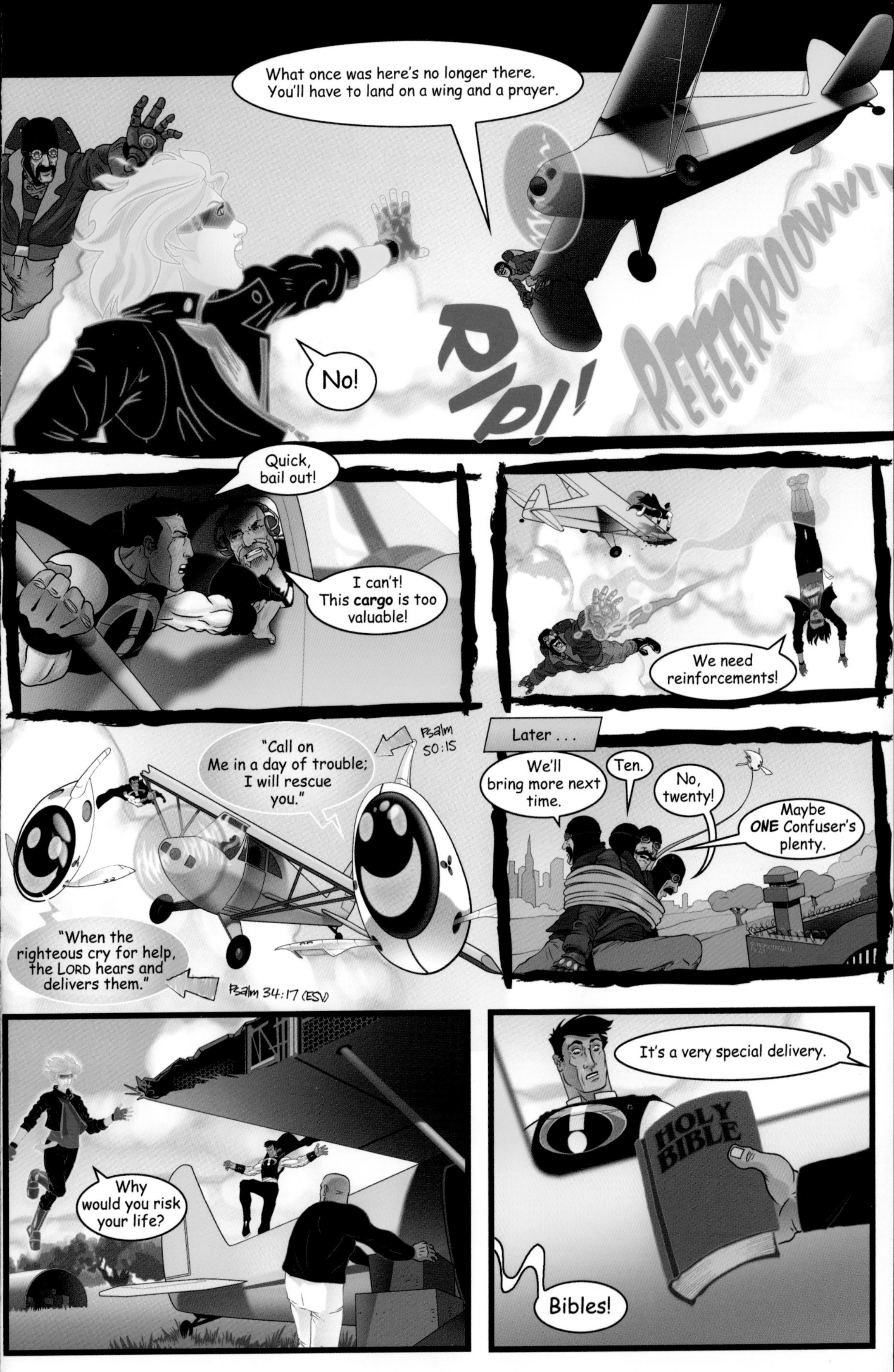

What once was here's no longer there. You'll have to land on a wing and a prayer.
No!
RIP!
REEEERROOWW!!
Quick, bail out!
I can't! This **cargo** is too valuable!
We need reinforcements!
"Call on Me in a day of trouble; I will rescue you."
Psalm 50:15
"When the righteous cry for help, the LORD hears and delivers them."
Psalm 34:17 (ESV)
Later . . .
We'll bring more next time.
Ten.
No, twenty!
Maybe **ONE** Confuser's plenty.
Why would you risk your life?
It's a very special delivery.
HOLY BIBLE
Bibles!

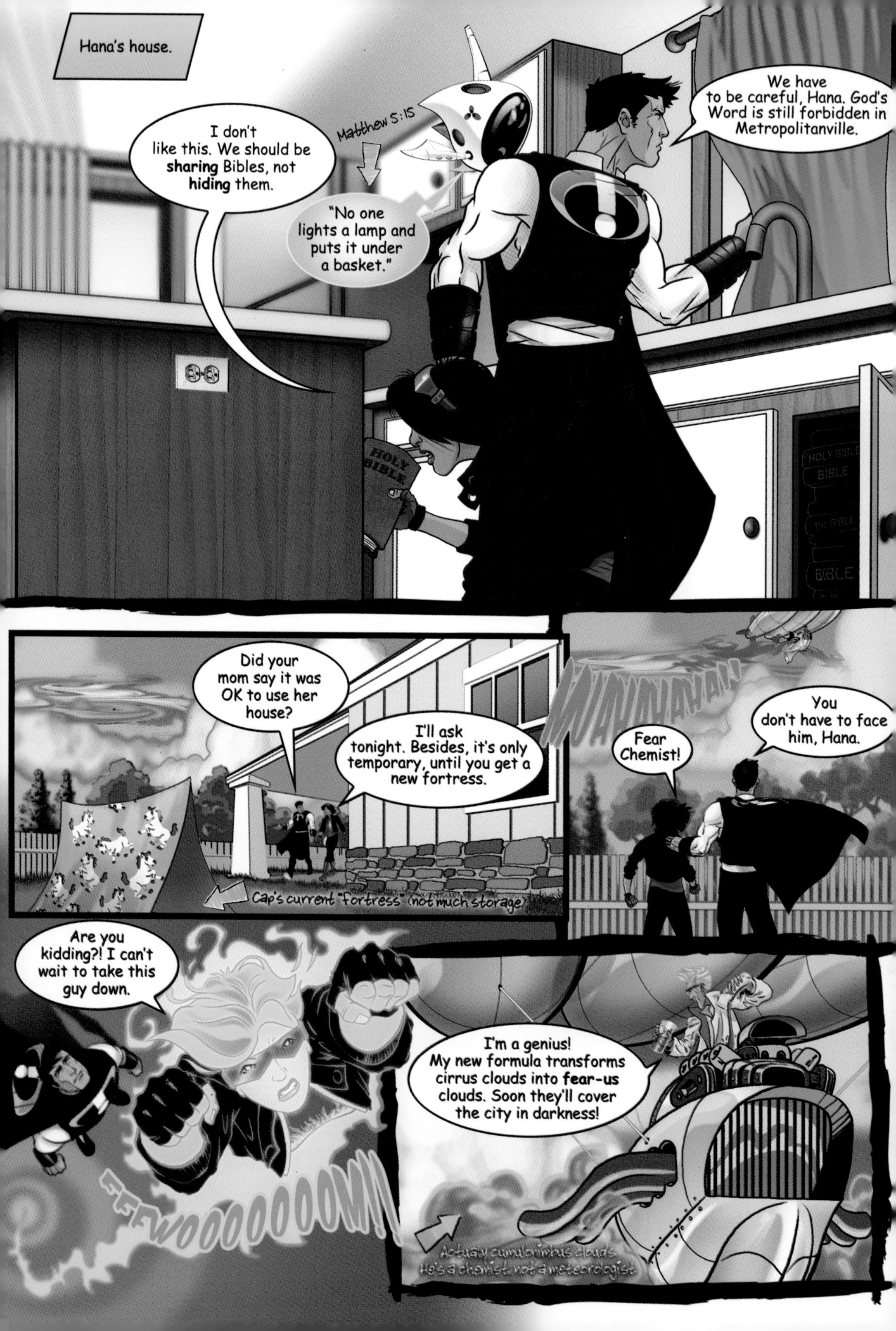
Hana's house.
I don't like this. We should be **sharing** Bibles, not **hiding** them.
Matthew 5:15
"No one lights a lamp and puts it under a basket."
We have to be careful, Hana. God's Word is still forbidden in Metropolitanville.
HOLY BIBLE
Did your mom say it was OK to use her house?
I'll ask tonight. Besides, it's only temporary, until you get a new fortress.
Cap's current "fortress" (not much storage)
Fear Chemist!
You don't have to face him, Hana.
Are you kidding?! I can't wait to take this guy down.
FFWOOOOOOOM!!
I'm a genius! My new formula transforms cirrus clouds into **fear-us** clouds. Soon they'll cover the city in darkness!
Actually cumulonimbus clouds. He's a chemist, not a meteorologist.

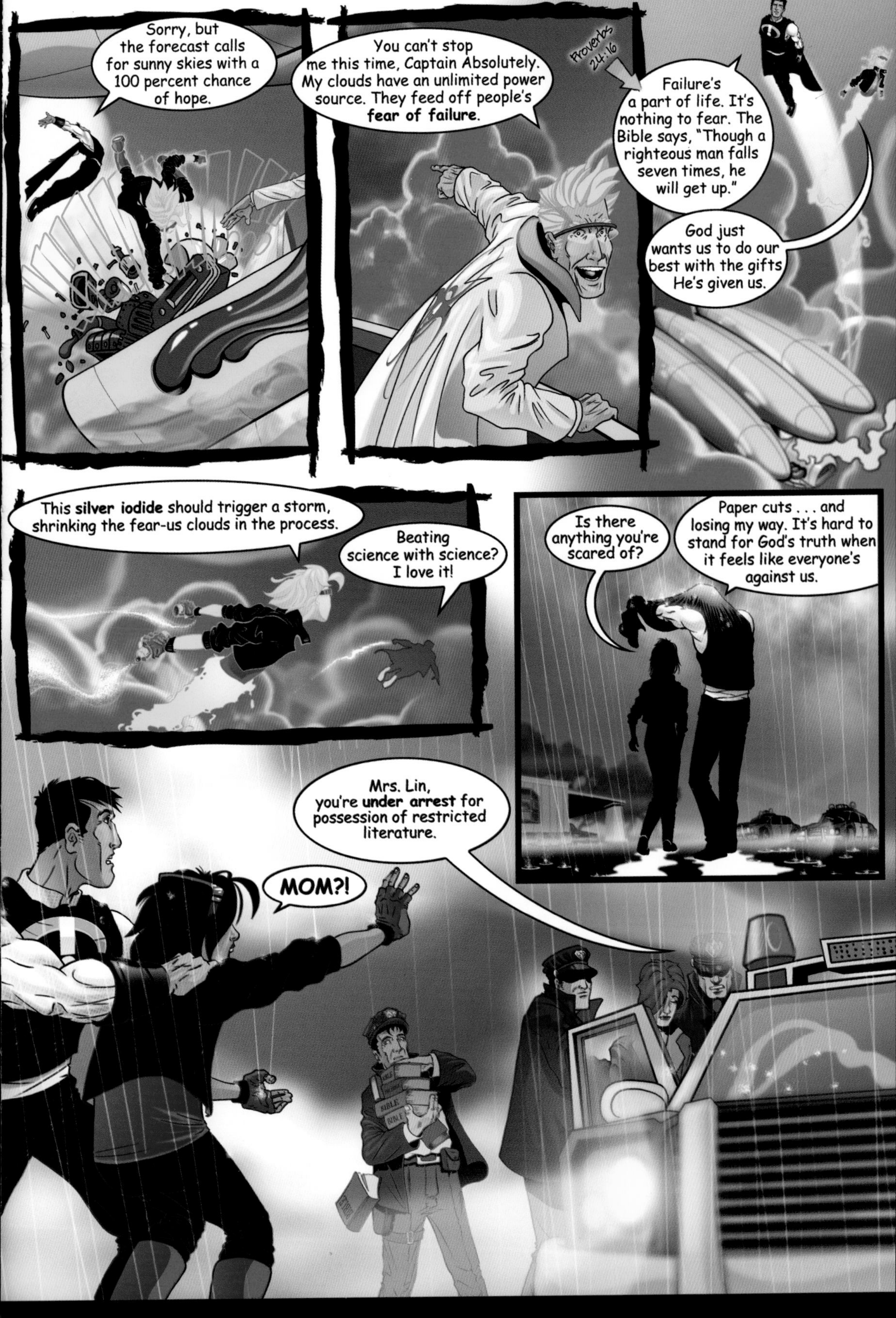
Sorry, but the forecast calls for sunny skies with a 100 percent chance of hope.
You can't stop me this time, Captain Absolutely. My clouds have an unlimited power source. They feed off people's **fear of failure**.
Proverbs 24:16
Failure's a part of life. It's nothing to fear. The Bible says, "Though a righteous man falls seven times, he will get up."
God just wants us to do our best with the gifts He's given us.
This **silver iodide** should trigger a storm, shrinking the fear-us clouds in the process.
Beating science with science? I love it!
Is there anything you're scared of?
Paper cuts . . . and losing my way. It's hard to stand for God's truth when it feels like everyone's against us.
Mrs. Lin, you're **under arrest** for possession of restricted literature.
MOM?!

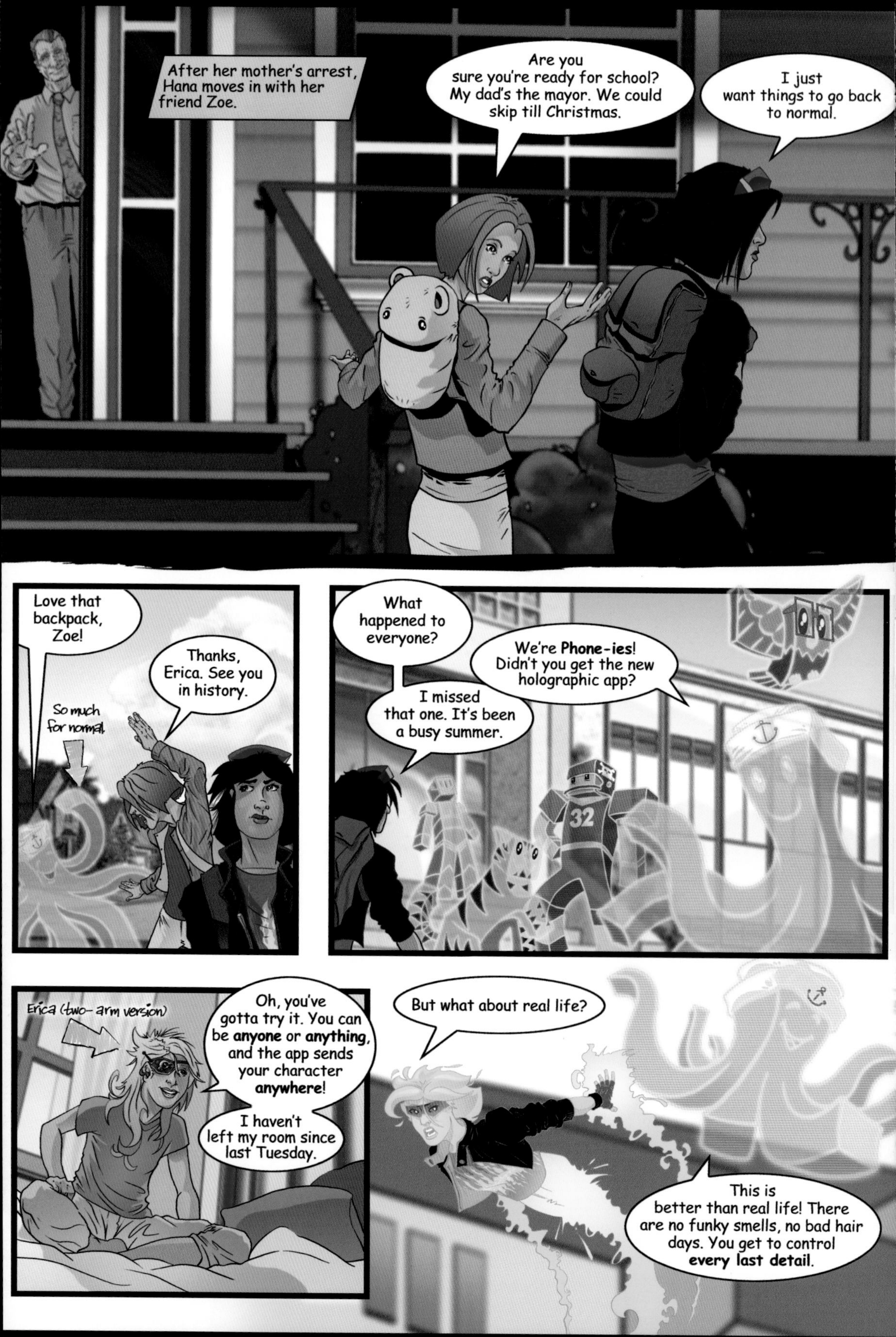
After her mother's arrest, Hana moves in with her friend Zoe.
Are you sure you're ready for school? My dad's the mayor. We could skip till Christmas.
I just want things to go back to normal.
Love that backpack, Zoe!
Thanks, Erica. See you in history.
So much for normal.
What happened to everyone?
We're **Phone-ies**! Didn't you get the new holographic app?
I missed that one. It's been a busy summer.
32
Erica (two-arm version)
Oh, you've gotta try it. You can be **anyone** or **anything**, and the app sends your character **anywhere**!
I haven't left my room since last Tuesday.
But what about real life?
This is better than real life! There are no funky smells, no bad hair days. You get to control **every last detail**.

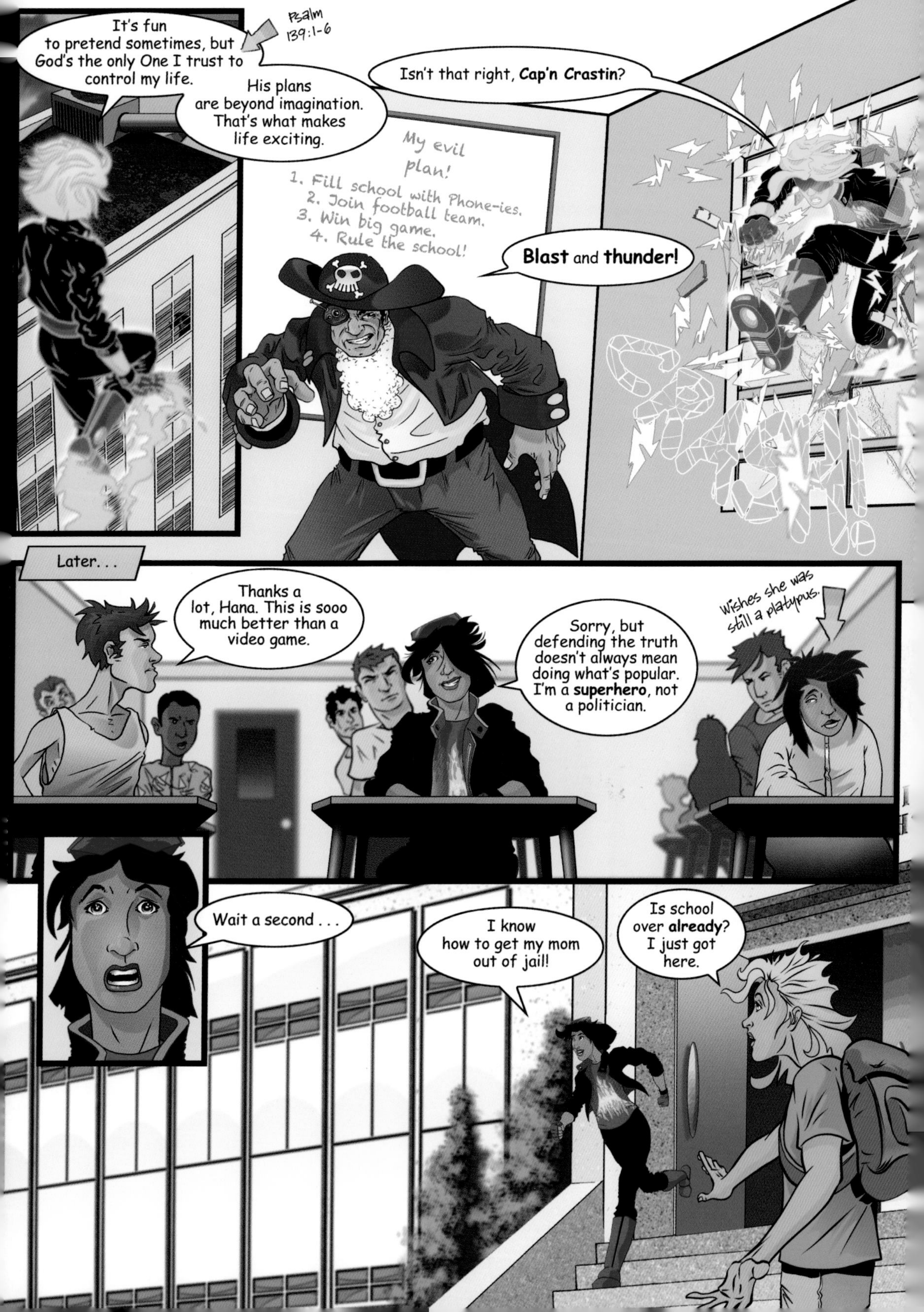
Psalm 139:1-6
It's fun to pretend sometimes, but God's the only One I trust to control my life.
His plans are beyond imagination. That's what makes life exciting.
Isn't that right, Cap'n Crastin?
My evil plan!
1. Fill school with Phone-ies.
2. Join football team.
3. Win big game.
4. Rule the school!
Blast and thunder!
SMASH!
Later. . .
Thanks a lot, Hana. This is sooo much better than a video game.
Sorry, but defending the truth doesn't always mean doing what's popular. I'm a superhero, not a politician.
Wishes she was still a platypus.
Wait a second . . .
I know how to get my mom out of jail!
Is school over already? I just got here.

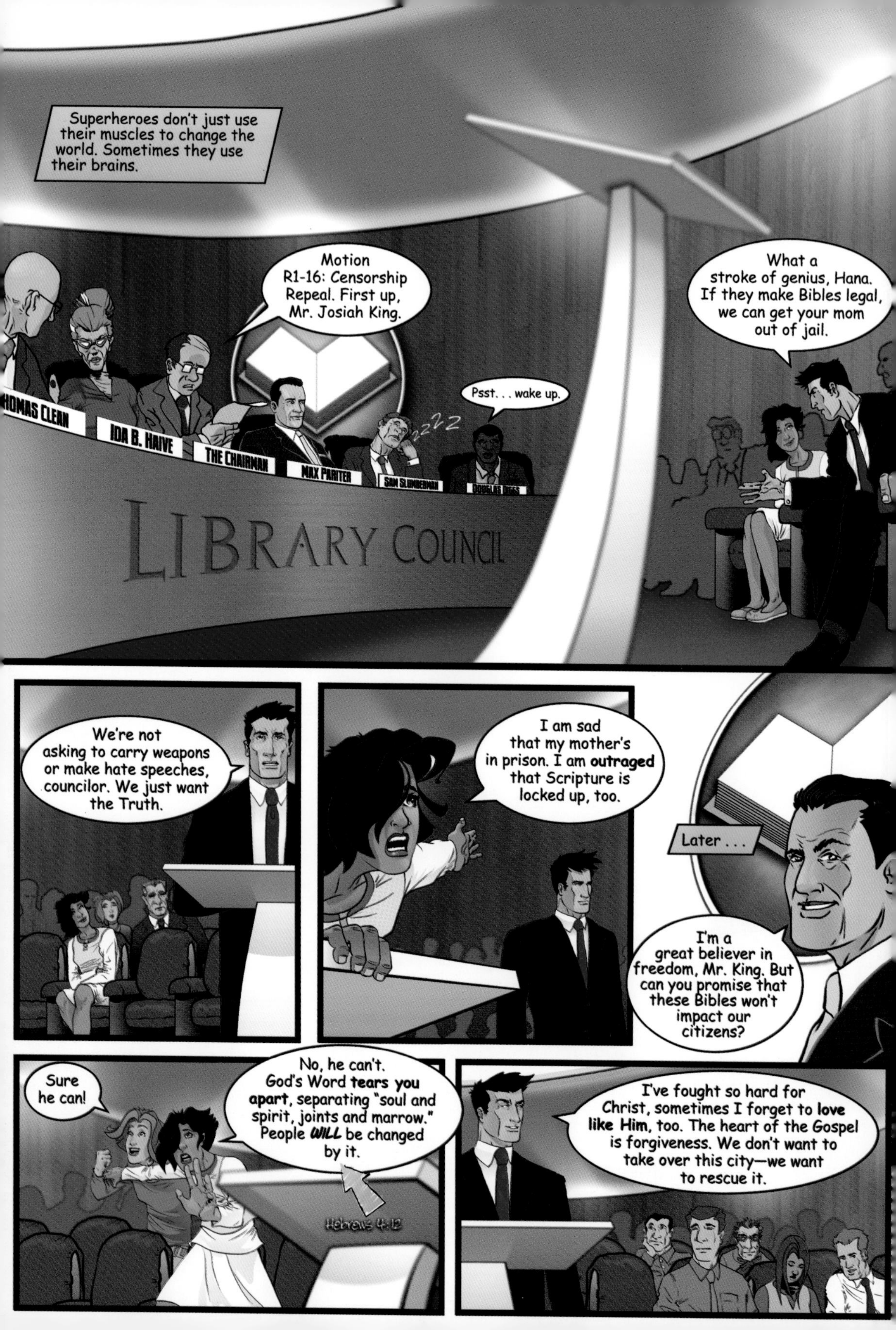
Superheroes don't just use their muscles to change the world. Sometimes they use their brains.
Motion R1-16: Censorship Repeal. First up, Mr. Josiah King.
HOMAS CLEAN
IDA B. HAIVE
THE CHAIRMAN
MAX PARITER
SAM SLUMBERMAN
DOUGLAS DIGGS
zzzZ
Psst. . . wake up.
What a stroke of genius, Hana. If they make Bibles legal, we can get your mom out of jail.
LIBRARY COUNCIL
We're not asking to carry weapons or make hate speeches, councilor. We just want the Truth.
I am sad that my mother's in prison. I am **outraged** that Scripture is locked up, too.
Later . . .
I'm a great believer in freedom, Mr. King. But can you promise that these Bibles won't impact our citizens?
Sure he can!
No, he can't. God's Word **tears you apart**, separating "soul and spirit, joints and marrow." People ***WILL*** be changed by it.
Hebrews 4:12
I've fought so hard for Christ, sometimes I forget to **love like Him**, too. The heart of the Gospel is forgiveness. We don't want to take over this city—we want to rescue it.

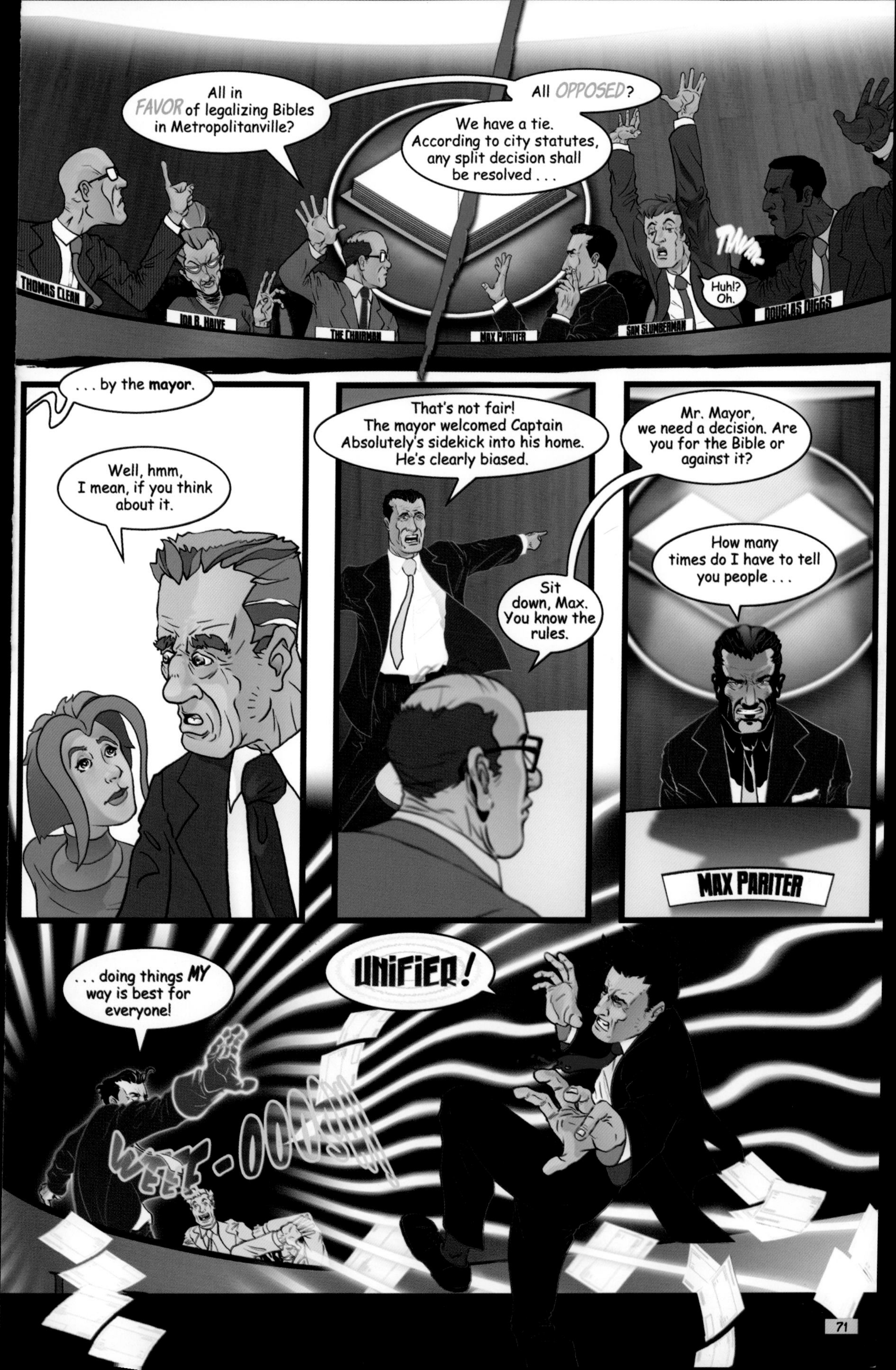
All in FAVOR of legalizing Bibles in Metropolitanville?
All OPPOSED?
We have a tie. According to city statutes, any split decision shall be resolved . . .
THOMAS CLEAN
IDA B. NAIVE
THE CHAIRMAN
MAX PARITER
Huh!? Oh.
SAM SLUMBERMAN
DOUGLAS DIGGS
. . . by the mayor.
Well, hmm, I mean, if you think about it.
That's not fair! The mayor welcomed Captain Absolutely's sidekick into his home. He's clearly biased.
Sit down, Max. You know the rules.
Mr. Mayor, we need a decision. Are you for the Bible or against it?
How many times do I have to tell you people . . .
MAX PARITER
. . . doing things MY way is best for everyone!
UNIFIER!

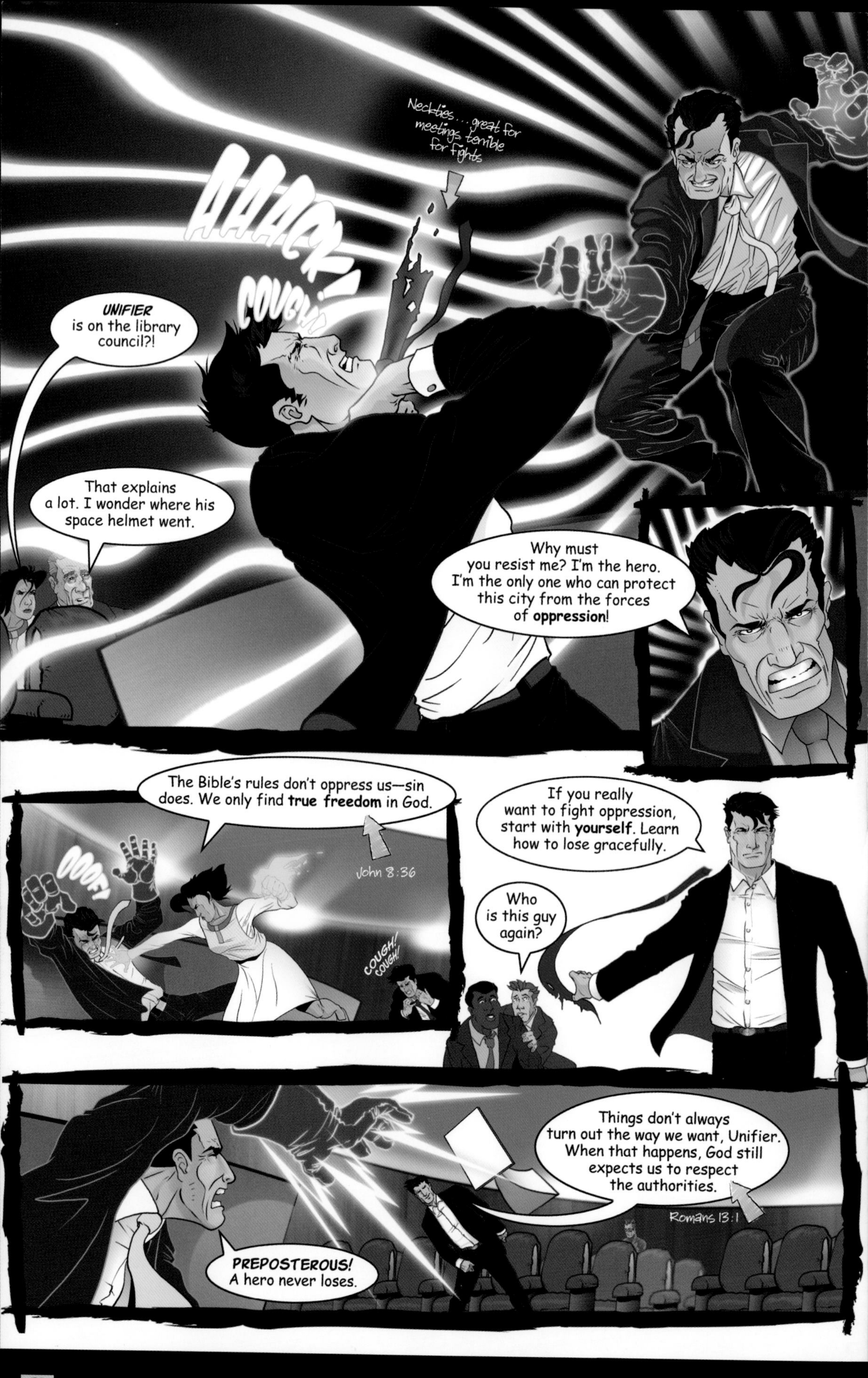
Neckties . . . great for meetings, terrible for fights
AAAACK!
COUGH!
UNIFIER is on the library council?!
That explains a lot. I wonder where his space helmet went.
Why must you resist me? I'm the hero. I'm the only one who can protect this city from the forces of **oppression**!
OOOF!
The Bible's rules don't oppress us—sin does. We only find **true freedom** in God.
John 8:36
COUGH! COUGH!
If you really want to fight oppression, start with **yourself**. Learn how to lose gracefully.
Who is this guy again?
PREPOSTEROUS! A hero never loses.
Things don't always turn out the way we want, Unifier. When that happens, God still expects us to respect the authorities.
Romans 13:1

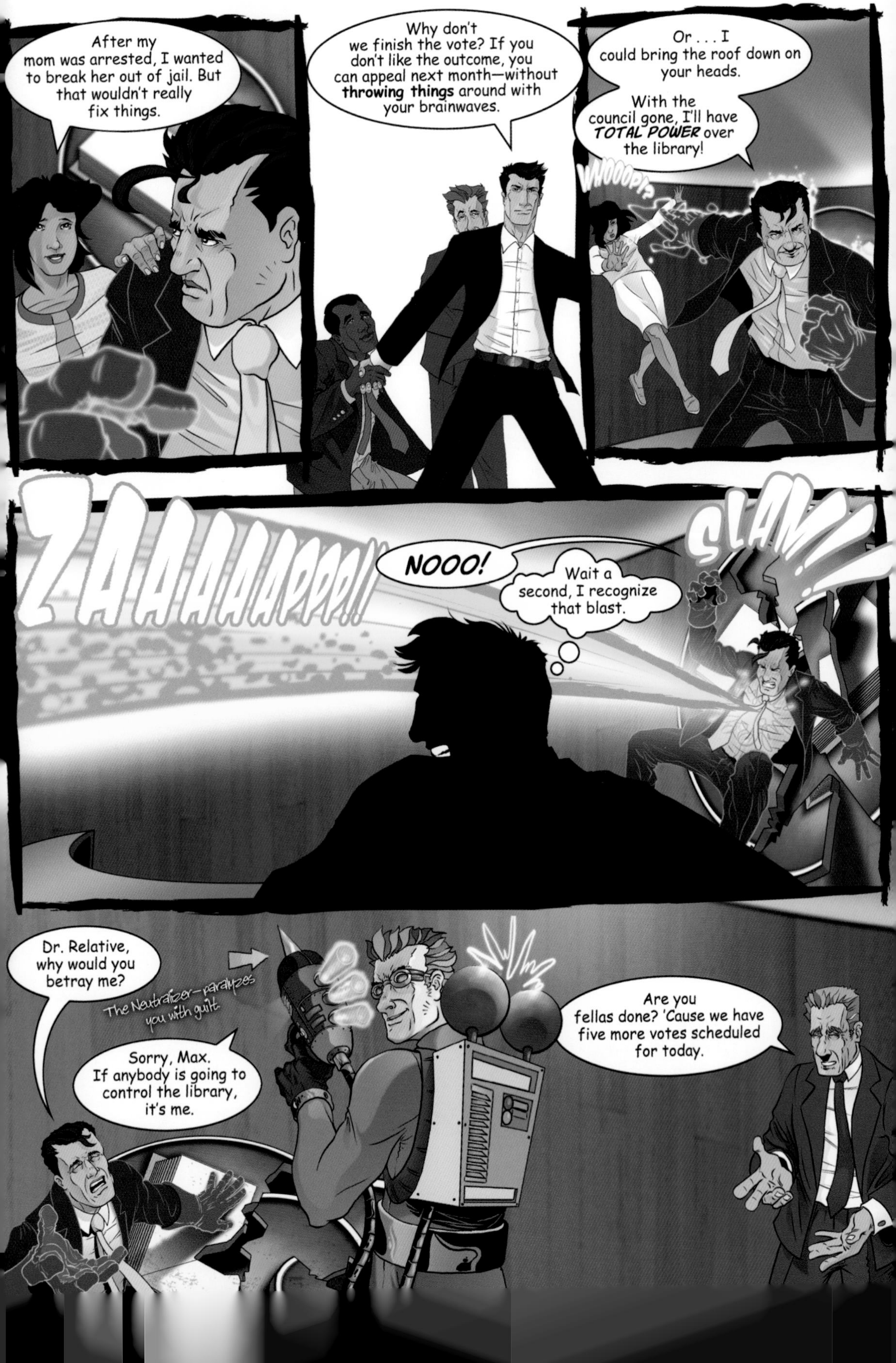
After my mom was arrested, I wanted to break her out of jail. But that wouldn't really fix things.
Why don't we finish the vote? If you don't like the outcome, you can appeal next month—without **throwing things** around with your brainwaves.
Or . . . I could bring the roof down on your heads.
With the council gone, I'll have ***TOTAL POWER*** over the library!
WHOOOP!?
ZAAAAAAPPP!!
NOOO!
Wait a second, I recognize that blast.
SLAM!!!
Dr. Relative, why would you betray me?
The Neutralizer—paralyzes you with guilt.
Sorry, Max. If anybody is going to control the library, it's me.
Are you fellas done? 'Cause we have five more votes scheduled for today.

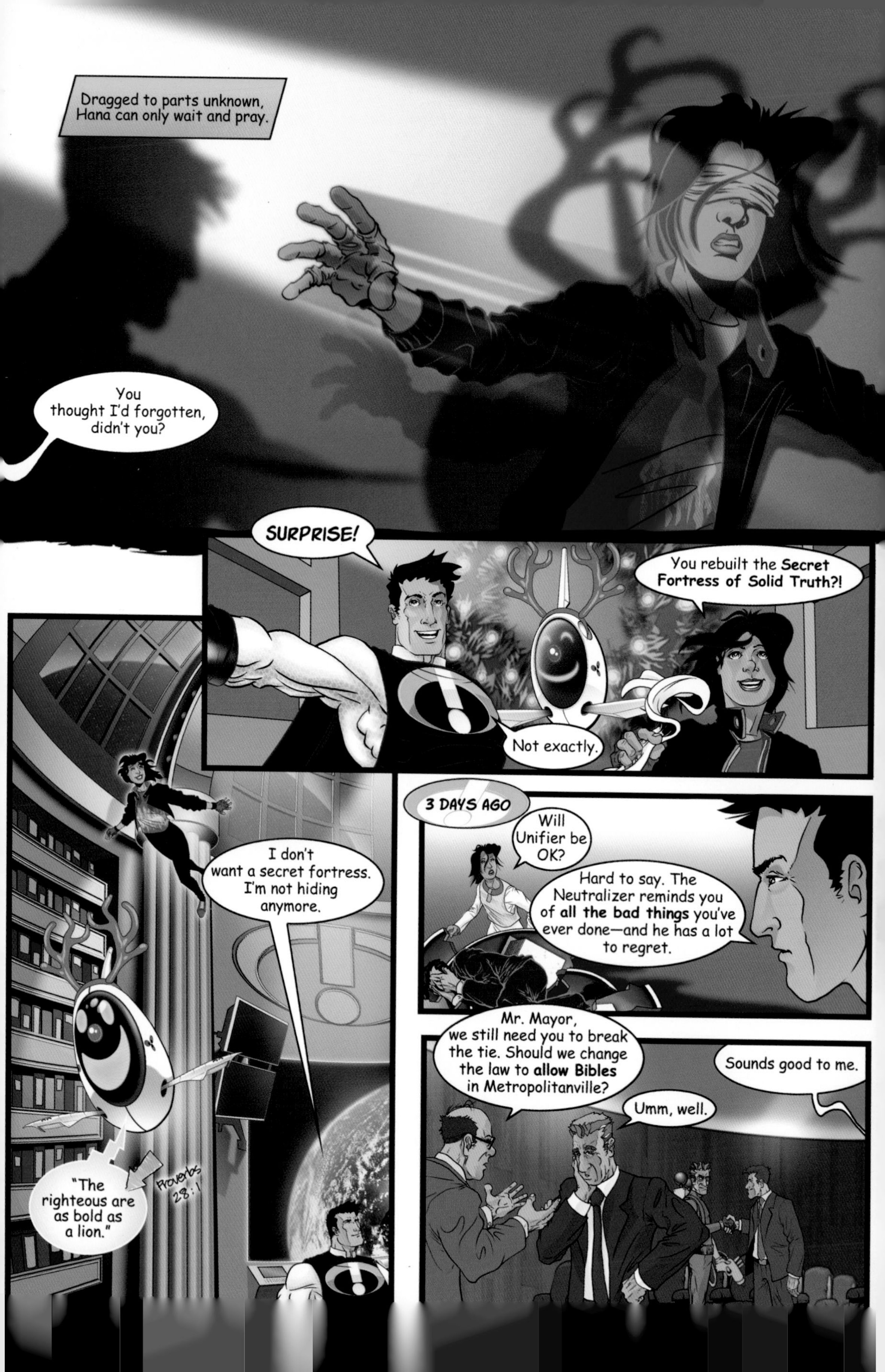
Dragged to parts unknown, Hana can only wait and pray.
You thought I'd forgotten, didn't you?
SURPRISE!
You rebuilt the **Secret Fortress of Solid Truth?!**
Not exactly.
I don't want a secret fortress. I'm not hiding anymore.
"The righteous are as bold as a lion."
Proverbs 28:1
3 DAYS AGO
Will Unifier be OK?
Hard to say. The Neutralizer reminds you of **all the bad things** you've ever done—and he has a lot to regret.
Mr. Mayor, we still need you to break the tie. Should we change the law to **allow Bibles** in Metropolitanville?
Umm, well.
Sounds good to me.

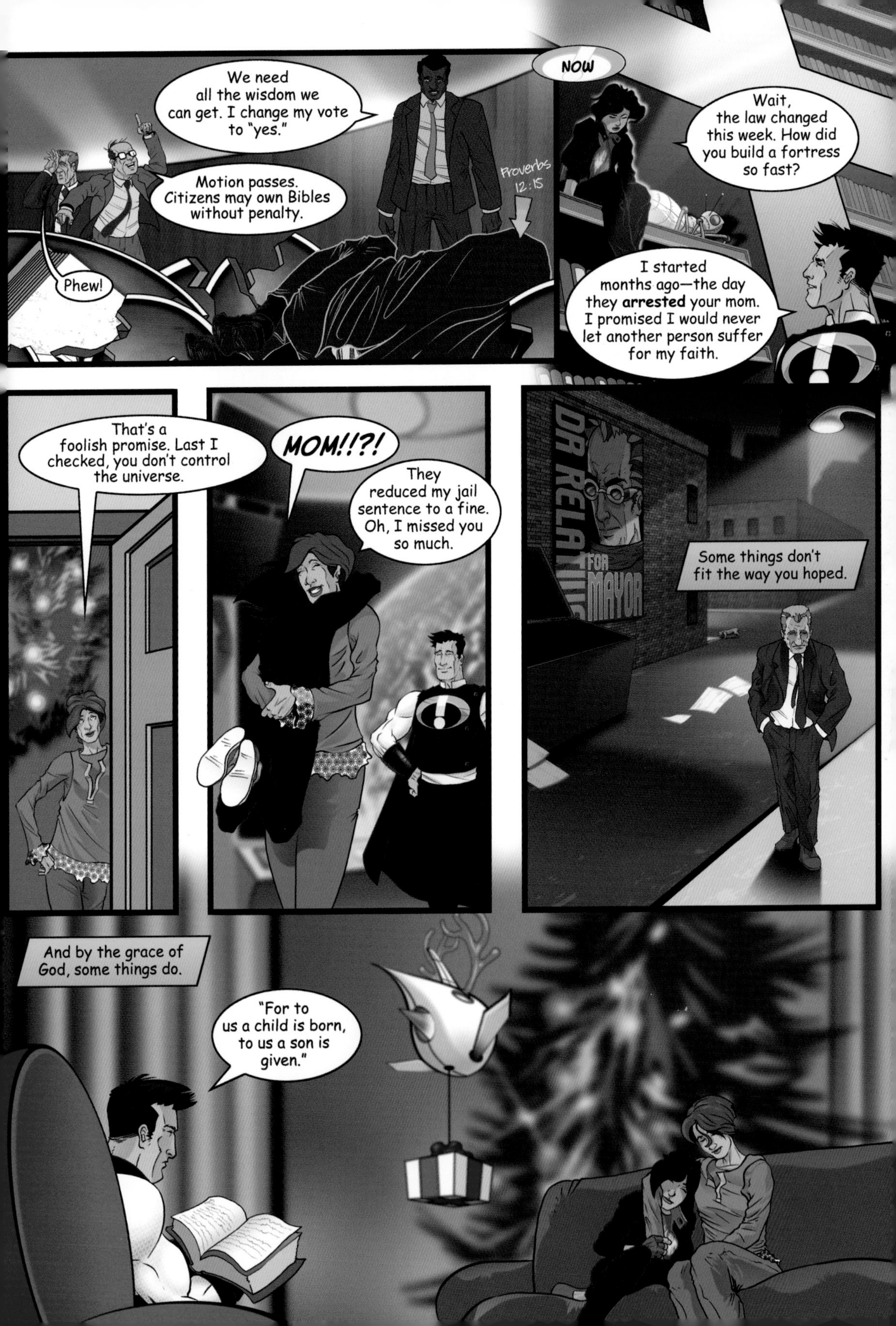

We need all the wisdom we can get. I change my vote to "yes."
Motion passes. Citizens may own Bibles without penalty.
Phew!
Proverbs 12:15
NOW
Wait, the law changed this week. How did you build a fortress so fast?
I started months ago—the day they **arrested** your mom. I promised I would never let another person suffer for my faith.
That's a foolish promise. Last I checked, you don't control the universe.
MOM!!?!
They reduced my jail sentence to a fine. Oh, I missed you so much.
DR RELATIVE FOR MAYOR
Some things don't fit the way you hoped.
And by the grace of God, some things do.
"For to us a child is born, to us a son is given."

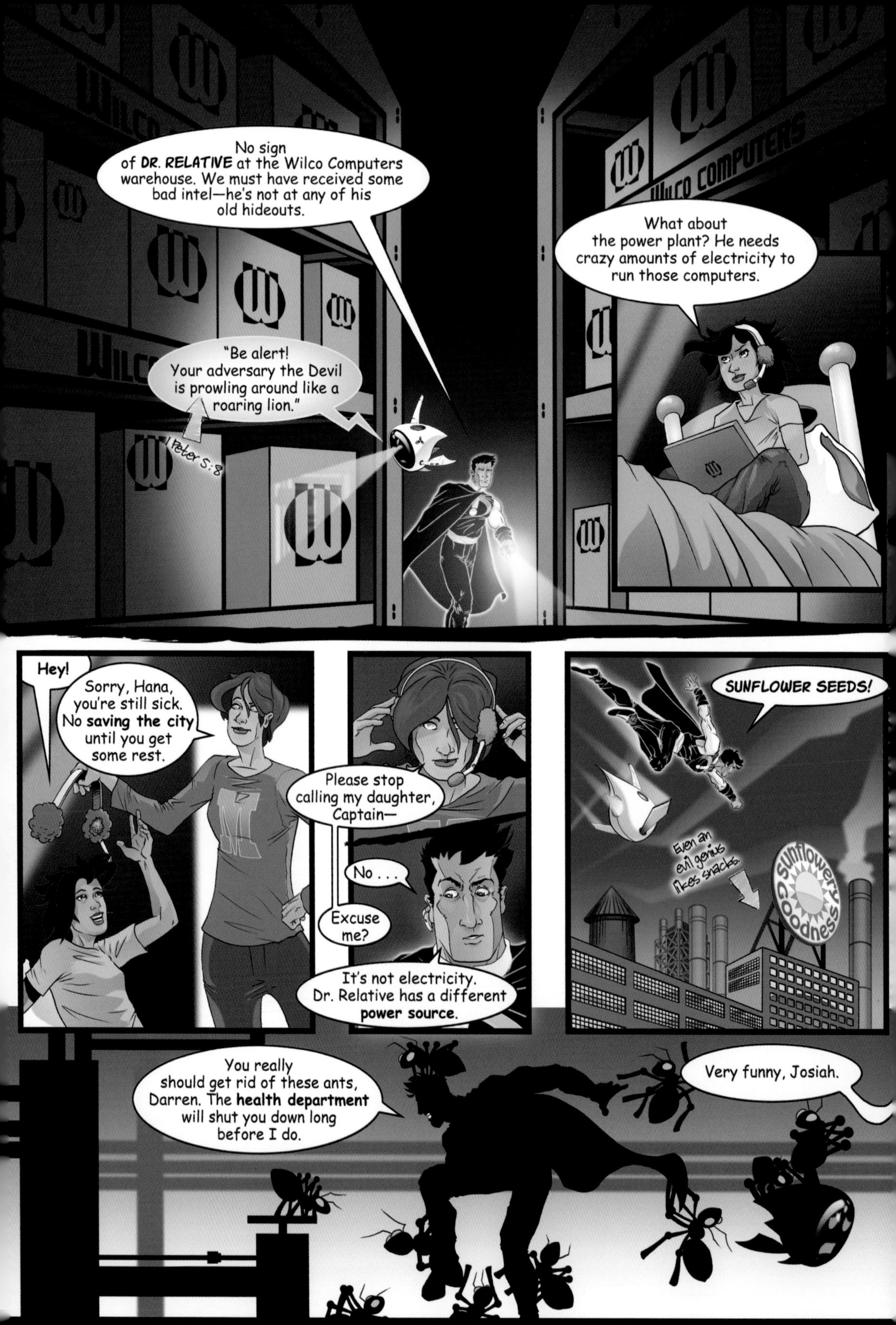
WILCO
No sign of DR. RELATIVE at the Wilco Computers warehouse. We must have received some bad intel—he's not at any of his old hideouts.
WILCO COMPUTERS
What about the power plant? He needs crazy amounts of electricity to run those computers.
"Be alert! Your adversary the Devil is prowling around like a roaring lion."
1 Peter 5:8
Hey!
Sorry, Hana, you're still sick. No saving the city until you get some rest.
Please stop calling my daughter, Captain—
No . . .
Excuse me?
It's not electricity. Dr. Relative has a different power source.
SUNFLOWER SEEDS!
Even an evil genius likes snacks.
Sunflowery Goodness
You really should get rid of these ants, Darren. The health department will shut you down long before I do.
Very funny, Josiah.

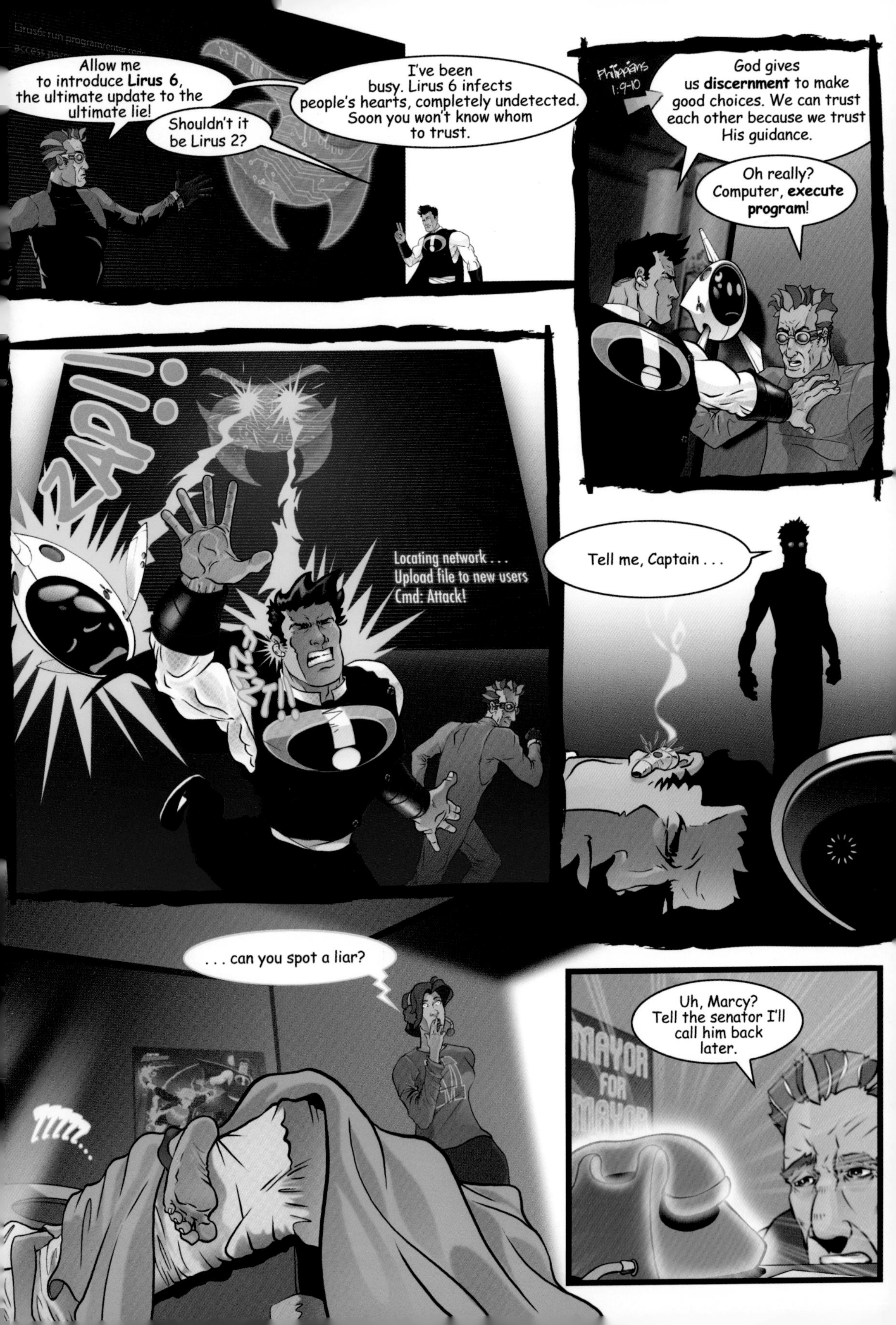

Lirus6: run program/enter code
Allow me to introduce **Lirus 6**, the ultimate update to the ultimate lie!
Shouldn't it be Lirus 2?
I've been busy. Lirus 6 infects people's hearts, completely undetected. Soon you won't know whom to trust.
Philippians 1:9-10
God gives us **discernment** to make good choices. We can trust each other because we trust His guidance.
Oh really? Computer, **execute program**!
ZAP!!
Locating network . . .
Upload file to new users
Cmd: Attack!
Tell me, Captain . . .
. . . can you spot a liar?
Uh, Marcy? Tell the senator I'll call him back later.
MAYOR FOR MAYOR

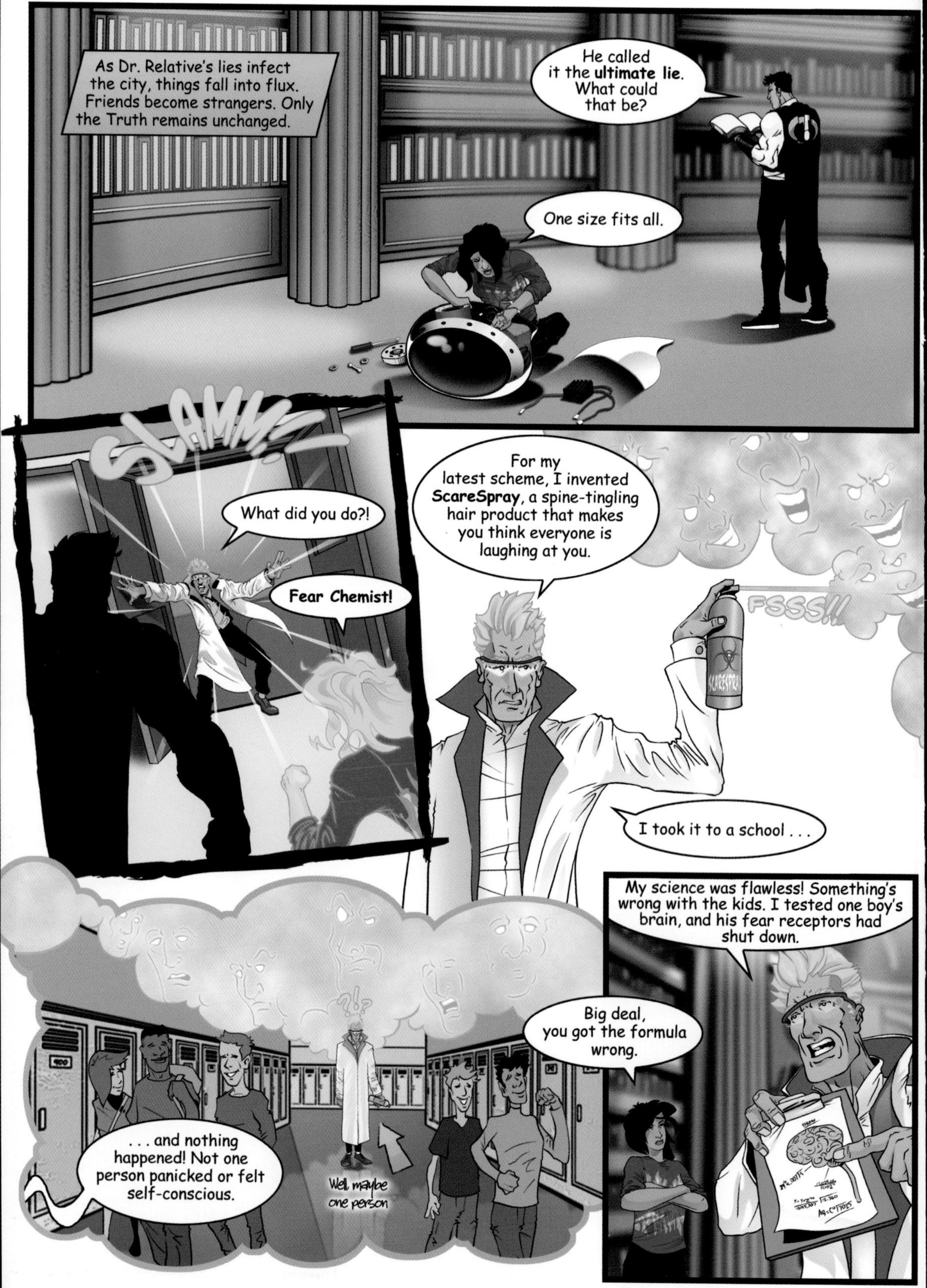
As Dr. Relative's lies infect the city, things fall into flux. Friends become strangers. Only the Truth remains unchanged.
He called it the **ultimate lie**. What could that be?
One size fits all.
SLAMM!!
What did you do?!
Fear Chemist!
For my latest scheme, I invented **ScareSpray**, a spine-tingling hair product that makes you think everyone is laughing at you.
FSSS!!
I took it to a school . . .
. . . and nothing happened! Not one person panicked or felt self-conscious.
Well, maybe one person
My science was flawless! Something's wrong with the kids. I tested one boy's brain, and his fear receptors had shut down.
Big deal, you got the formula wrong.

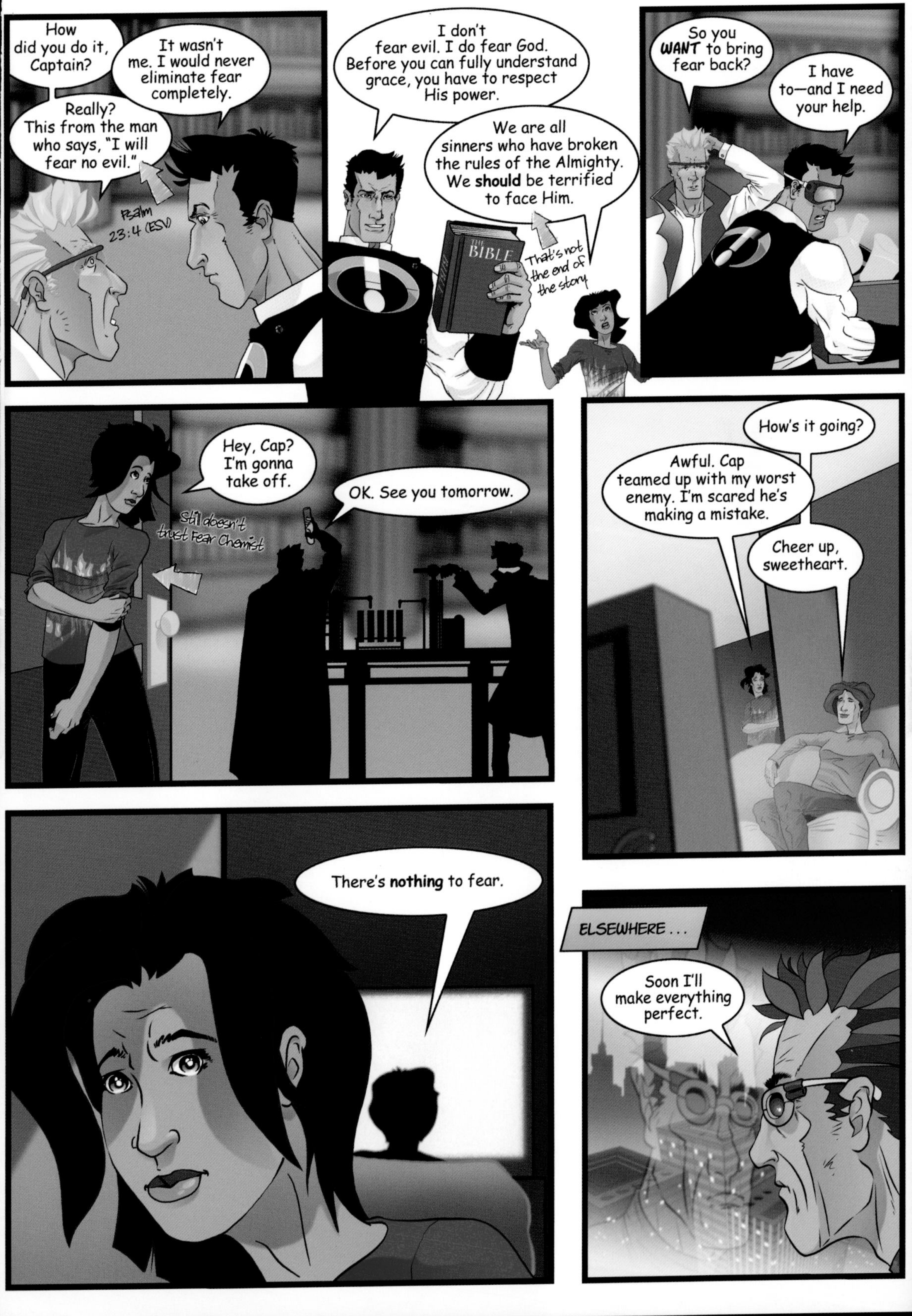
How did you do it, Captain?
It wasn't me. I would never eliminate fear completely.
Really? This from the man who says, "I will fear no evil."
Psalm 23:4 (ESV)
I don't fear evil. I do fear God. Before you can fully understand grace, you have to respect His power.
We are all sinners who have broken the rules of the Almighty. We **should** be terrified to face Him.
THE BIBLE
That's not the end of the story
So you **WANT** to bring fear back?
I have to—and I need your help.
Hey, Cap? I'm gonna take off.
Still doesn't trust Fear Chemist
OK. See you tomorrow.
How's it going?
Awful. Cap teamed up with my worst enemy. I'm scared he's making a mistake.
Cheer up, sweetheart.
There's **nothing** to fear.
ELSEWHERE . . .
Soon I'll make everything perfect.

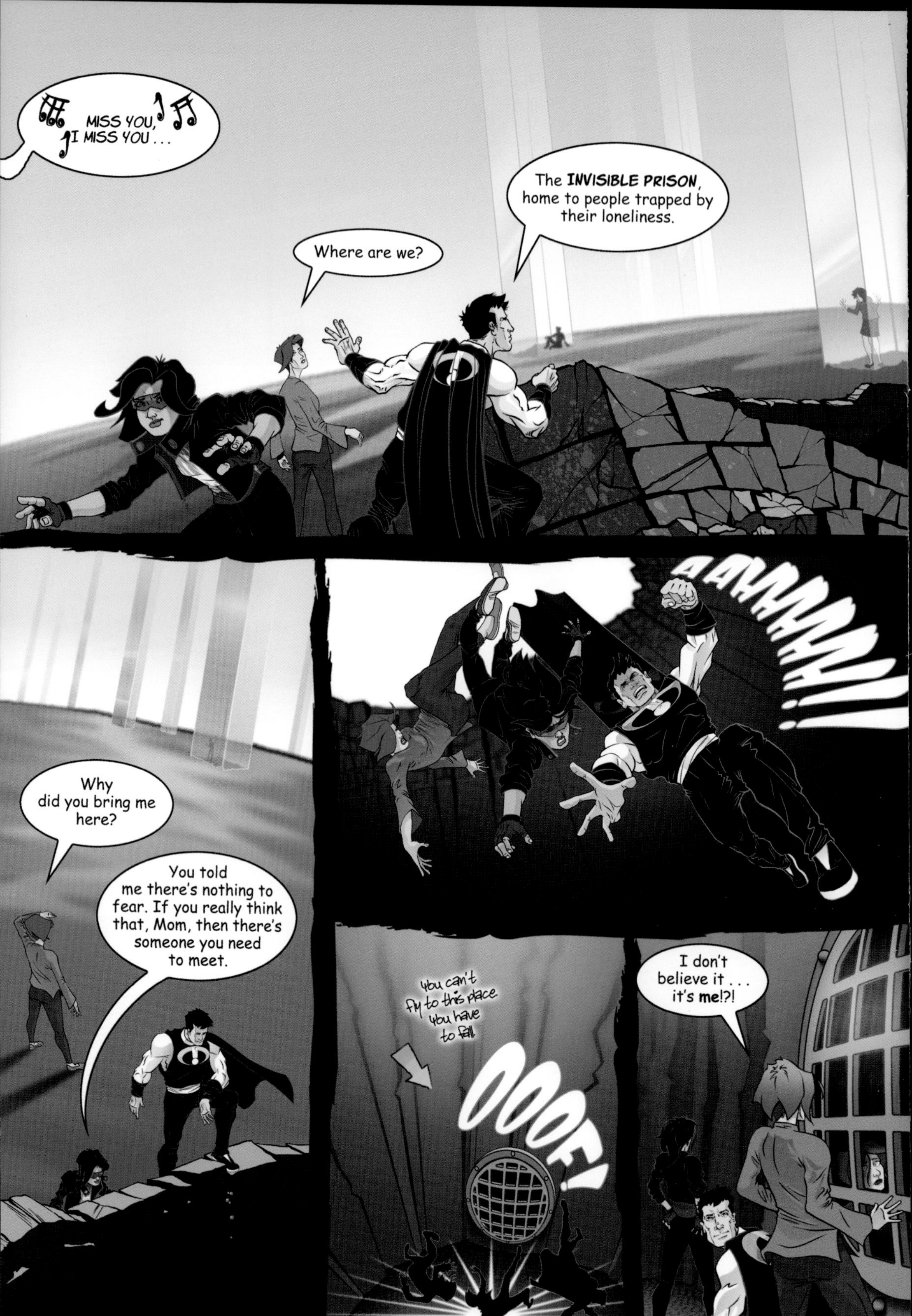

MISS YOU, I MISS YOU . . .
Where are we?
The INVISIBLE PRISON, home to people trapped by their loneliness.
AAAHHHH!!!
Why did you bring me here?
You told me there's nothing to fear. If you really think that, Mom, then there's someone you need to meet.
You can't fly to this place. You have to fall.
OOOF!
I don't believe it . . . it's me!?!

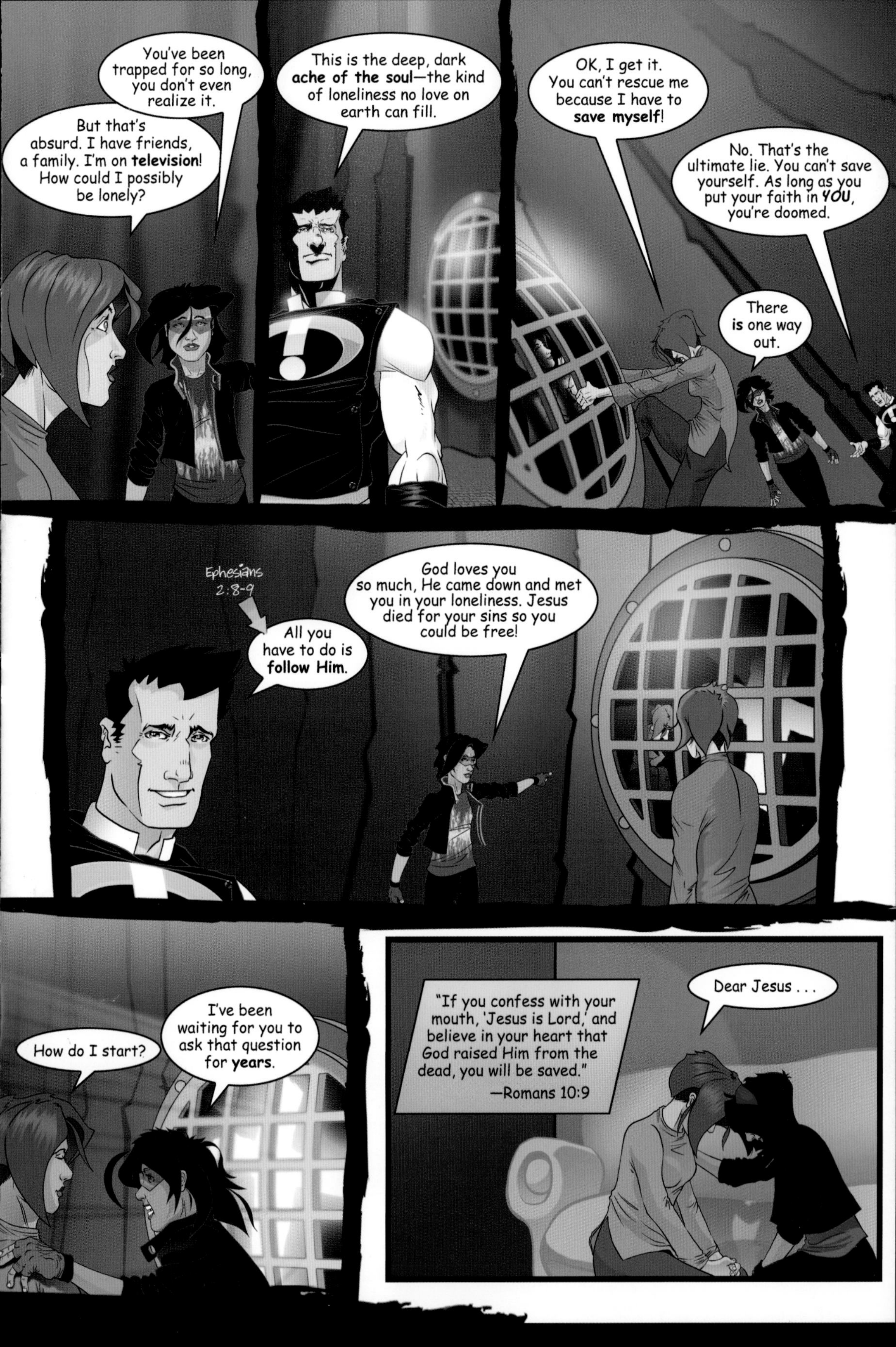
You've been trapped for so long, you don't even realize it.
But that's absurd. I have friends, a family. I'm on **television**! How could I possibly be lonely?
This is the deep, dark **ache of the soul**—the kind of loneliness no love on earth can fill.
OK, I get it. You can't rescue me because I have to **save myself**!
No. That's the ultimate lie. You can't save yourself. As long as you put your faith in ***YOU***, you're doomed.
There **is** one way out.
God loves you so much, He came down and met you in your loneliness. Jesus died for your sins so you could be free!
Ephesians 2:8-9
All you have to do is **follow Him**.
How do I start?
I've been waiting for you to ask that question for **years**.
"If you confess with your mouth, 'Jesus is Lord,' and believe in your heart that God raised Him from the dead, you will be saved."
—Romans 10:9
Dear Jesus . . .

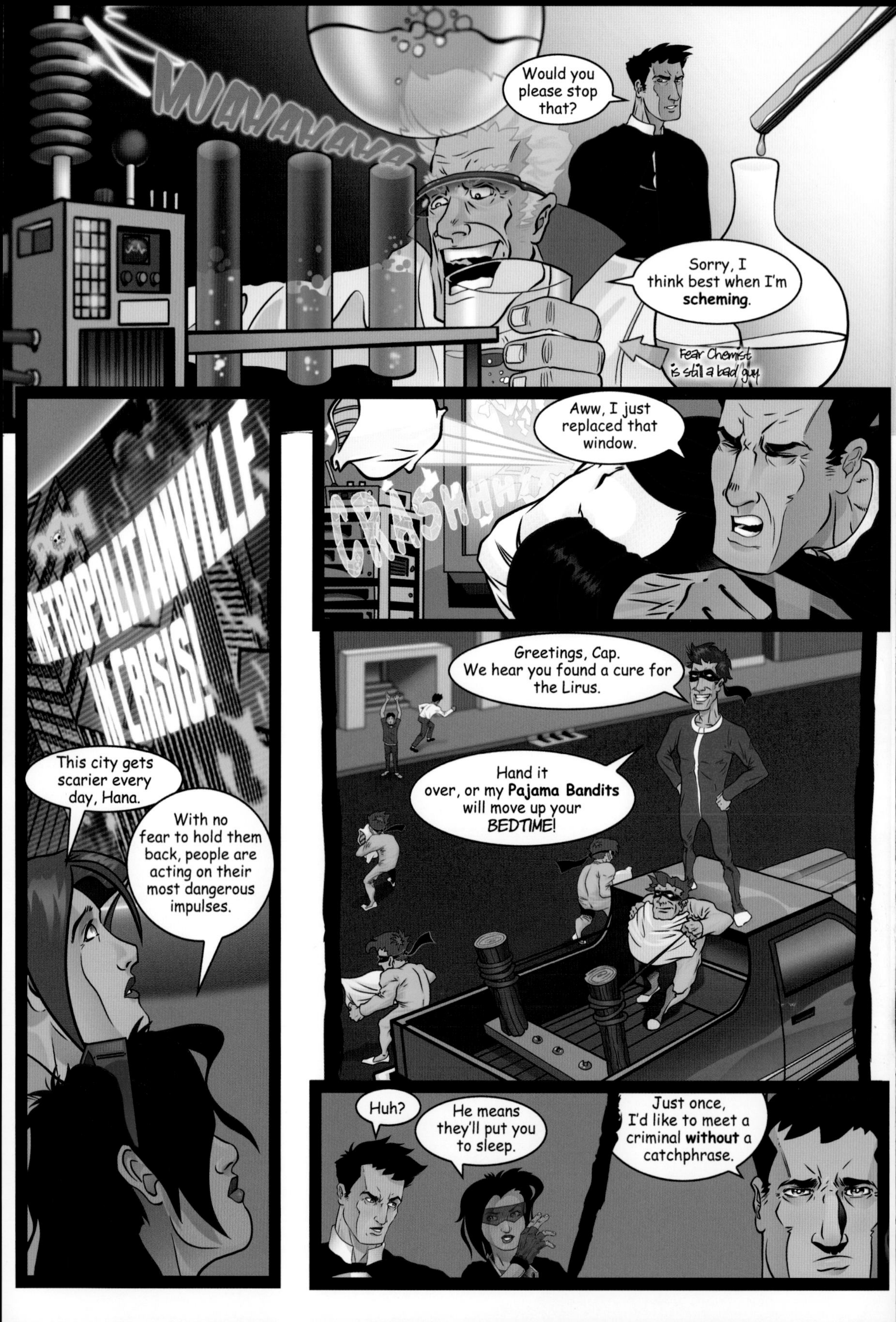

MUAHAHAHAHA
Would you please stop that?
Sorry, I think best when I'm **scheming**.
Fear Chemist is still a bad guy.
METROPOLITANVILLE IN CRISIS!
This city gets scarier every day, Hana.
With no fear to hold them back, people are acting on their most dangerous impulses.
CRASHHH
Aww, I just replaced that window.
Greetings, Cap. We hear you found a cure for the Lirus.
Hand it over, or my **Pajama Bandits** will move up your *BEDTIME*!
Huh?
He means they'll put you to sleep.
Just once, I'd like to meet a criminal **without** a catchphrase.

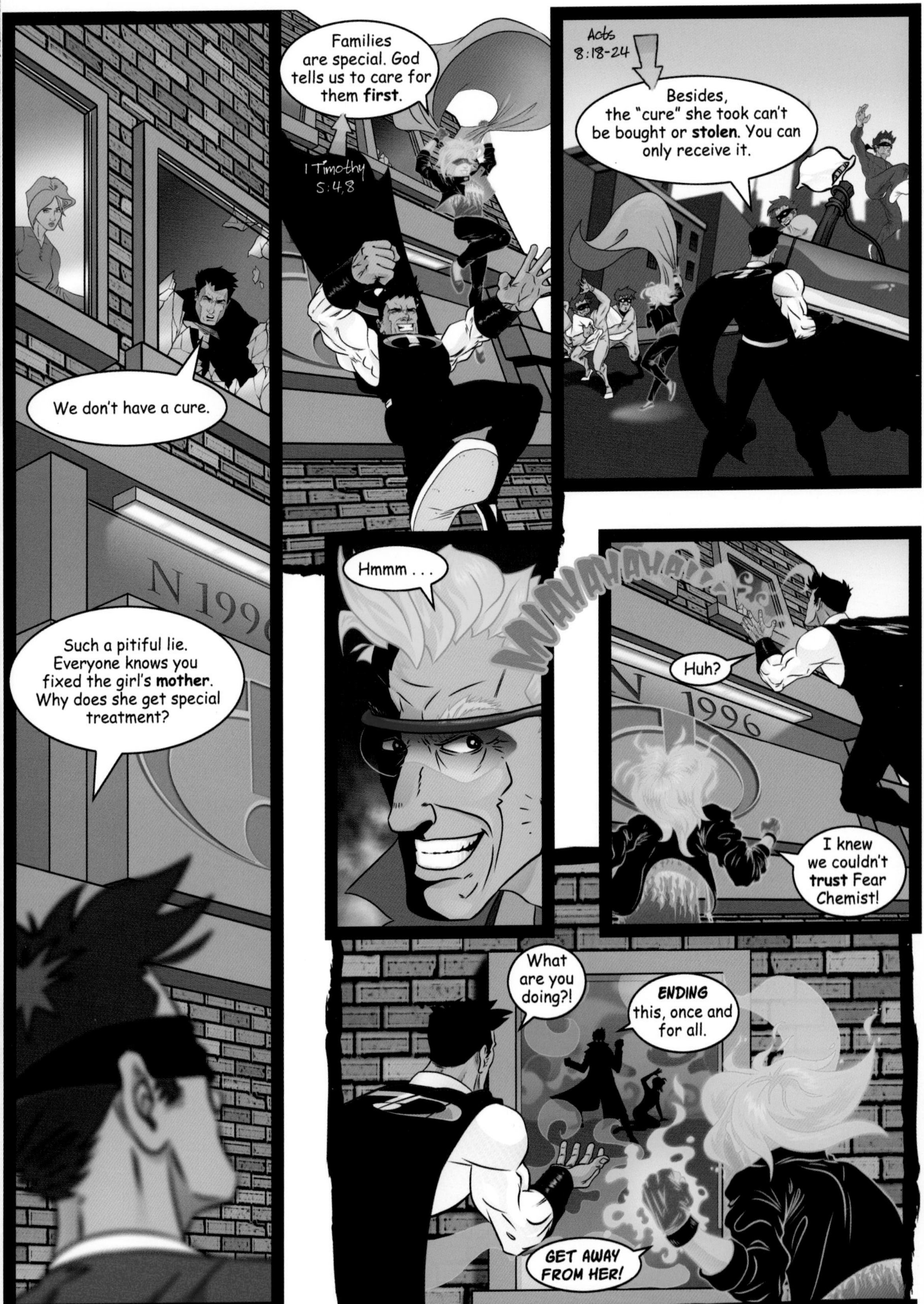
We don't have a cure.
Such a pitiful lie. Everyone knows you fixed the girl's **mother**. Why does she get special treatment?
N 1996
Families are special. God tells us to care for them **first**.
1 Timothy 5:4,8
Acts 8:18-24
Besides, the "cure" she took can't be bought or **stolen**. You can only receive it.
Hmmm . . .
Huh?
N 1996
I knew we couldn't **trust** Fear Chemist!
What are you doing?!
ENDING this, once and for all.
GET AWAY FROM HER!

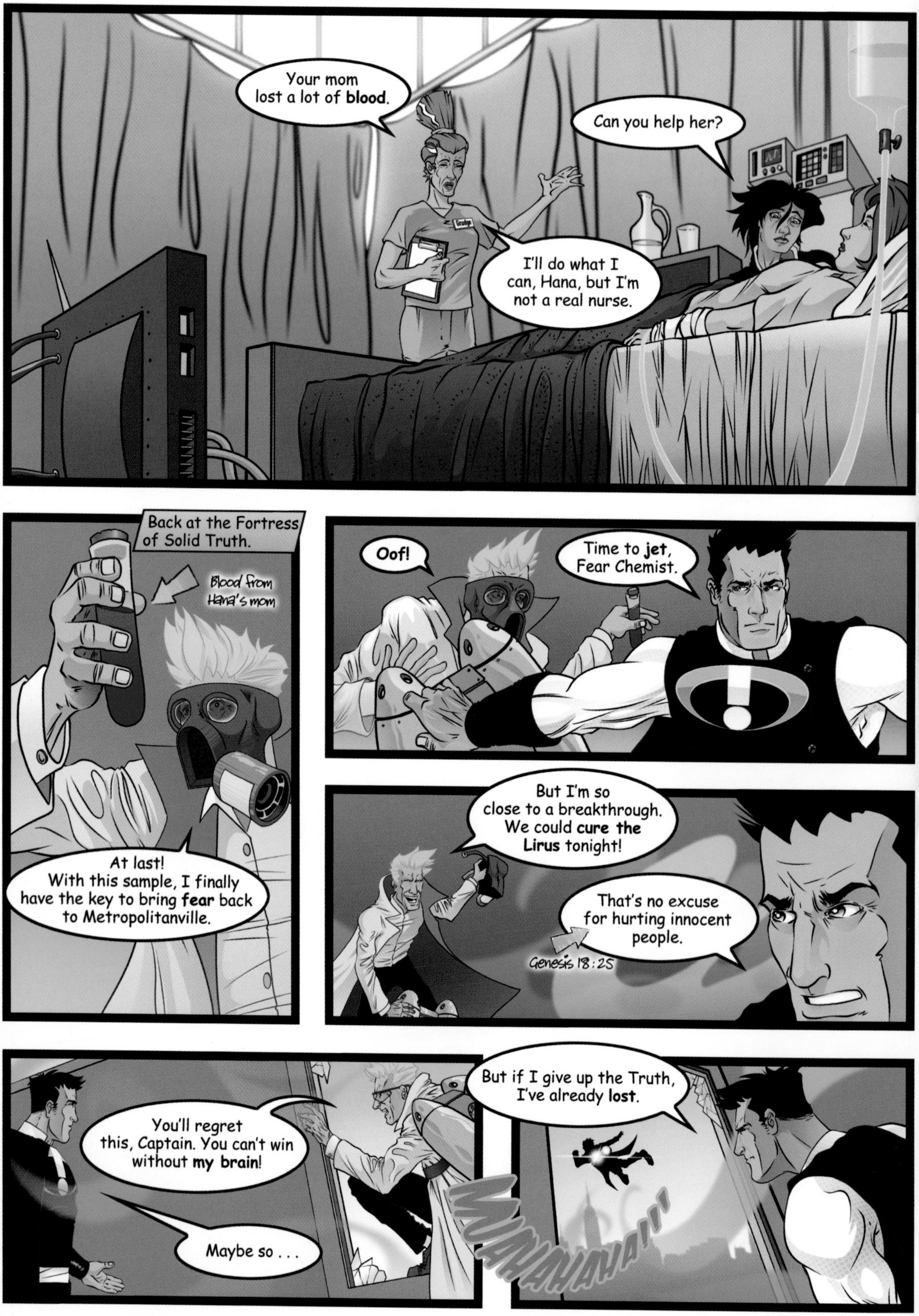
Your mom lost a lot of **blood**.
Can you help her?
I'll do what I can, Hana, but I'm not a real nurse.
Back at the Fortress of Solid Truth.
Blood from Hana's mom
At last! With this sample, I finally have the key to bring **fear** back to Metropolitanville.
Oof!
Time to **jet**, Fear Chemist.
But I'm so close to a breakthrough. We could **cure the Lirus** tonight!
That's no excuse for hurting innocent people.
Genesis 18:25
You'll regret this, Captain. You can't win without **my brain**!
Maybe so . . .
But if I give up the Truth, I've already **lost**.
MUAHAHAHAHA!!!

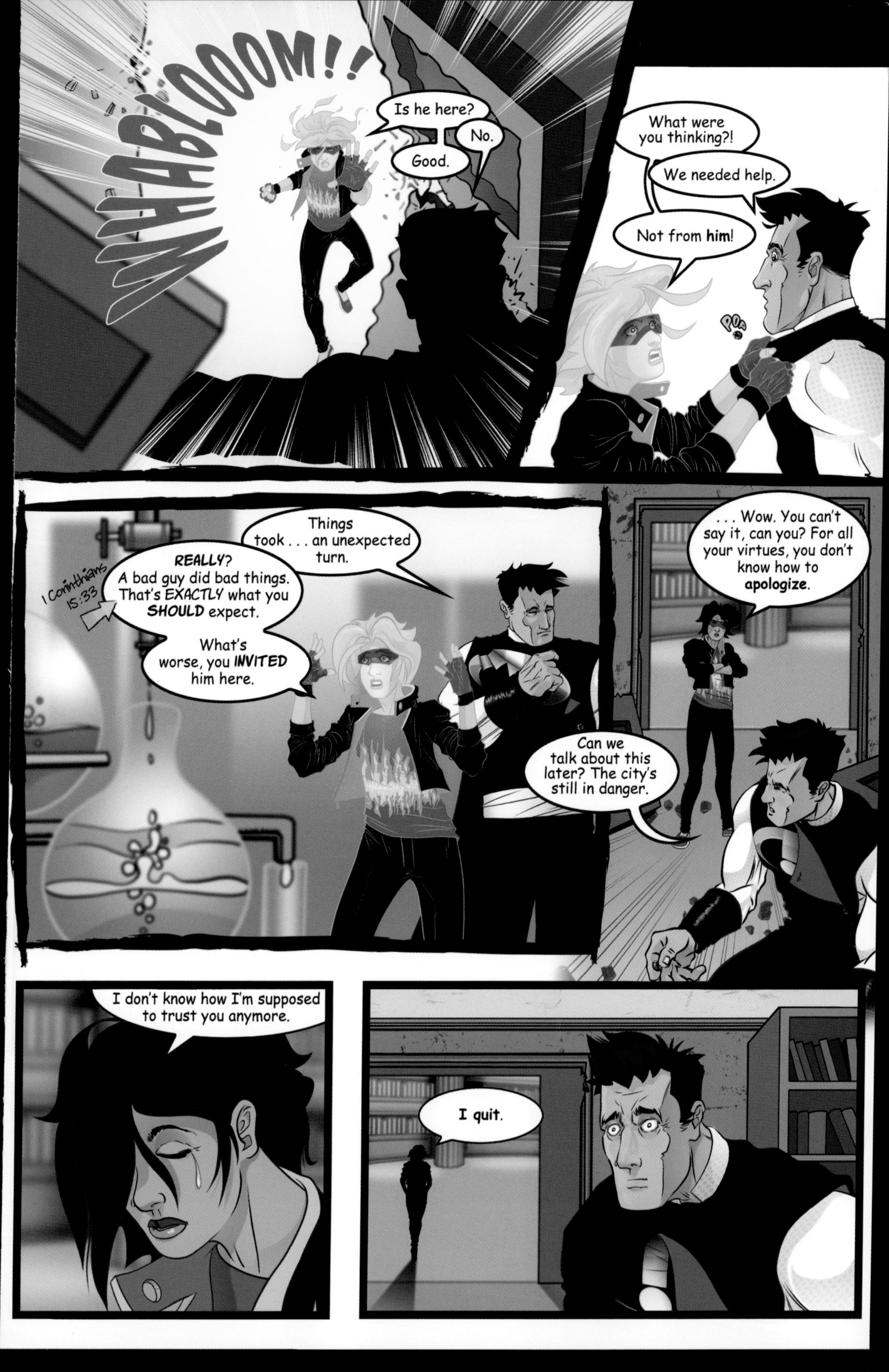
WHABLOOOM!!
Is he here?
No.
Good.
What were you thinking?!
We needed help.
Not from him!
POP
Things took . . . an unexpected turn.
REALLY? A bad guy did bad things. That's EXACTLY what you SHOULD expect.
1 Corinthians 15:33
What's worse, you INVITED him here.
. . . Wow. You can't say it, can you? For all your virtues, you don't know how to apologize.
Can we talk about this later? The city's still in danger.
I don't know how I'm supposed to trust you anymore.
I quit.

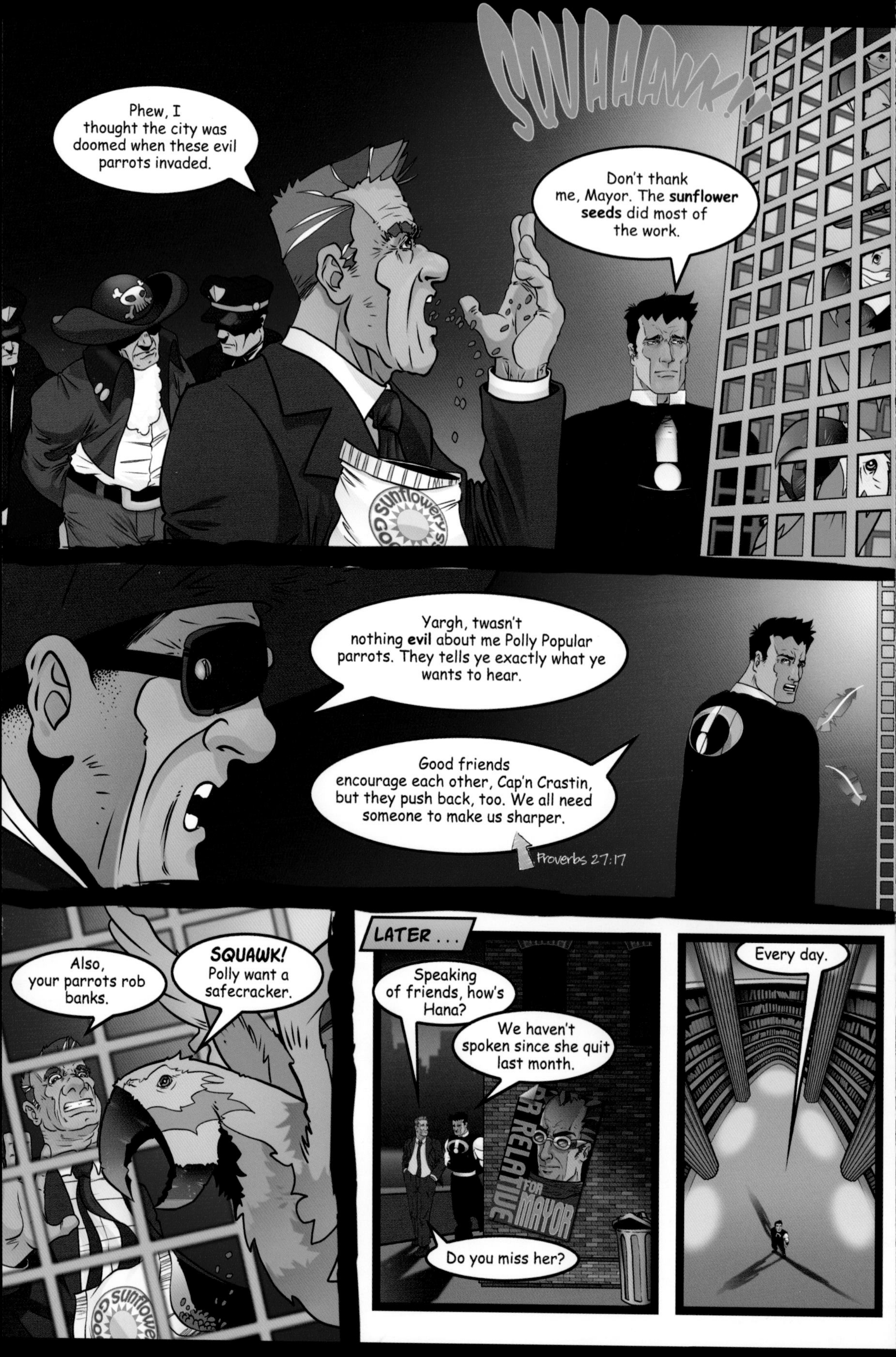
SQUAAAAWK!!
Phew, I thought the city was doomed when these evil parrots invaded.
Don't thank me, Mayor. The **sunflower seeds** did most of the work.
Sunflower Seeds Good
Yargh, twasn't nothing **evil** about me Polly Popular parrots. They tells ye exactly what ye wants to hear.
Good friends encourage each other, Cap'n Crastin, but they push back, too. We all need someone to make us sharper.
Proverbs 27:17
Also, your parrots rob banks.
SQUAWK! Polly want a safecracker.
LATER . . .
Speaking of friends, how's Hana?
We haven't spoken since she quit last month.
Do you miss her?
FOR MAYOR
Every day.

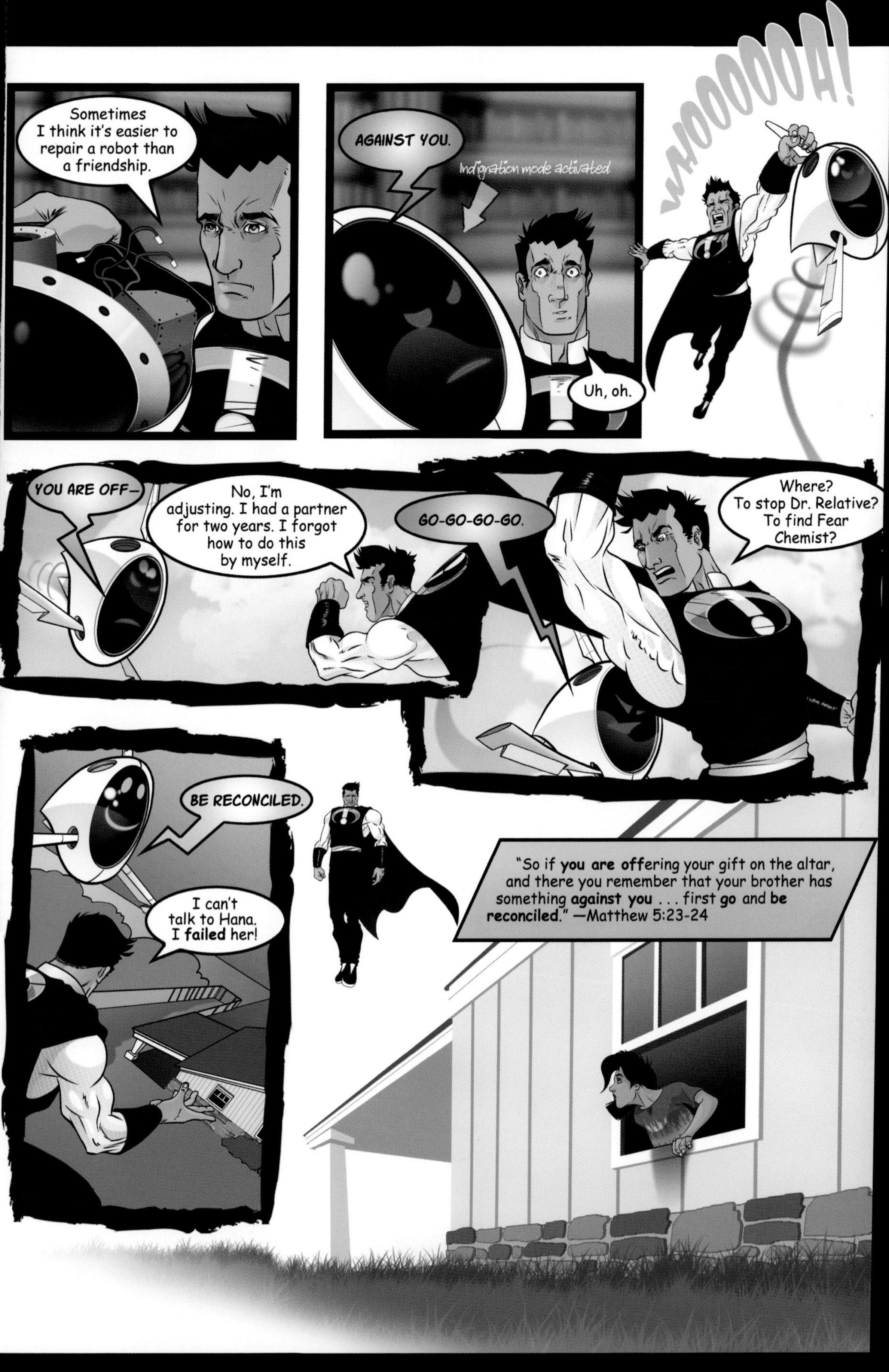

Sometimes I think it's easier to repair a robot than a friendship.
AGAINST YOU.
Indignation mode activated
Uh, oh.
WHOOOOOA!
YOU ARE OFF—
No, I'm adjusting. I had a partner for two years. I forgot how to do this by myself.
GO-GO-GO-GO.
Where? To stop Dr. Relative? To find Fear Chemist?
BE RECONCILED.
I can't talk to Hana. I **failed** her!
"So if **you are off**ering your gift on the altar, and there you remember that your brother has something **against you** . . . first **go** and **be reconciled**." —Matthew 5:23-24

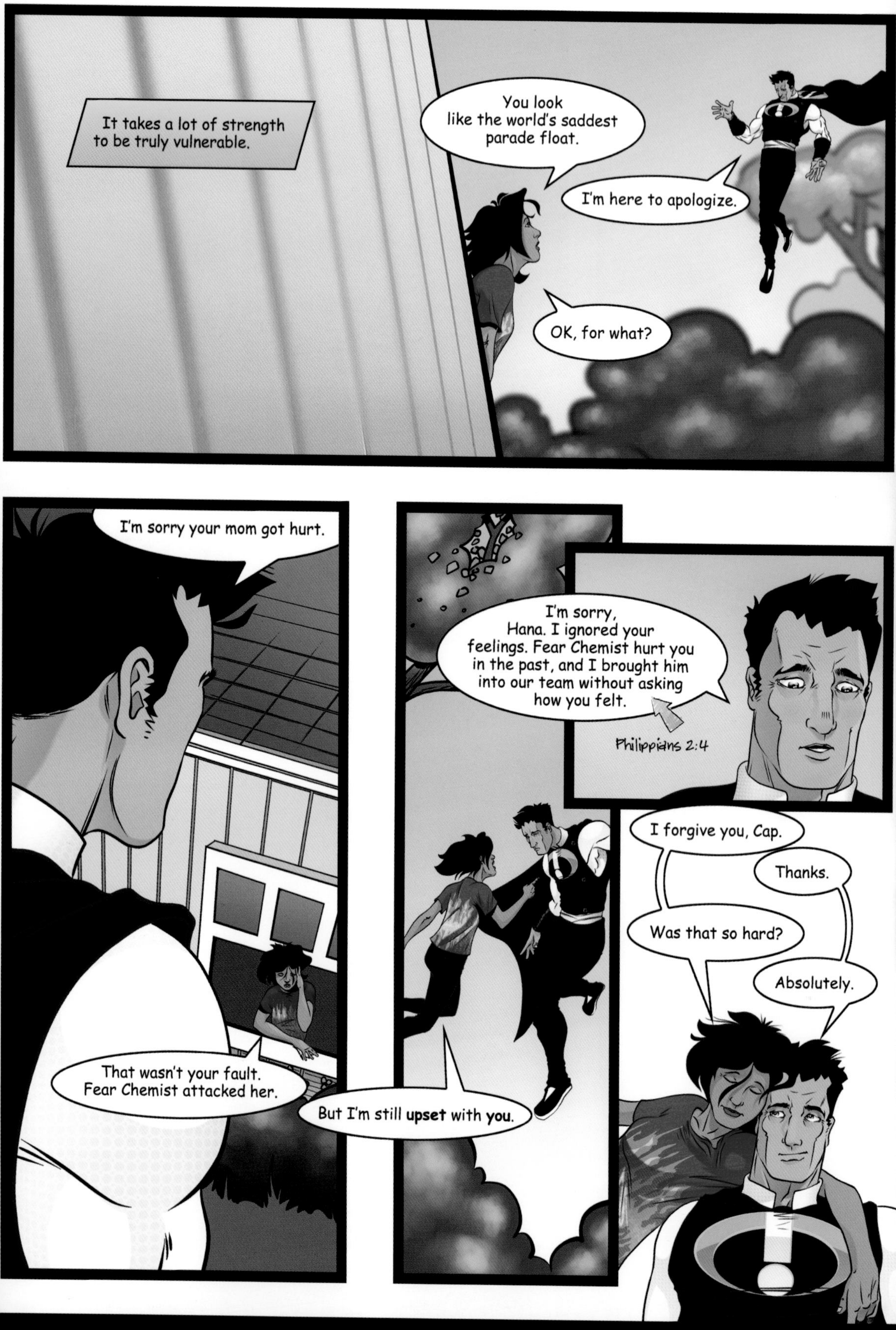

It takes a lot of strength to be truly vulnerable.
You look like the world's saddest parade float.
I'm here to apologize.
OK, for what?
I'm sorry your mom got hurt.
That wasn't your fault. Fear Chemist attacked her.
But I'm still **upset** with **you**.
I'm sorry, Hana. I ignored your feelings. Fear Chemist hurt you in the past, and I brought him into our team without asking how you felt.
Philippians 2:4
I forgive you, Cap.
Thanks.
Was that so hard?
Absolutely.

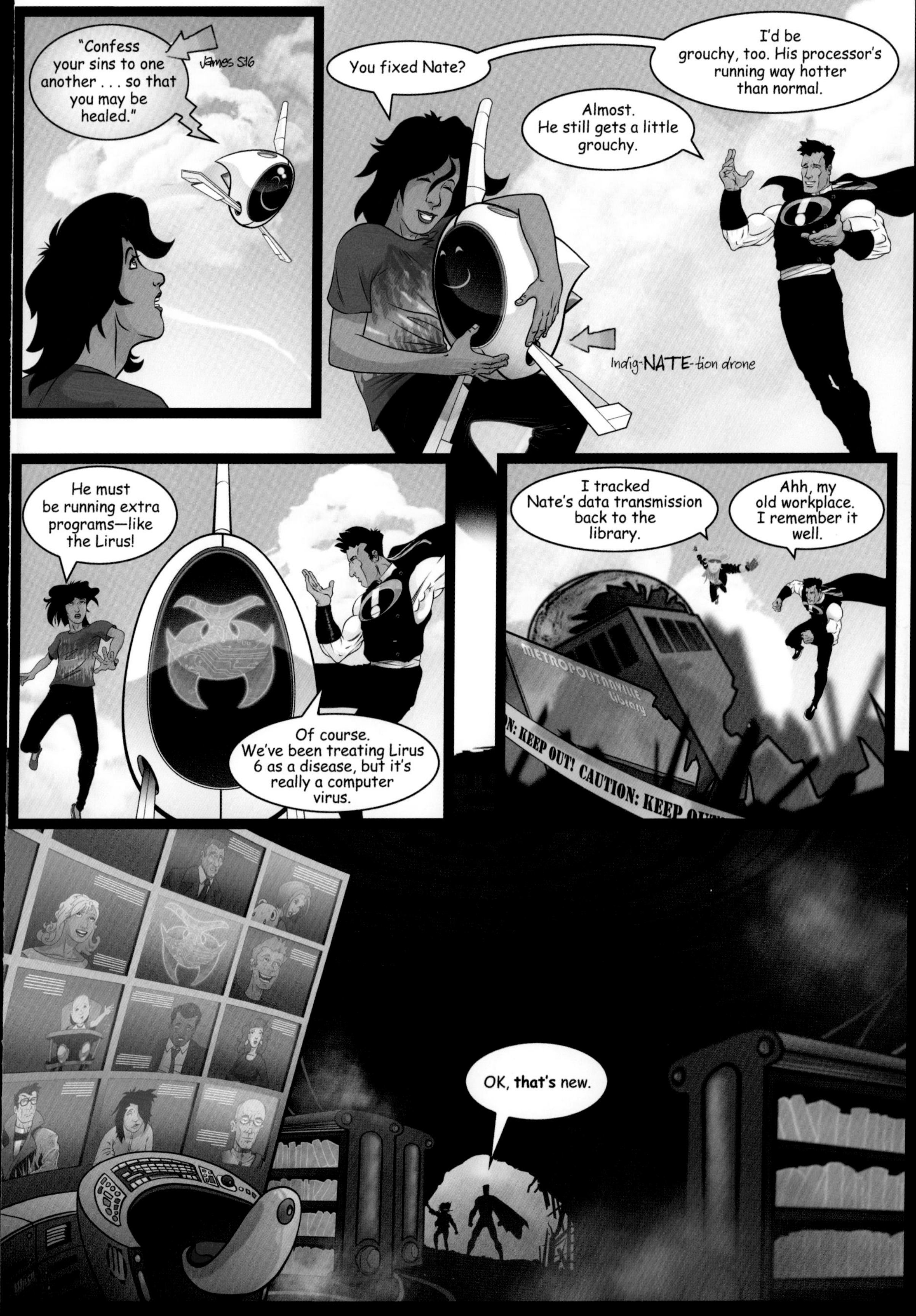

"Confess your sins to one another . . . so that you may be healed."
James 5:16
You fixed Nate?
Almost. He still gets a little grouchy.
I'd be grouchy, too. His processor's running way hotter than normal.
Indig-NATE-tion drone
He must be running extra programs—like the Lirus!
Of course. We've been treating Lirus 6 as a disease, but it's really a computer virus.
I tracked Nate's data transmission back to the library.
Ahh, my old workplace. I remember it well.
METROPOLITANVILLE library
N: KEEP OUT! CAUTION: KEEP OU
OK, that's new.

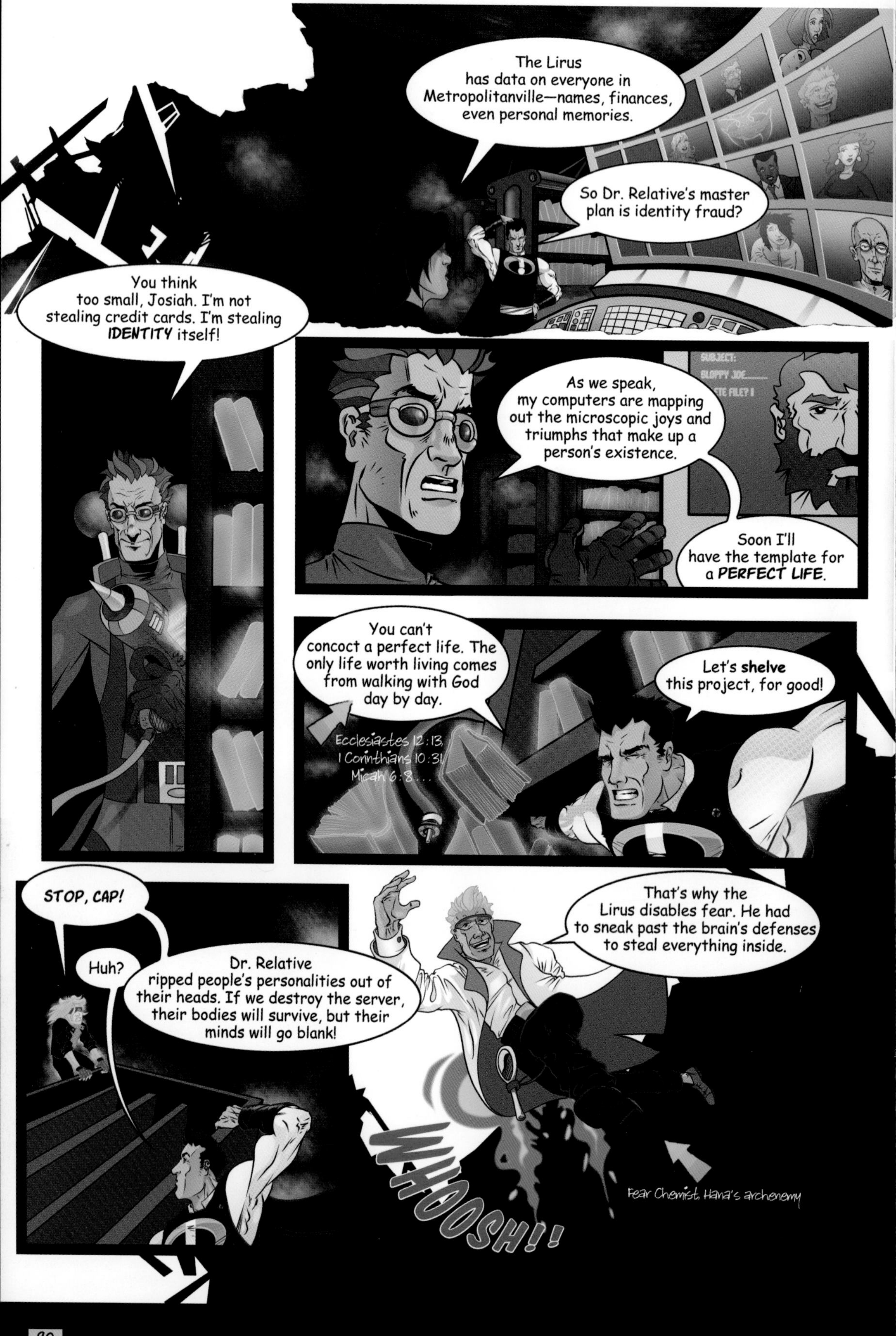
The Lirus has data on everyone in Metropolitanville—names, finances, even personal memories.
So Dr. Relative's master plan is identity fraud?
You think too small, Josiah. I'm not stealing credit cards. I'm stealing IDENTITY itself!
As we speak, my computers are mapping out the microscopic joys and triumphs that make up a person's existence.
Soon I'll have the template for a PERFECT LIFE.
You can't concoct a perfect life. The only life worth living comes from walking with God day by day.
Ecclesiastes 12:13, I Corinthians 10:31, Micah 6:8 . . .
Let's shelve this project, for good!
STOP, CAP!
Huh?
Dr. Relative ripped people's personalities out of their heads. If we destroy the server, their bodies will survive, but their minds will go blank!
That's why the Lirus disables fear. He had to sneak past the brain's defenses to steal everything inside.
WHOOSH!!
Fear Chemist, Hana's archenemy

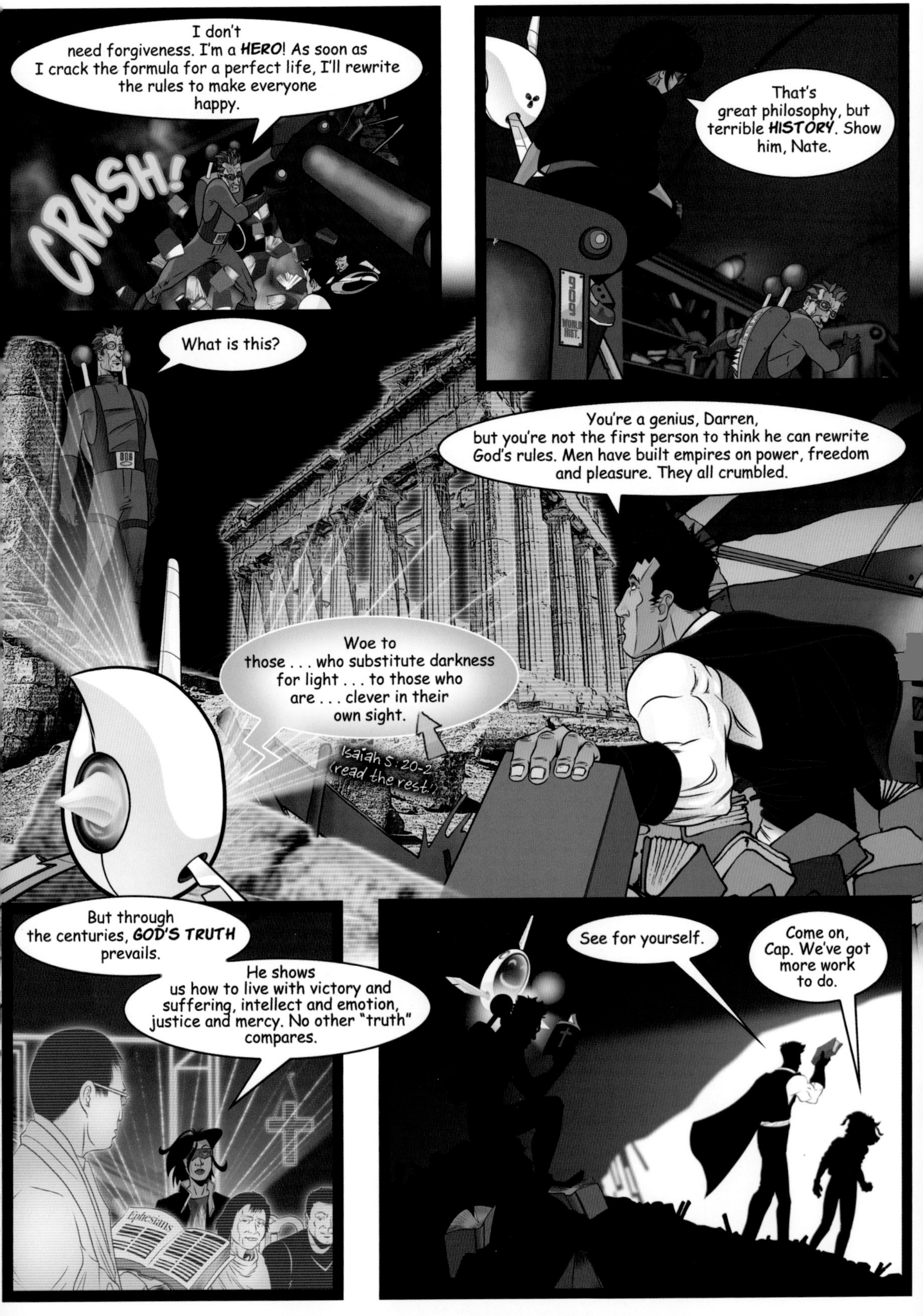
I don't need forgiveness. I'm a **HERO**! As soon as I crack the formula for a perfect life, I'll rewrite the rules to make everyone happy.
CRASH!
That's great philosophy, but terrible **HISTORY**. Show him, Nate.
909 WORLD HIST.
What is this?
You're a genius, Darren, but you're not the first person to think he can rewrite God's rules. Men have built empires on power, freedom and pleasure. They all crumbled.
Woe to those . . . who substitute darkness for light . . . to those who are . . . clever in their own sight.
Isaiah 5:20-2
(read the rest!)
But through the centuries, **GOD'S TRUTH** prevails.
He shows us how to live with victory and suffering, intellect and emotion, justice and mercy. No other "truth" compares.
Ephesians
See for yourself.
Come on, Cap. We've got more work to do.

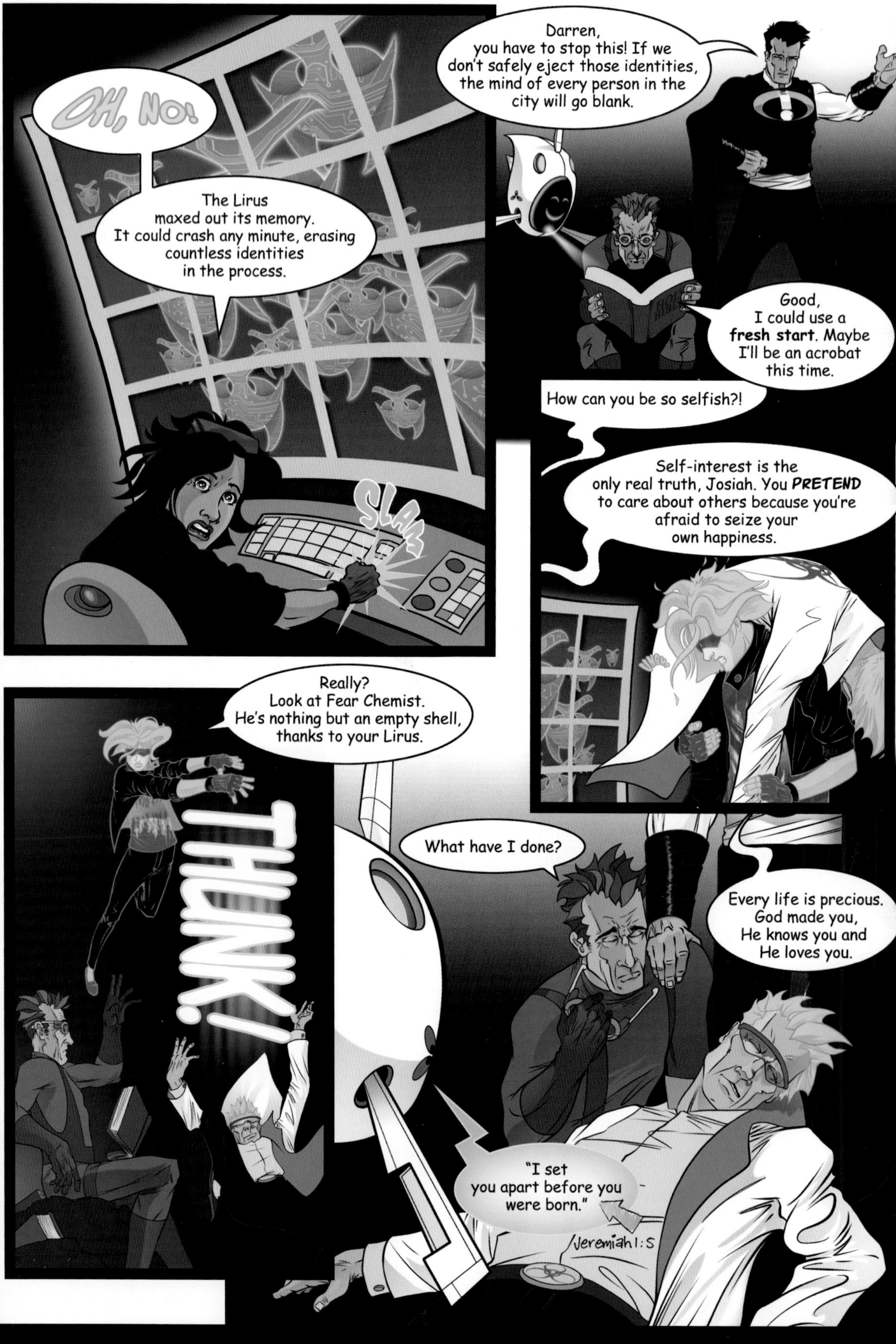
OH, NO!
The Lirus maxed out its memory. It could crash any minute, erasing countless identities in the process.
SLAM
Darren, you have to stop this! If we don't safely eject those identities, the mind of every person in the city will go blank.
Good, I could use a **fresh start**. Maybe I'll be an acrobat this time.
How can you be so selfish?!
Self-interest is the only real truth, Josiah. You **PRETEND** to care about others because you're afraid to seize your own happiness.
Really? Look at Fear Chemist. He's nothing but an empty shell, thanks to your Lirus.
THUNK!
What have I done?
Every life is precious. God made you, He knows you and He loves you.
"I set you apart before you were born."
Jeremiah 1:5

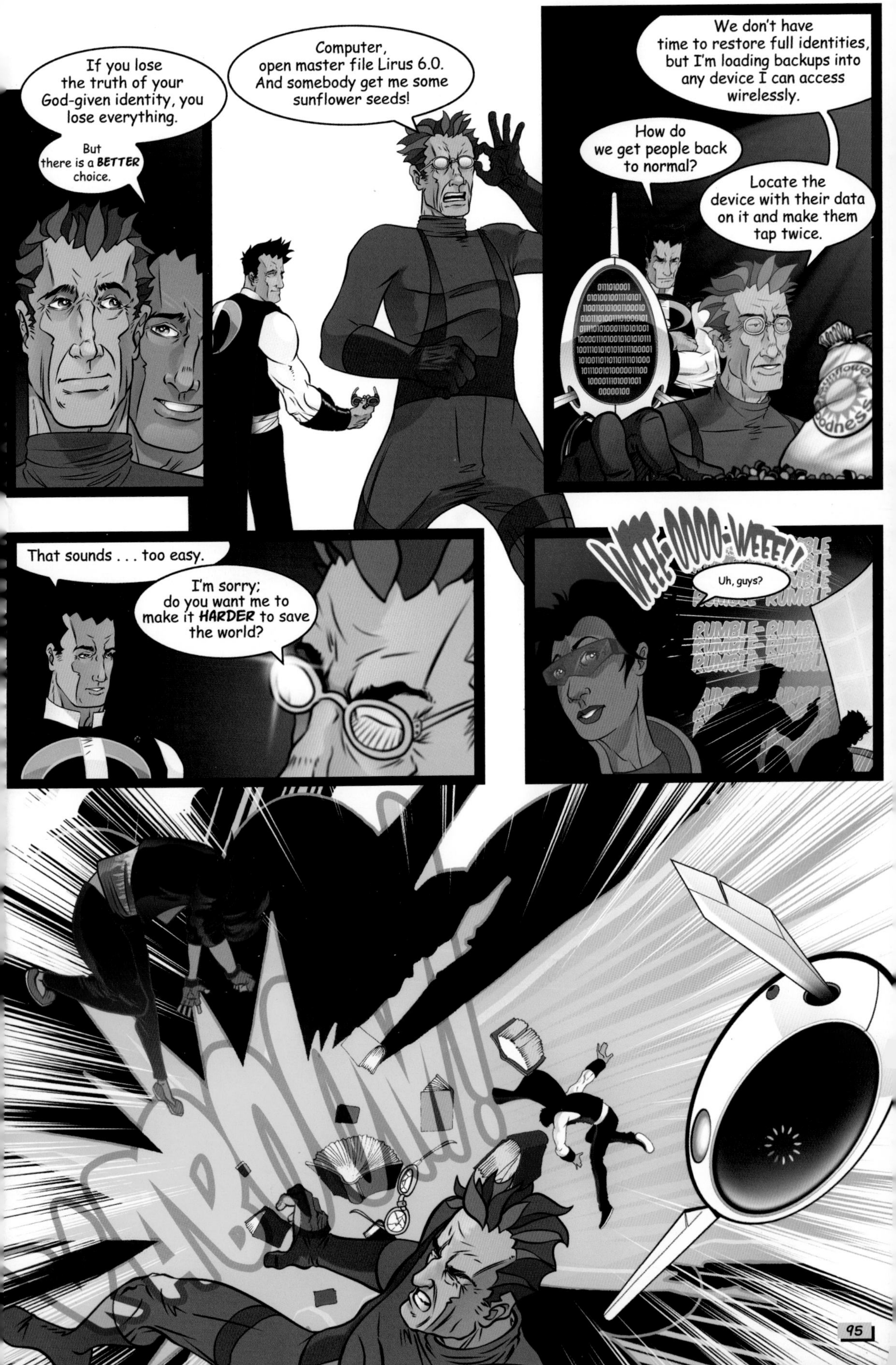
If you lose the truth of your God-given identity, you lose everything.
But there is a **BETTER** choice.
Computer, open master file Lirus 6.0. And somebody get me some sunflower seeds!
We don't have time to restore full identities, but I'm loading backups into any device I can access wirelessly.
How do we get people back to normal?
Locate the device with their data on it and make them tap twice.
That sounds . . . too easy.
I'm sorry; do you want me to make it **HARDER** to save the world?
WEEE-OOOO-WEEE!!
Uh, guys?
RUMBLE-RUMBLE

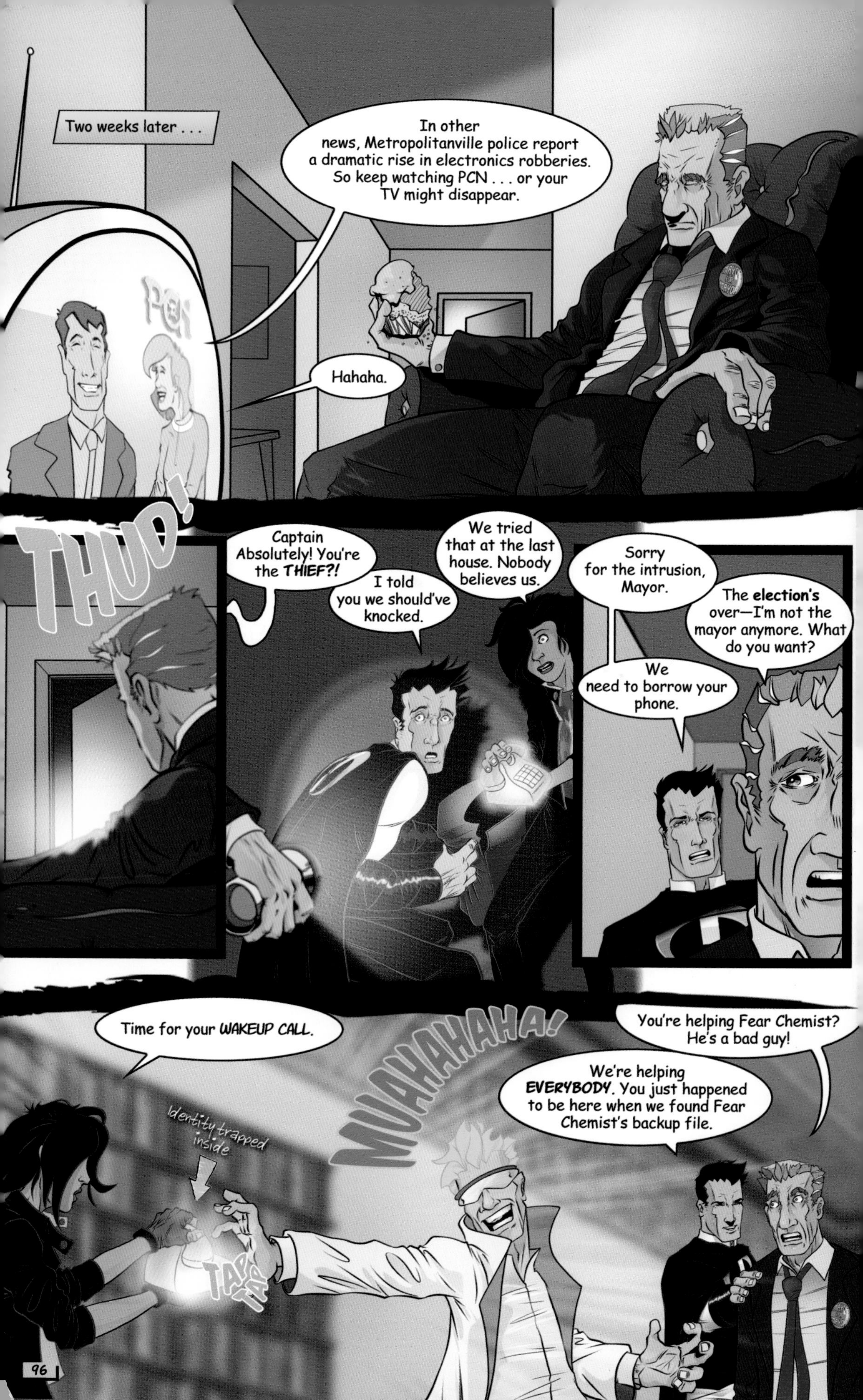

Two weeks later . . .
In other news, Metropolitanville police report a dramatic rise in electronics robberies. So keep watching PCN . . . or your TV might disappear.
Hahaha.
THUD!
Captain Absolutely! You're the THIEF?!
I told you we should've knocked.
We tried that at the last house. Nobody believes us.
Sorry for the intrusion, Mayor.
The election's over—I'm not the mayor anymore. What do you want?
We need to borrow your phone.
Time for your WAKEUP CALL.
MUAHAHAHAHA!
Identity trapped inside
TAP TAP
You're helping Fear Chemist? He's a bad guy!
We're helping EVERYBODY. You just happened to be here when we found Fear Chemist's backup file.

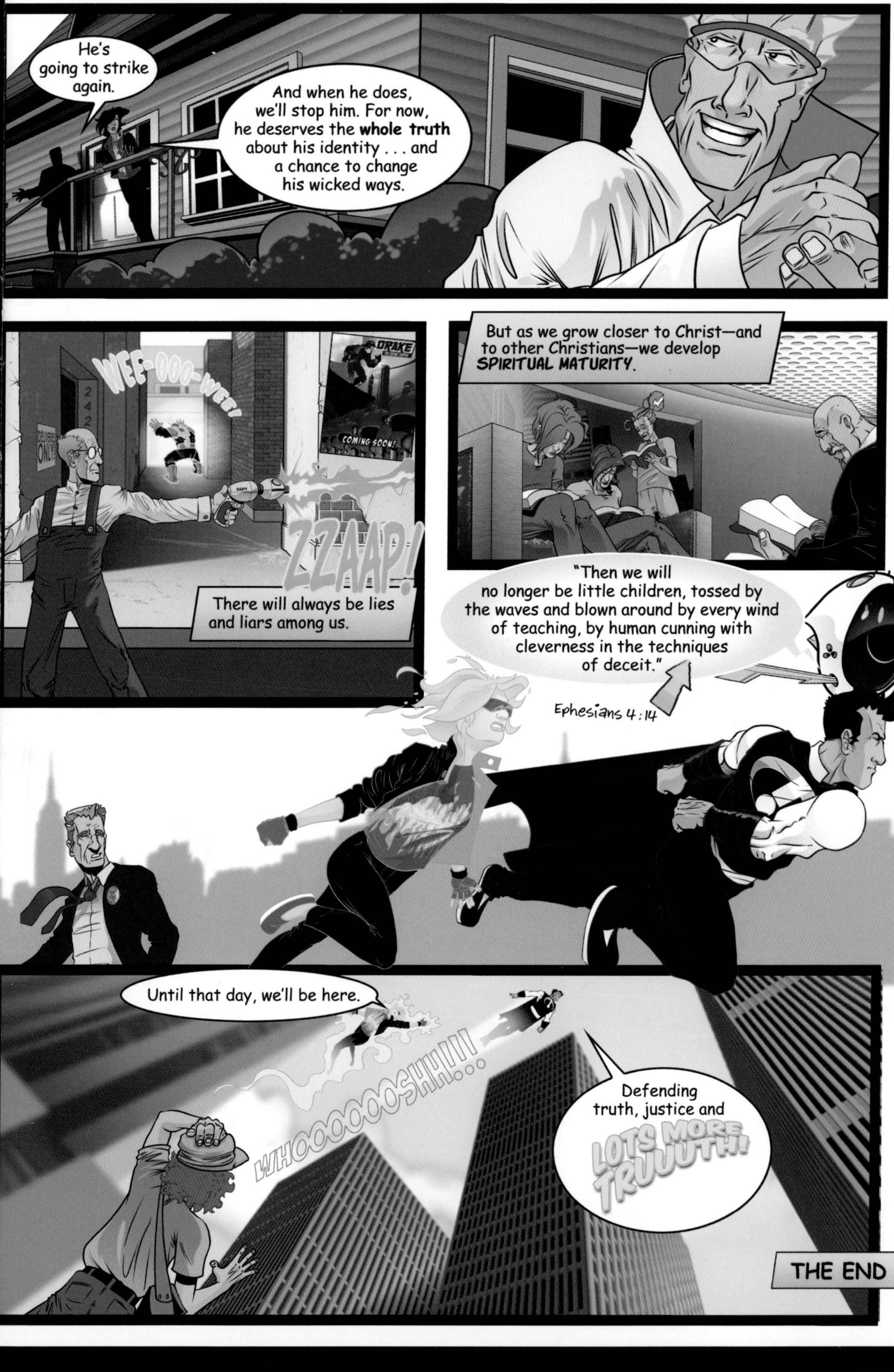
He's going to strike again.
And when he does, we'll stop him. For now, he deserves the **whole truth** about his identity . . . and a chance to change his wicked ways.
WEE-OOO-WEE!
DRAKE
COMING SOON!
ZZAAP!
There will always be lies and liars among us.
But as we grow closer to Christ—and to other Christians—we develop **SPIRITUAL MATURITY**.
"Then we will no longer be little children, tossed by the waves and blown around by every wind of teaching, by human cunning with cleverness in the techniques of deceit."
Ephesians 4:14
Until that day, we'll be here.
WHOOOOOOOSHHH!!!...
Defending truth, justice and
LOTS MORE TRUUUTH!
THE END

CAPTAIN ABSOLUTELY

Mild-mannered librarian Josiah King had never heard of the Bible . . . until a massive explosion revealed a chamber full of banned books. That night, Josiah read God's Truth for the first time, and it—along with mysterious radioactive fumes—changed his life forever.

Worldview: The Bible contains Absolute Truth—timeless, God-given wisdom on how to live.
Superpowers: Strength; Flight
Height: 6 feet 1 inch
Eyes: Pale Blue
Favorite Sport: Wrestling
Biggest Problem: Paper Cuts

He reads a lot of books.

"You will know the truth, and the truth will set you free." —John 8:32

HANA

Seeing Cap's heroics inspired Hana Lin to put her faith into action. Sometimes this teenage inventor's zeal for God leads her to take shortcuts, like the time she stole Bibles from the library. However, Hana's courage, intellect and heart make her a terrific sidekick.

Worldview: The Bible changes lives; we need to share its truth with as many people as possible.
Inventions: Rocket Boots; Fire Suit
Height: 5 feet 4 inches
Eyes: Green
Favorite School Subject: Science
Biggest Problem: Fear Chemist

"For the word of God is living and effective and sharper than any double-edged sword, penetrating as far as the separation of soul and spirit, joints and marrow." —Hebrews 4:12

DR. RELATIVE

Darren Gray was a computer programmer and Josiah's friend. After the explosion, Darren discovered relative truth—the idea that everyone makes their own rules. Since then, he's tried to take over Metropolitanville and destroy God's Truth once and for all.

Worldview: Right and wrong can change, depending on what's best for me at the moment.
Weapons: Neutralizer Laser; Shackles of Selfishness; Lirus 1-6
Height: Size Is Just a Number
Eyes: Green
Favorite Snack: Sunflower Seeds
Biggest Problem: Instruction Manuals

Nobody tells Dr. Relative what to do!

"A fool's way is right in his own eyes, but whoever listens to counsel is wise." —Proverbs 12:15

Hear Dr. Relative in the episode "The Truth Be Told" on The Truth Chronicles or at OAClub.org.

Adventures in
ODYSSEY

THE REAL JOSIAH KING

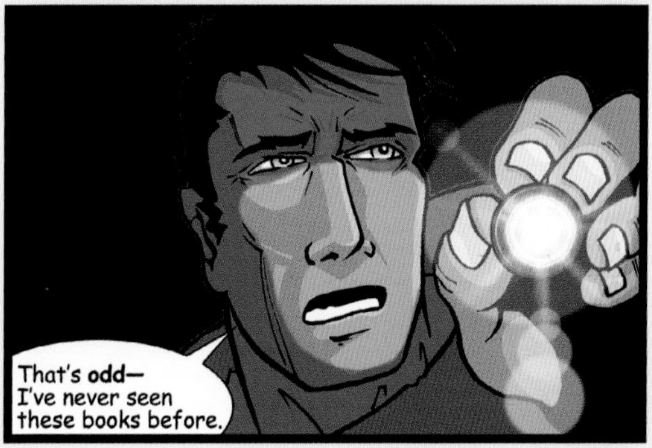
That's **odd—**
I've never seen
these books before.

Does Captain Absolutely's origin story remind you of anyone? Sure, the sunflower seeds and exploding computers are unique to this comic, but Josiah King isn't the first Josiah to completely change his life after finding God's Truth in a forgotten room.

According to 2 Kings 22:1, "Josiah was **eight years old** when he became king" of Judah. His father's reign had been wicked and short. And Josiah's grandfather, Manasseh, was basically a supervillain. Still, the boy king had a heart for God.

Josiah hired workers to repair the temple. They emptied the treasury and put that money to work. Once they cleared away the junk, the high priest discovered the long-lost book of the law—Scriptures written down by Moses himself.

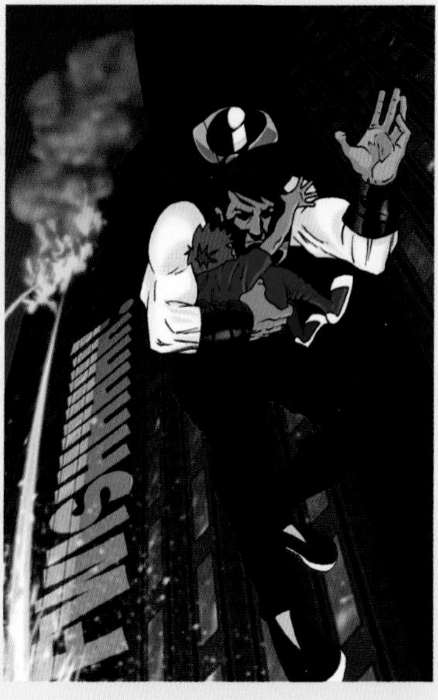

When Josiah heard the Word of God, he tore his clothes in sorrow. He knew his ancestors had been evil, but he had no idea how far they had fallen!

Josiah ordered the people of Jerusalem to gather inside the temple. "As they listened, he read **all the words** of the book" (2 Kings 23:2). Then Josiah promised to follow the Lord with all his mind and with all his heart.

From that day on, Josiah was a fearless champion for God's Truth. He traveled the kingdom, destroying idols and getting rid of corrupt priests. He brought back Passover for the first time in centuries. He even rescued children from human sacrifices.

Talk about a real-life superhero!

FEAR CHEMIST

Frederick Olben worked at a chemical plant, developing environmentally friendly cleaning supplies. Constant exposure to experimental compounds gave him terrible nightmares. One day, Olben discovered the chemical formula for fear. Now he uses his genius to terrify others.

Worldview: Fear is power.
Inventions: Scary Clean; Fear Toxin; Fear-us Clouds; Scare Spray
Height: 6 feet 3 inches ⟵ *If you count his hair*
Eyes: Blue
Favorite Elements: Iron and Argon
Biggest Problem: Hana

"Do not fear, for I am with you; do not be afraid, for I am your God." —Isaiah 41:10

UNIFIER

Max Pariter was an aspiring politician on the library council. He found a mysterious space helmet that allowed him to control objects using his brain. The power went to Max's head, and soon his massive "rezoning" projects endangered the whole city.

Worldview: People should stop arguing and accept the obvious truth—doing things *my way* is best for everyone!
Superpower: Moves Objects With His Mind
Height: 6 feet 8 inches
Eyes: Black
Favorite Game: Simon Says ⟵ *As long as he's in charge*
Biggest Problem: Democracy

"All things have been created through Him and for Him. He is before all things, and by Him all things hold together." —Colossians 1:16-17

Hear Unifier in the episode "Three in One" on The Truth Chronicles or at OAClub.org.

BARON VON CONFUSER

Richard Von Confuser, 14th Baron of Whichway, squandered his family fortune on puzzling contraptions. Although a member of the Legion, he often wanders off to cause mischief. He insists on speaking in rhyme.

Worldview: Life is chaos and confusion; nobody really knows what they're doing, so why pretend otherwise?
Contraptions: Cropduster; Mecha-Knight; Confuser Clones
Height: 60 inches ⟵ *Never takes off his goggles*
Eyes: Brown?
Favorite Activity: Mazes
Biggest Problem: Landing

"Your word is a lamp for my feet and a light on my path." —Psalm 119:105

CAP'N CRASTIN

For years, Davey Crastin worked as a mascot for PCN (Pirate Cable News). Through a clerical error, he was promoted to CEO and soon transformed the television network into a hypnotic propaganda arm of the Legion.

Worldview: Stop working so hard and just relax. Real life can wait.
Projects: PCN Network; Phone-ies App
Height: 5 feet 8 inches
Eyes: Green
Favorite Show: Reruns
Biggest Problem: Finding the Remote

> "The one who is truly lazy in his work
> is brother to a vandal."
> —Proverbs 18:9

FARMER VILE

Toxic fumes from the library explosion poisoned Grant Vile's crops, leaving the farmer penniless—and angry. Dr. Relative helped Vile build rage-inducing robot ants out of old tractor parts.

Worldview: You'll never win until you fight for what you want.
Tools: Vile Ants; Hypnotic Radishes
Height: 6 feet 2 inches
Eyes: Gray
Favorite Vegetable: Kohlrabi
Biggest Problem: Hurtful Stereotypes in Broadway Musicals

> "The one who sows injustice will reap disaster,
> and the rod of his fury will be destroyed."
> —Proverbs 22:8

MR. MAYOR

Saul Rey Jr. ran for mayor because it sounded less stressful than his dad's job as a federal judge. He served 15 years without making any tough choices . . . until the library exploded.

Worldview: It's easier to let people decide things for themselves.
Talent: High Approval Ratings
Height: 5 feet 10 inches
Eyes: Green
Favorite Animal: Cats
Biggest Problem: Reelection

> "How long will you go limping between two different opinions?
> If the Lord is God, follow him."
> —1 Kings 18:21 (ESV)

HANA'S MOM

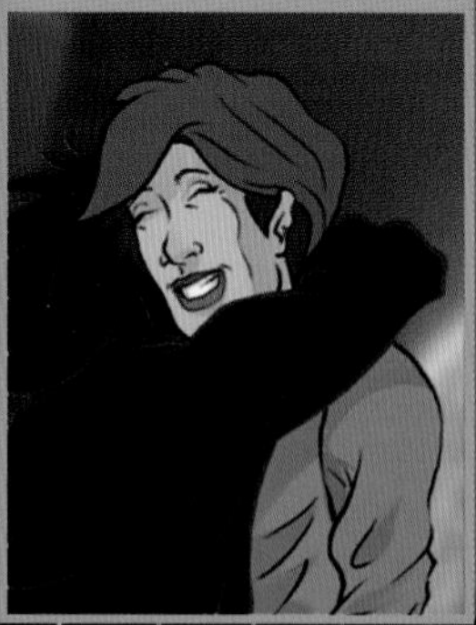

After her husband's death, Anita Lin had to raise their daughter alone. She is very protective of Hana, although her job as a PCN news anchor keeps her away from home most nights.

Worldview: Christianity is too dangerous for my daughter.
Superpower: Mom
Height: 5 feet 7 inches
Eyes: Pale Blue
Favorite Hobby: Photography
Biggest Problem: Works for Cap'n Crastin

"In this world you will have trouble. But take heart! I have overcome the world." —John 16:33 (NIV)

LORD FOULSPLEEN

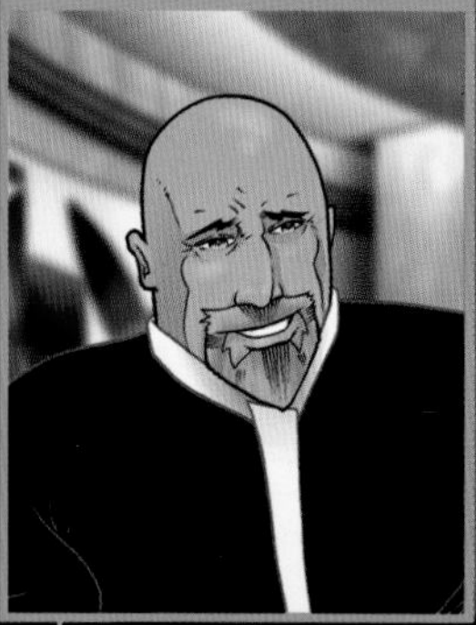

Hear Lord Foulspleen in the episode "Push the Red Button" on The Grand Design or at OAClub.org.

A former time-traveler who destroyed priceless works of art, Gargantuan Foulspleen changed his life after going to prison. Now he works for the museum and supports Captain Absolutely.

Worldview: Everyone deserves a second chance.
Skills: Grappling; Flying Small Aircraft
Height: 5 feet 2 inches
Eyes: Hazel
Favorite Art Style: Renaissance
Biggest Problem: Can't Time Travel Anymore

"Therefore, if anyone is in Christ, he is a new creation; old things have passed away, and look, new things have come." —2 Corinthians 5:17

NURSE GRUDGE

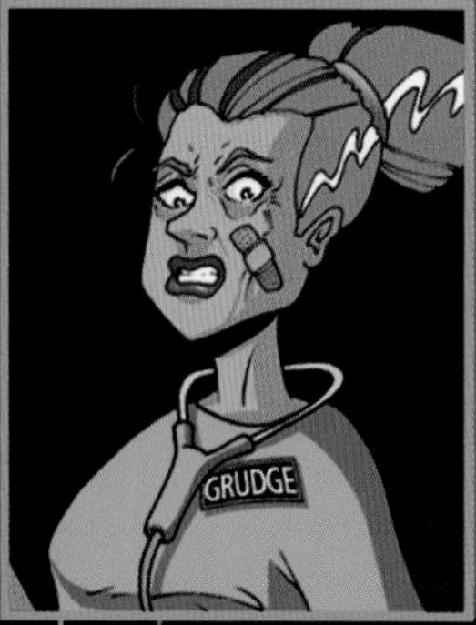
GRUDGE

The oldest of seven daughters, Emilia Grudge wrote down every mistake her sisters made, hoping her parents would recognize how much better she was.

Worldview: It's ***my*** job to make sure rule-breakers get the punishment they deserve.
Profession: Not a real nurse (I can't stress that enough)
Height: 5 feet 6 inches
Eyes: Brown
Favorite Clothes: Scrubs
Biggest Problem: Forgiveness

"Why do you pass judgment on your brother? . . . We will all stand before the judgment seat of God." —Romans 14:10 (ESV)

Blue Cupid is the top-selling band in Metropolitanville. Their brokenhearted lyrics appeal mostly to lonely teenagers.

Worldview: Life's not worth living if I can't be with you.
Superpower: Music Transports Listener to Invisible Prison
Height: 18 feet 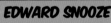 Split three ways
Eyes: Unknown
Favorite Feeling: Despondence
Biggest Problem: Album Sales

> "Remember, I am with you always,
> to the end of the age." —Matthew 28:20

BLUE CUPID

Joe Michaels was a school cafeteria chef who decided to become a superhero. His plans are more misguided than evil, but he still makes a big mess.

Worldview: As long as you have good intentions, you will always do the right thing.
Superpowers: None
Height: 5 feet 11 inches
Eyes: Green
Favorite Meal: Second Breakfast
Biggest Problem: Soap

> "If you love Me, you will keep My commands."
> —John 14:15

SLOPPY JOE

Leader of the Pajama Bandits, Edward Snooze has spent more than half his life in prison. He loves to test Captain Absolutely's commitment to his ideals.

Worldview: People only pretend to be good so othes won't judge them.
Weapon: Pillows
Height: 6 feet 4 inches
Eyes: Gray
Favorite Holiday: Mardi Gras
Biggest Problem: Alarm Clocks

> "How happy are those who uphold justice, who practice
> righteousness at all times." —Psalm 106:3

EDWARD SNOOZE

BIG QUESTIONS

God's Word is true, but it's not always simple. Discuss these questions with a parent or youth pastor as you dig deeper into *Captain Absolutely*.

- Why should you clean up your own messes? p.2
- Why can't you decide good and evil for yourself? p.6
- What makes the Bible different from other books? p.8
- How do you control your anger? p.10

- Has television ever distracted you from making better choices? p.12
- What do you fear most? p.14
- What does the Bible say about fear? (Start with Psalm 27:1.) p.16
- How does God's Word put you on "solid ground"? p.18

- How does reading the Bible change you? p.4

- Have you ever felt outnumbered? What did you do? p.20

- How do *you* share the truth in your neighborhood? p.22
- Why does obeying God sometimes make you unpopular? p.24
- Should Christianity be fun? p.26

- How can you "light the way" for your friends and classmates? p.28
- Are you willing to suffer for God? p.30
- Is it OK to steal Bibles? p.32

- What do you do when you feel lonely? p.34
- Why do Christians care about hygiene and appearance? p.36
- Which qualities should you look for in a godly sidekick (or friend)? p.38

• Who inspires you to be a better person? p.40
WHOOOOOOOSHH!!!...

• Have you ever felt tempted to sin "just this once"? What did you do? p.42

• Does holding a grudge ever make things better? p.44

• What does it mean to "waste" your freedom? p.46

• Is fantasy better than reality? p.68
32

• Why can't you scare people into following God? p.48

• When was the last time you thanked your parents? p.50

• Have you ever stood up to a bully? What did you say? p.52

• Have you "outgrown" an idea like you outgrow clothes? (Read 1 Corinthians 13:11.) p.54

• Why is teamwork important? p.56

• How does it feel when God calls you to serve? Can you be sure it's really Him? p.58

• Without judgment, how does anybody improve? p.60

• What do you do when your parents make a mistake? p.62

• When was the last time you asked God for help? p.64

• Has someone you love ever suffered because you made a hard choice? p.66

• Do you know who makes the rules at your school? How do the rules change? p.70

• If God is always with you, why do you still lose some battles? p.72

• Why is church important? p.74

• How do you decide whether to trust someone? p.76

• Is God scary? p.78

• Are you "trapped" in sin? Do you want Jesus to set you free? p.80

• How do you put family first? p.82

• Why do Christians still sin? p.84

• Why did Hana make Cap *explain* his apology? p.88

• When was the last time you apologized? p.86

• What makes you truly happy? p.90

• What's the difference between cleverness and wisdom? p.92

• Does God love bad people? p.94

• What is spiritual maturity? p.96

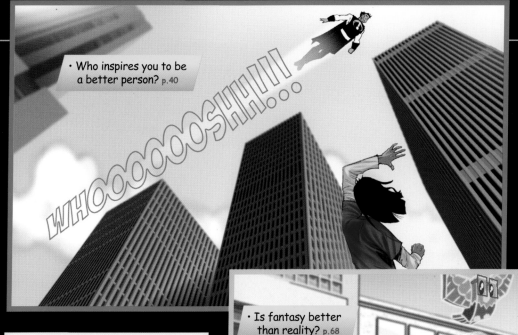

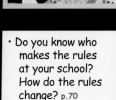

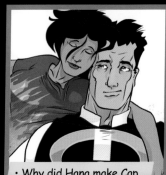

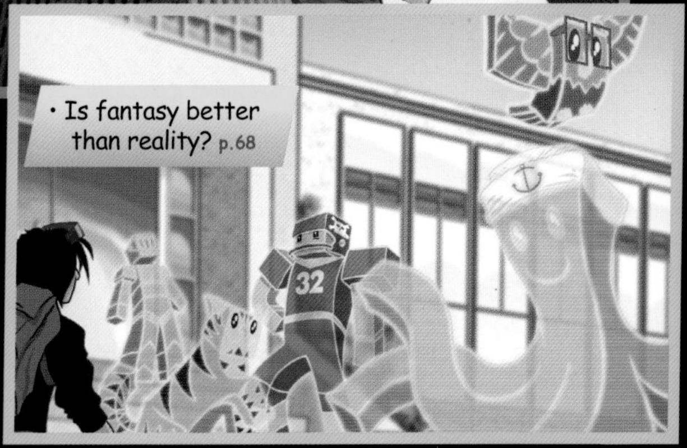

ODYSSEY
ADVENTURE CLUB™

The Great Adventure Awaits™!

Help the Kids in Your Life Get Engaged with Their Faith!

With your membership, you get:

- Over 800 *Adventures in Odyssey* episodes to stream
- Members-only stories and content
- A free subscription to *Focus on the Family Clubhouse*® Magazine (U.S. residents only)
- A monthly web quest of activities
- Exclusive product discounts

Plus—A portion of all subscription proceeds will benefit alliance organizations helping others in need!

Amazing Value!
$9.99/month

Join today at OAClub.org

Call 1-800-A-FAMILY (232-6459) for technical information only.

WAIT ... THERE'S MORE!

Find action-packed comics, jokes, stories and more every month in *Focus on the Family Clubhouse*®—the official magazine of Adventures in Odyssey. Created for kids ages 8 to 12, *Clubhouse* will make you laugh and grow closer to God. Check out an exclusive offer and sample more exciting adventures at **WhitsEnd.org/comics**.

DISCOVER. IMAGINE. GROW.

Adventures in Odyssey 90 Devotions for Kids

Join your friends from the exciting world of Odyssey and discover biblical truths from the book of Matthew. Through historical stories and key scenes from Adventures in Odyssey® audio dramas, you'll imagine what it's like to walk with Jesus.

The devotions feature a Bible passage that will help you grow in your faith along with a creative daily challenge to encourage life application. Plus there are fun activities to do alone or with your family.

Get your copy today!

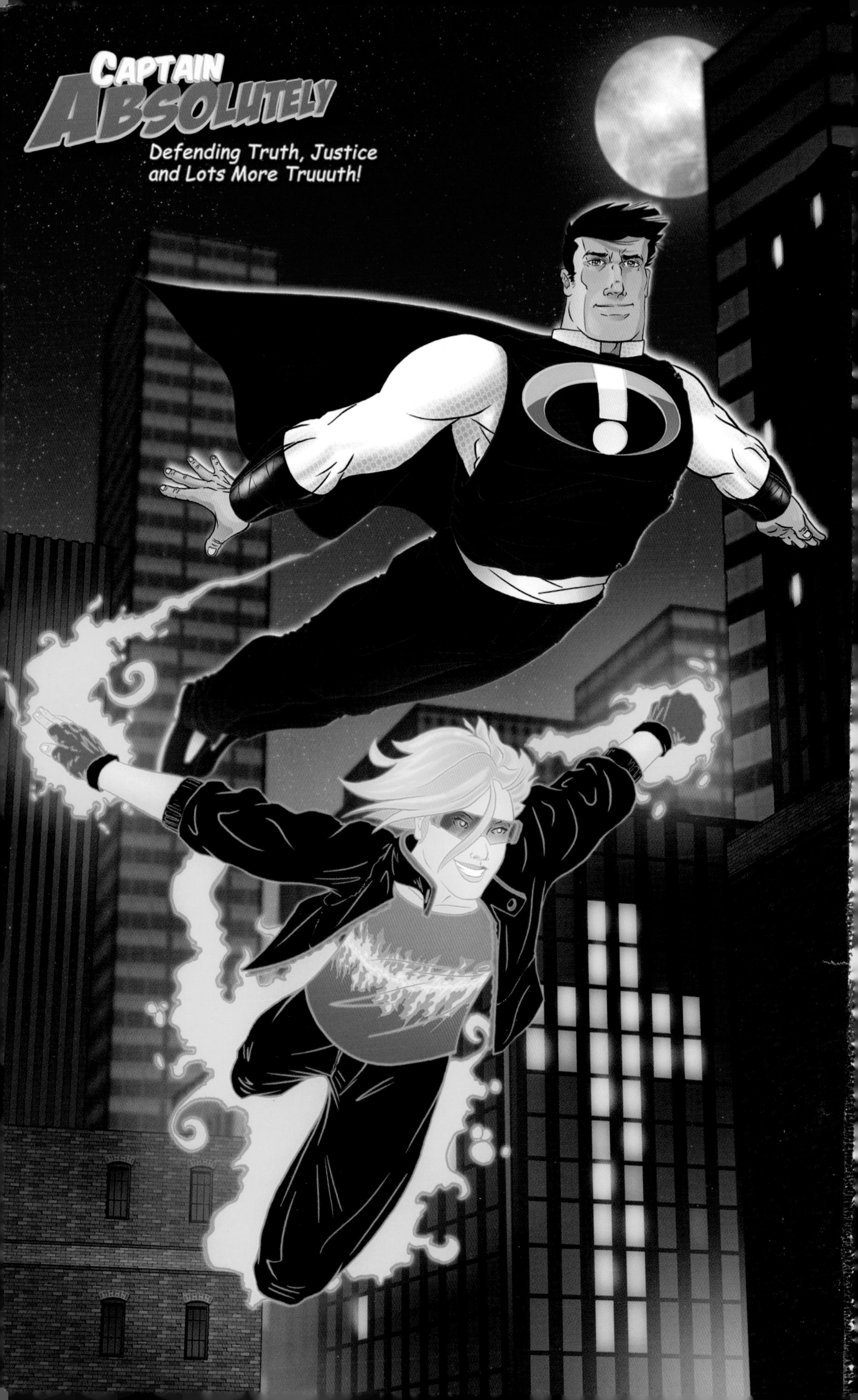
Captain Absolutely
Defending Truth, Justice and Lots More Truuuth!